DANGEROUS VOWS

AVA PARKER

TABLE OF CONTENTS

ACKNOWLEDGEMENTS

Thank you to all of my friends and family for your love and support.

To my dad for teaching me to be pragmatic, to my mom for teaching me be idealistic, and to Paula for showing me how to just be. I love you all.

To my friends and beta readers for suffering through the early drafts and encouraging me to persevere. To Tauni, Thomas, Christopher, Will, and of course B, for always being so wonderful and inspiring.

To Mara White for holding my hand.

To Daniela Medina for making me look like a real author.

To my editor, Stephanie Dagg, for seeing everything that I didn't.

And to all the boys I've loved before....

Thank you.

PROLOGUE

TUESDAY MORNING SHERIFF TOM GRIER stood on the South Carolina shore, adjusting his hat against the sudden rain, and thinking to himself that now there were two things to make this day extraordinary: a morning sun shower, and a dead body.

"Damn," he said aloud to no one in particular, though both of his deputies startled at the sudden noise. "Get a tarp!" he yelled and the younger of the two ran off to his cruiser to find something to prevent the rain from washing away any evidence.

While the two deputies fashioned a tent over the body, Sheriff Grier called the county coroner's office and explained that they had a dead man on the beach just outside of Graceful Bay and it looked like foul play. When the man on the other end of the line admonished him not to touch anything, he growled and hung up.

The call had come from a manager at one of the resort hotels along the water. Evidently, a staff member had been sent down to pick up garbage along the beach and had seen the man lying there. At first he'd thought the man was sleeping or passed out. That happened occasionally, partiers crashing on the beach, but when he called out to him and finally walked up and gave him a little shake, he realized that the man's body was stiff and icy. He ran, hollering like a banshee, according to the manager, back up to the hotel where it had taken the desk manager another few minutes to figure out what he was hollering about.

That same Tuesday morning, a mile down the beach Lucy Walker woke feeling refreshed and motivated. She'd been back home in Graceful Bay for only two days, and yet the peace and quiet of her childhood home was already soothing her nerves and relieving her stress. She went down to the kitchen to start her coffee before returning to the master bathroom to wash her face and brush her teeth. *A shower can wait until the afternoon*, she thought as she examined her long dark hair before taking a brush to it. Her skin was smooth and glowing, her blue eyes bright and shiny She felt beautiful and fresh this morning, and she thought again how gray and tired her stay in Miami's Metropolitan Hospital had made her. Even after she had recovered from her injuries, the Miami Dade police department had kept her in a discreet airport hotel near the clinic where she underwent rehabilitation treatment for the muscle damage to her left leg. She had spent weeks going from the stale air of the three-star hotel to the rarified air of the hospital.

Even though different make-up and a return to her natural hair color had changed her appearance significantly from the glossy, highlighted, South Beach bimbo look she'd had when she was an undercover agent, it was important to remain anonymous in the weeks after the operation had been blown. Since she hadn't had a real home of her own or a family, it had been easier just to stash her in the one-room suite with a kitchenette near the hospital.

Even before her hospitalization, the overpopulated beaches and the smog of the city had never felt like the same Atlantic Ocean she'd known as a child. Lucy was sure that, if she'd thought about it, she had always known that Miami was not a permanent home for her. It was during those endless weeks at Metropolitan Hospital that she had longed for the wet salty air of home and her decision to return to Graceful Bay had been solidified.

THE PREVIOUS SUNDAY

THE SUN WAS JUST SETTING when Lucy Walker pulled up alongside the Shaker house she had inherited from her grandparents nearly ten years ago. Her old Volvo station wagon had made the drive from Miami admirably, and surprisingly, considering how tired she'd been when she'd packed it up and pulled away from her high-rise apartment building near South Beach, so had Lucy. The open road had lifted her spirits as she drove further away from a lot of bad memories and closer to her childhood home.

Lucy got out of her car, stretched, took a deep breath of salty air and seaweed, and did a little dance on the gravel driveway that made her wounded leg ache and her heart swell.

"Hey, Lucyfer! Get your butt up here and give me a hug!"

Lucy spun around so fast she almost fell over, but when she saw her oldest friend coming around from the beach side of the porch and her childhood nickname finally registered, she laughed. "Carolina! You almost gave me a heart-attack!"

Caroline Lamont swaggered down the porch steps and gave Lucy the once-over. "Were you reaching for your gun?"

Self-consciously, Lucy moved her gripped hand away from her hip. "Old habits...."

Caroline smiled. "Leave 'em in Miami. You're home now. Safe and sound." The two friends hugged each other tightly. "You don't look too bad for a girl who was stabbed in the leg. I thought you'd be bruised and battered with a permanent snarl on your face after spending so much time with drug dealers and gun-runners and whoever else you had to live with."

"Drug dealers and gun-runners live pretty well, my dear, and I wiped that snarl off of my face as soon as I came out from under cover."

"Came out? Got yanked out is more like it." At Lucy's expression, Caroline relented. "Well, you're pretty as ever, that's for sure."

"Me?" She looked Caroline over from head to foot. Her friend was as beautiful as always, from her honey blonde hair and bright blue Valkyrie eyes, to her long legs. "You're stunning!"

"Oh, you're just saying that because it's true!" She gave Lucy a wink. "C'mon, let's get your things inside."

They each took two bags from the back and headed up the porch steps. Caroline unlocked the door with the keys Lucy had left with her after she'd inherited the house and moved to Miami. Once they'd set the bags in the foyer, she handed them over to Lucy with ceremony. "You're home now, so you'd better take these back."

Lucy hefted the key ring: one for the front and back doors, one for the little storage shed, and one for the garage. "Don't worry," said Caroline, I've still got the spare at home in case you lose these. More to the point, in case you go out of town, so I can have wild parties."

"Yeah, sure," Lucy laughed.

They finished unpacking her car and left everything in the foyer. Gesturing toward the small stack of suitcases and boxes, she said, "I'll take care of those later." Then she walked into the living room and looked around. "It's spotless! Not a speck of dust."

"Sarah comes in and dusts once a month, but I asked her to come in a few days ago and give it a proper scrub for your homecoming. The fridge is stocked for a couple of days. Chunky Monkey in the freezer for your hips. I have to head home. Daniel sent me a text message a few minutes before you pulled in. He came home suddenly to surprise me."

When Caroline trailed off and didn't say anymore, Lucy asked, "Everything okay?"

She looked startled, "Oh, of course! Hey, why don't you join us for dinner tonight? I'm sure Daniel would love to see you, and we could catch up."

Lucy wasn't so sure about that. She and Daniel Lamont had never been very comfortable around each other. "Thank you, Caroline, but I'm not fit for anything but a hot bath and a game of Solitaire. "Tomorrow?"

"Tomorrow it is. It might just be the two of us. I'm not sure how long my darling husband will be home. He usually spends the workweek in Atlanta. Right now you just settle in and call me in the morning, or sooner, if you need anything. We're only five minutes away."

"Caroline, you are the best friend in the world! How did I ever find you?"

"Dumb luck." She hugged Lucy again and, with a flourish, strutted out the door and down the drive.

Lucy looked at the small stack of suitcases and boxes and mentally kissed herself for having packed an overnight bag with everything she would need for at least the next twelve hours. She grabbed her little suitcase and headed upstairs to her childhood bedroom. The en suite had a shower and tub, but Lucy opted for expediency and turned on the shower. The hot water and steam rinsed away the long drive and she began to relax.

With her hair wrapped in a towel, she slathered herself with a lavender scented lotion she had treated herself to in Miami and padded around the second floor of the house naked, pulling on her cotton jersey pajamas and smoothing the covers on the double bed in her old bedroom. *No sense sleeping in here,* she thought suddenly. This was her house. In fact, it had been her house for many years now, though she hadn't lived in it since the death of her grandparents.

She picked up her overnight bag and walked across the hall to her grandparents' bedroom suite. As she opened the door, the failing evening light coming through two walls of windows and the scent of fresh lilies washed over her. "Oh, Caroline!" she exclaimed when she saw the crystal vase of fresh flowers on the nightstand. Lucy jumped onto the king size bed and mentally made a point of calling it her own.

She went downstairs and pulled out the plate of cut veggies and cheese her friend had left for her. She opened a box of water crackers and arranged it all on a tea tray. When her grandparents bought the house there had been a wall dividing this room into a medium-sized parlor and a medium-sized living room, but Lucy's grandmother had made short shrift of the dividing wall. Now the entire ocean side of the house was one great big room framed with bookcases on one side, a fireplace on the other, and nothing but windows and French doors in between. It was a dramatic view for guests coming in through the foyer or sitting in the dining room. The kitchen was the only room on the first floor that didn't share the view, but it faced the drive and the road beyond. As her grandmother said, "All you need to see when you're cooking is who is coming to dinner."

Lucy set her simple dinner on a low table in the library section of the wide living room that swept across the entire front of the beach house, sat down on the thick Afghani rug beneath it and ate with utter contentment. It was the first time in a long time that she had been able to just be. Years as an undercover cop in Miami had created a survival instinct completely based on lies and mistrust, and although she had put away a few really bad people, the job had taken its toll on her ability to relax. *Among other things*, she thought with some irritation. These last few days, every time she realized how relaxed she was, Lucy remembered how vigilant she had had to be for so long, and the awareness popped her out of her reverie.

"Enough of that!" she said out loud and took her tray into the kitchen where she set the dishes in the sink, put the rest of the cheese back into the fridge, wrapped a kitchen towel around her pint of Ben and Jerry's so that her hand wouldn't get cold, and, armed with a spoon headed to the foyer for the leftover crossword puzzle in her purse. Back in her seat in the living room under the bookshelves, she had just finished it off, along with half of the ice cream, when her phone chirruped, announcing a text message.

In the foyer, somewhere in the clutter of her belongings she found her phone and read the message from Caroline. 'Forgot to tell you that you have a new neighbor.' Then there was a smiley face and an 'xo' followed by a capital 'C'.

The neighbor was a man, of course. *That's the last thing that I need,* thought Lucy, even though, what she wouldn't let herself think was that a man might be just exactly what she needed to help her relax.

Climbing the stairs felt like a ten-mile run and by the time she was in bed, it was all Lucy could do to switch off the bedside lamp before she was sound asleep.

With the curtains still wide open, Lucy woke with the sun in the bright room. She felt good: ready to start the day. Throwing open one of the windows, she backed up a step when the cold morning air hit her bare arms, but left it open. She bounded down the stairs to start a pot of coffee, which, thanks to Caroline, she found in a paper bag in the freezer. The aroma as it began brewing picked her up another notch. It was seven a.m. but she had slept over nine hours, and she felt wonderful. *There is no place like home*, she thought as she climbed the stairs to dress and unpack her suitcases.

Coffee in hand, Lucy spent the next couple of hours unpacking the things she had brought with her and airing out the house as the temperature outside climbed to a velvety sixty-five degrees. The clean salty air was familiar and comforting, and it occurred to her that sometimes home is the only place a girl can really heal.

NEW MAN IN TOWN

UNPACKING HADN'T TAKEN LONG: SHE had few possessions to show for nearly eight years in Miami. When she moved down there a few years out of college to begin the police academy, she had sublet a furnished room in a cramped not-quite South Beach condo with two other women. For the next couple of years she had bounced around similar living situations, buying a mattress with a wire frame at one point and a used lounge chair at another, but never bothering with anything else. At the time she thought it was because she was too busy. By the time she got her own place, she had joined the narcotics division and busy didn't cover it.

When she'd finally gone deep under cover, she'd been living like a nomad for so long, she had no problem subletting her little apartment and its meager furnishings to new police cadets for the interim. And when she came out – was forced to come out – she signed over the lease, donated everything that didn't fit in her car, and left. It was like she was never there. Now, Lucy wondered if she'd never made a home for herself in the Florida city because she knew that the soil in Miami wasn't deep enough to put roots in. Not for her, anyway.

No use wondering about it now, she thought, looking around the old house.

Her cell phone rang and jolted Lucy out of her musings. "I bet it's Caroline," she said aloud and then thought; *I'm going to have to stop talking to myself.*

"Have you had lunch yet?" was Caroline's greeting.

Trying to remember if she'd even had breakfast yet and suddenly aware that her stomach was growling, Lucy answered, "No."

"Want to go to LaValle's for a sandwich and a little walk through town afterward? I managed to keep my mouth shut about your coming home, but I bet everyone knows by now anyway. No way that your old hippie-mobile went unnoticed."

Lucy laughed, "Let's do it!"

"I'll swing by and pick you up in fifteen minutes."

Then she was gone. Lucy ran upstairs, brushed the coffee taste out of her mouth, and changed into a fiery peach T-shirt that showed off her olive skin, left the jeans on, brushed her hair, powdered her nose and pinched her cheeks when she couldn't find any blush. *Still a little pale*, she thought, *but not bad.*

By the time she'd finished primping she heard Caroline pull up on the gravel drive. Lucy snatched up a wrinkled linen blazer and her purse and ran out the door. Putting on her seat belt and kissing Caroline's cheek in one fluid motion, Lucy realized she had not felt so good in a long time.

"There's blush in here," Caroline said as she set her purse in Lucy's lap and grinned at her.

Lucy gave her arm a little slap and laughed as she dug into her friend's make-up bag.

"Sorry, girl, but after a month in the hospital it takes a little more than a pinch to make those cheeks glow."

"God, I missed having a girlfriend, Caroline."

"I missed you too," Caroline replied as she deftly u-turned out of the drive.

Looking around the sleek leather and wood interior of Caroline's black BMW two-seater, Lucy commented, "Still driving fast cars, Carolina?"

"What did you expect? Hey, did you get a chance to walk along the beach today?"

"No, I did not. Can I assume my new neighbor is a man?"

"Oh yeah. And a very fine specimen of a man at that! I'm not kidding, Lucy, he's the prettiest boy to come to town in a while."

Lucy laughed, but said seriously, "I'm not interested."

"You haven't even seen him! Don't you turn into an old maid on me, Lucy. I know you've been living a life in which distrust is what kept you alive, but you're safe now, girl. Time to take a leap!"

Lucy hoped Caroline was right and wished it were so easy. "I worry that I can't, Caroline. Right now I need to figure out who I am again."

Caroline looked thoughtful, then she said, "That is probably not a bad start."

Two minutes later, Caroline squeezed the BMW into a tiny parking spot on Main Street. The early afternoon was a typical bustling Monday in Graceful Bay. In fact, it was typical of every weekday in

Graceful Bay. The affluent South Carolina town was always vibrant with townspeople drinking coffee, strolling its streets, waving hello or goodbye to each other and gathering to gossip in its restaurants, shops and cafés. Even during the tourist season, when the resorts and hotels surrounding the beaches were packed with people, the lazy pace of Graceful Bay never wavered. The frenetic energy of its visitors was mitigated by the natural ease with which these South Carolinians moved through their lives, and if that didn't do the trick, the heat and humidity slowed visitors down in spite of themselves. Lucy always suspected this relaxed atmosphere was the main appeal for tourists, and now that she was back, she felt herself ease into the luxurious lassitude of Graceful Bay with a smile and a sigh of relief.

The two women got out of the car. Caroline dutifully dropped quarters into the meter, and then they strolled twenty paces to LaValle's. The bakery and café had been an institution in Graceful Bay for thirty years. Originally opened by Sandy LaValle, and now run by his son, Sandy LaValle Junior, the bread and pastries were homemade, the sandwiches, omelets and salads were fresh and the portions were big. Now Sandy Senior was a permanent fixture in the front of the house, either helping out behind the counter during a rush, or seated with a cup of coffee and a cigar that he never, ever lit. *In fact*, thought Lucy now as she grinned at him from the door, *it may be the exact same cigar he had been waving around since she was old enough to notice that it was never lit.*

Both Sandy LaValles were tall, strong men with

thick hair and brows, strong arms and flat bellies that belied their trade.

Sandy Senior stood up, gave Lucy the once-over and said, "Well, you're no worse for the wear, Miss Walker." Then he marched over and gave her a bear hug.

Hearing his father, Sandy Junior stuck his head out from the kitchen and said, "'Bout time you got back where you belong, Lucy Walker!"

And with that, Lucy was lavished with greetings and hugs from the lunch crowd in the packed restaurant, most of whom she knew, and some of whom she figured she would know soon enough. They deluged her with questions but the most important answer was that Lucy was here for good, so everyone would have plenty of time to ask her what happened in Miami and whether she had a boyfriend. In the meantime, they could speculate. And speculation, at least in Graceful Bay, was as important as eventually hearing the real story.

At last, Sandy Senior ushered Lucy and Caroline to a table and got their order.

When she took the first bite of her grilled cheese and tomato sandwich, followed by a forkful of cucumber and dill salad, Lucy thought she had just about died and gone to heaven.

"You look like you're having an orgasm," Caroline deadpanned quietly, before tucking into her French onion soup.

Lucy laughed happily and looked around the restaurant. Warm greetings aside, she knew she was going to be the subject of some hot gossip for a while to come, but gossip in Southern towns was rampant and rarely malicious – merely a necessary part of the organism. After a couple of years under deep cover, living someone else's life, in a city too big to hope for this kind of openness and familiarity, Lucy figured she could graciously trade the forced privacy of isolation in Miami for the chatter of family in Graceful Bay.

As they were finishing lunch, Sally and Susan O'Connor, sisters in biology and intrigue, pulled up two chairs to the small table where Lucy and Caroline ate. The two women were a couple of years apart in age but could've passed for fraternal twins. They had always looked very similar, even for siblings, but now in their fifties, they had taken to dressing alike, styling their platinum hair the same way, and even painting their fingernails the same color: bright pink today. They were married to two brothers and lived directly across the street from each other. As they situated their teacups between empty plates and water glasses, Lucy thought what it must be like to be part of that mess of siblings and in-laws and felt grateful that she could appreciate their eccentricities from afar.

Sally began, "Here is our little hometown hero! Lucy, you are fit as a fiddle! I didn't know what to think when I heard about the fiasco in Miami!"

Lucy's injuries and the catastrophic end of the undercover operation she had been working had made national headlines during a slow news week. The coverage was good, in a way, because it meant she wouldn't have to explain what happened in Miami, but also bad, because it didn't afford her much anonymity to anyone who'd happened to pay attention to the news during her fifteen minutes of fame.

Susan jumped in, "Well, she's been in the hospital for a month! Of course she looks fine now. Oh, dear, you must have been a fright."

"Oh, she was a fright!" said Caroline, with a little smile for Lucy's benefit. "Not to mention they had her dolled up like a drug dealer's ho for two years. I told her to get a haircut and fix her teeth before she went back out into the real world or she'd have children running scared. Not to mention men!"

"*Ho*?" asked Susan.

"Speaking of men," Sally didn't seem to hear her sister as her eyes nearly rolled back in her head with this little morsel, "have you met Gabriel Black?" She seemed to be directing this at Lucy.

Shaking her head, not sure she liked where this was going, Lucy replied, "No. Is he new to town since I left?"

Susan jumped in, "Oh, he's our most recent addition, dear. In fact, he's almost your neighbor," now her eyes lit up, "and he is just so handsome!"

"Are you planning on going back to Miami, Lucy?" Sally asked innocently.

"Actually, I think I'm home for good, Mrs. O'Connor."

"Well, then you have to meet Gabriel." Susan drew the name out thoughtfully while she sized Lucy up. "Don't you think so, Caroline?"

"Well, I think so," said Sally, a little irritated that her sister had asked Caroline and not her. "He is single. Is he divorced or never married? Well, doesn't matter. He moved here from New York, but that's not where he's originally from. He moved into the Westin-Harrison house when they decided to spend the winter in the Caribbean." She paused and looked at Lucy. "Gay couple, dear. Very stylish. Anyway, Gabriel is a little evasive about how much time he plans to spend in Graceful Bay. No one knows if he's renting the house or just using it while the Westin-Harrison's are away, but we do know that they're coming back for the summer. Maybe you can find out when you meet him, dear. I didn't want to seem too nosy." She smiled and nodded her head to indicate she was done.

Susan took the opportunity to lay out the important things, "He's about your age. Handsome as ever! And he was with the military police, so you have law enforcement in common. Now he's some kind of consultant like everybody else. Very well-off."

"I was getting to that," her sister snapped. Then, looking pointedly at Lucy's empty ring finger, she said sweetly, "We don't even know if Lucy is taken. She might have a fella in Miami."

Lucy felt more like an observer than a participant in the conversation and blinked a few times when she realized that she was expected to reply. "Nope, no fellas in Miami, but I have a lot of settling in to do before I start looking for one in Graceful Bay."

Caroline's phone chirped, and even before she read the message she was announcing their departure to the sisters O'Connor.

"Time to head out. We have some errands to run. So good to chat!" she said as she headed to the counter to pay for lunch.

"Yes, so lovely to see the two of you!" Lucy said

to Sally and Susan, wondering how long it would be before they dropped by with a pack of townswomen in tow to fill her kitchen with casseroles and cakes and sit her down to sing for her supper.

Outside, she said to Caroline, "Some things never change," and she smiled, genuinely happy that they hadn't.

HEY STRANGER

AFTER CAROLINE DROPPED HER OFF at home, Lucy hung her purse on a hook in the foyer, changed her ballet flats for her bright green Puma soccer shoes and headed through the house to the family room. She surveyed the beach through the wall-to-wall row of windows; it had been calling her. She went out through the French doors in the center of the room and stopped again on the beach side of the wraparound house. She smiled as she thought, *Yes, Grandma, I will be sure to go through the mudroom when I come home.*

Going down the half flight of stairs and then walking the wood plank path that led through the saw grass and sand, she could feel herself easing completely into the sensations of the South Carolina shore: the briny smell of the water tinged from a distance with the smell of shrimp boats off-loading their catches, the friction of the sand as it made room for her feet, the bright reflection of the sun off of the water, the sound of seabirds calling, the salty taste of the wind on her tongue as she inhaled deeply. Lucy threw her arms out and spun around until she was a little dizzy. Then, facing the water, she scanned the beach on either side and took off left.

She had been walking at a leisurely pace for

about ten minutes when she saw him. Actually, she saw the cat first. A big orange tabby sat languidly, watching her from its perch on the low stone wall that surrounded the house and about an acre of land. Just a few paces down from the cat, the ex-military man who had every woman in town weak at the knees, was standing at the edge of his new property where the saw grass ended and the real beach began. He seemed to be fixing the gate and damned if he wasn't wearing a tool belt! Lucy's tummy fluttered a little and she felt a little weak-kneed herself. *My goodness, Lucy, if ever there was ever a reason to jump into a man's arms...* Suddenly, she realized that he was turning around.

Scolding herself for weakness, and simultaneously wondering if there was anywhere to hide on the deserted beach, Lucy put on her best nonchalant face and gave a little wave.

Without a word, Lucy's new neighbor holstered his screwdriver and waved back, and, Lucy was sure, gave her the once-over! Then a slow smile spread across his face and he said, "Beautiful day," but he never took his eyes off of hers.

Lucy nodded and asked, "New in town?" Even she could hear the coyness in her tone. Oh well.

"I am. And you?" When Lucy looked at him quizzically, he continued, "I ask because I was pretty sure I had met every single resident of Graceful Bay, and I *know* that you and I have not met."

The sparkle in those eyes is going to do me in, she thought. "Not new, just back. I live about ten minutes that way," she pointed the way she'd come. Lucy realized she was still standing about thirty feet away. She quickly found her manners and walked up the sand toward him. "I'm Lucy. Lucy Walker."

She extended her hand and when he took it, she felt a surge of desire so strong it left her gaping for a second.

"Gabriel Black. It's a pleasure."

"Likewise."

When Lucy realized that their hands were still entwined she abruptly loosened her grip and stuck her hand in the pocket of her jeans, as if to prevent any further contact. *Very smooth, Lucy. Very, very smooth!*

Gabriel looked bemused but went on, "And this is Baxter, aka Big Cat." He gestured at the giant orange tabby who acknowledged him with a yawn and something between a meow and a growl. He then licked one paw, looked down the beach and started walking along the stone wall in their direction. About halfway, he stopped short and turned his nose up to catch a scent. "He's really friendly inside the house, but out here there's too much going on to pay attention to people who might pet him."

"Just this morning I was thinking I should have a cat to keep me company," Lucy replied with a long look at Baxter.

"I'm sure there's better company out there for you than a cat." Lucy turned back to him and the moment lingered as they looked at each other. "In the meantime, Baxter is home most evenings. Eating his kibbles, purring, snoring – hard to tell the difference sometimes – generally just being a cat. He probably wouldn't mind some extra attention."

"I'm sure he gets plenty from his owner." Lucy

shivered a little. Standing still the wind was chilly. "I should let you get back to your gate. It was nice to meet you, Gabriel."

"You too, Lucy Walker."

As she walked away, Lucy thought how nice it would be to let Mr. Black warm her up with his big strong arms. She had just about swooned when they shook hands. A sudden urge to turn around gripped her but Lucy controlled herself. *I can still at least pretend to play it cool. Besides,* she thought, *I'll have to walk past his house again on my way home.* Thick, dark hair, sparkling brown eyes, and a smile that hit her right in her center... *Take a deep breath, girl!*

Lucy wasn't sure she'd be able to trust a man to get close to her. It wasn't that she'd been left broken-hearted. The problem, as Lucy saw it, was that she had been surrounded by really bad guys for a couple of years with only one exception. Her undercover partner, who had also played her "big brother", was a good guy, but while she was with him he was pretending to be an up-and-coming drug kingpin. Otherwise, every guy around really was a drug dealer or a killer, or both. Sure, some of them had families or girlfriends and loved them very much, but at the end of the day, the men Lucy had been surrounded by in the last few years were pretty awful. Not to mention that she had been play-acting for all that time. Could she really trust herself to be honest with a man? Was she even capable anymore?

The worst of it was when, after years of building trust with lies, Lucy had to break cover to save her partner's life and all hell had broken loose. Lucy had almost died, but the things she would never forget were the looks of shock and betrayal from the gangsters she'd been living with for so long. Then, despite the medals the police gave her to make sure the public believed everything had gone according to plan, the ultimate rebuke from the Miami Dade brass. She had broken protocol, ruined the operation, and rendered herself useless as a cop.

I'm hopeless, she concluded. *Maybe time will help, but right now, I'm not fit for male companionship.* A cat, on the other hand, a little kitty-cat, might be the very thing. Right on cue, Baxter mewed at her and she realized that she was about to pass Gabriel Black's house again.

As if the fates were letting her know that she could wallow forever, but her heart would still do what it wanted, she saw Gabriel coming down the walk with a bottle of beer in his hand. He saw her and smiled broadly. He'd lost the tool belt and Lucy noticed how his jeans caught his waist and his rust-streaked white T-shirt clung to his muscles. *This is ridiculous*, she chided herself.

Gabriel's eyes never left hers as he continued down the path. *Lucy Walker, you are a beautiful woman*, he thought as he watched her approach. In spite of what he thought might be a slight limp, there was something liquid about the way she moved, her long dark hair flowing behind her, cheeks flushed, Mona Lisa smirk on her face. What did that look mean?

They met at the gate. "Hello again, Lucy. Would you like something to drink?"

"Thanks, but I need to get home before dark,"

she replied, even as she realized that sunset was still a couple of hours away.

Gabriel glanced at the bright sky, which belied Lucy's time concerns, but graciously said nothing. "Let me know if you change your mind," and he tipped the bottle of dark beer toward her before taking a slow sip.

Lucy was clearly uncomfortable around him, but Gabriel wasn't sure why. He hoped it was because she was as crazily attracted to him as he was to her, but for all he knew it was because he had been flirting and she had a boyfriend. She wasn't married; there was no ring on her finger. He decided to tone it down.

There were two wide steps down to the beach from the gate and he sat on the top one, gesturing for Lucy to join him.

She hesitated for a second and then sat down next to him. *Why not?* Her injured leg was beginning to ache from the long walk and just because she wasn't going to date the guy didn't mean she had to avoid him completely. "Finished the gate?"

"I replaced the hinges, but I think the whole wall is going to fall into the sand before long."

Lucy took a look at the stone wall. It was mostly decorative, only about two feet high and hand stacked, more New England than Mid-Atlantic. The stones were all different shapes and she couldn't see any mortar between them. "I don't know about that. It looks like an original. If you walk the border each year and replace the stones that fall out, it might last forever."

"I'll leave that to the couple who own the house. I just couldn't stand the squeaking gate anymore."

This time when Gabriel smiled at her, she was disappointed to see that his gaze was no longer flirtatious but held only a friendly invitation. "So, Lucy, where did you come back from?"

She looked out toward the sea. "Miami. I moved there about eight years ago and finally wore out my welcome."

When she turned back to him, Gabriel had a look of slow recognition on his face. The Miami Dade police department had managed to keep most pictures of her out of the paper. The media had an official police academy graduation photo and the picture from her police ID, both of which were a matter of public record. Mercifully, and probably thanks to the Miami Dade brass, the media didn't get enough steam out of the story to keep airing it. It wasn't simply good luck that no one had ever recognized her from the grainy versions of those photos that ended up in the papers, on the internet and very briefly on the news. Media liaisons from the police department had kept a lid on as many of the details as they could without appearing as if they were hiding anything. Though her name and photos were released, in both official pictures she was in full uniform and not immediately recognizable. She was sold as a hero, but kept out of the limelight. Unless you were looking. Unless you knew her name, had read the stories, and were looking straight at her.

"Ah," was Gabriel's simple reaction. "You were an undercover cop in Florida." At her quizzical look, he explained, "I have a friend in the Miami Dade police department who likes to gossip, and I recognize your picture from the *Herald*." Taking another pull from his beer he looked into the distance. "You did a brave thing down there. Saved your partner's life and probably your own too."

Lucy looked at him for a second. She thought, *He seems more empathetic than curious.* When he looked at her again she saw that the desire had returned to his eyes, and before she could stop herself, felt it flutter across her gaze as well.

"Until a few years ago I was an MP overseas and I supervised some undercover projects. Gun running, mostly."

"And now?" she asked even though the O'Conner sisters had already told her he was some sort of consultant.

"I have a securities firm called Special Securities Provisions. It's out of New York but we do mostly electronic protection, so I can work from Graceful Bay for a couple of months." He made a sweeping gesture from the beach to the house behind them. "Anyway, I have some idea about what you went through in Florida if you ever want to talk about it."

Right then, Lucy decided it was fine to flirt a little with this gorgeous guy sitting next her. Maybe, she had been anxious about having to explain where the last eight years of her life had gone. But Gabriel didn't seem to need an explanation.

"Story for another time, perhaps," she said, standing up and brushing the sand off of her butt. When she turned back to him, she distinctly saw Gabriel look up from her behind. He didn't even seem to be hiding it! *A little cocky aren't you? Two can play at that game.*

"Thanks for the sit-down, Gabriel. See you around." Lucy winked at him before turning gracefully and walking away.

Alone on the stairs, Gabriel couldn't take his eyes off of her. The papers had said she'd been stabbed, but not how badly. Rick Mortimer, one of his oldest friends from West Point, was now the Chief of Police of Miami Dade County and Gabriel knew a lot more about Lucy's situation than had been in any of the papers. Lucy Walker was a hero. He figured narcotics brass in Miami had spent a good part of what had probably been an excruciatingly long debriefing making her feel like she'd messed up. He was certain that if press coverage had gone on much longer, they would have thrown her to the wolves instead of letting it come out that a new Vice Captain – hired for his politics and not his experience – had screwed up big time. Every cop out there knew Lucy did the right thing. When it's a question of the sting or your partner's life, you choose your partner. No questions asked. As it turned out, another cheating congressman scandal took the spotlight off of the bloodshed in Florida and Lucy emerged unscathed in the headlines. Still, knowing your bosses are holding you by a string, willing to drop you in a heartbeat to save themselves, can be devastating.

He watched Lucy's long strides until she disappeared along the curve of the beach, a little slower now, but just as graceful. She definitely had a limp. Left side. The walk down the beach had probably exaggerated it, and now he knew where it had come from. *I never would have guessed that the woman causing such a stir in Miami would turn out to be such a beauty – and my neighbor.* Gabriel smiled. Lucy Walker had lit him up from the inside.

He felt Baxter brush against his arm and looked down at him. "You could help out a little, buddy. You know, rub up against her, sit in her lap, make her think we're gentlemen." Baxter replied with a plaintive cry. "I know, I know. It's dinnertime. It's always about food with you."

With a last contemplative look down the beach, Gabriel Black picked up his empty beer bottle and he and Baxter walked up the path to find something to eat.

ORPHANED

WHEN LUCY GOT HOME SHE found some ibuprofen in her purse and swallowed it with a long drink of cold water. She knew she should sit down and rest her leg, but she wanted to do something productive. First, she called Caroline and asked her whether she should bring anything to dinner.

"Just be here with bells on at seven," was her friend's response.

Next Lucy busied herself around the kitchen for a few minutes and realized that she would have to do some serious grocery shopping. *The cupboard is bare, to say the least*, she thought. All of the kitchen staples one took for granted were demonstrably missing. There was no sugar or flour, and except for a familiar blue cardboard cylinder of Morton's iodized salt, no spices for baking or cooking. Caroline had supplied basic perishables like milk and butter and cream, but no condiments. Lucy was a firm believer that she could make anything taste like a meal if she had enough varieties of mustard, pickles, salad dressings and bottled sauces on hand.

She sat down at the breakfast bar in the kitchen to write a grocery list, but paused when it occurred to her that it had been nine years since anyone had lived in the house. When her grandparents had been alive this big old house had been brimming with life.

Lucy had been orphaned shortly before her fifth birthday. Lucy's father had been a prominent financial investor on Wall Street. He and her mother were on their way to a client's Blue Ridge lodge for a business-social weekend when the small plane carrying them and two other couples, including their hosts for the weekend, went down. They had flown from New York City into Charleston, where her grandparents had picked Lucy up, and then they took a private plane the rest of the way. That had been the plan anyway; they never made it through the Appalachian Mountains. Lucy's grandparents later told her it had been the first time her mother and father had left her alone for more than half a day, but, to Lucy, that had only made it seem worse.

She remembered her parents like a five-year-old would. She had never experienced teenage rebellion or the moment of realization that they were not perfect. Lucy's parents had died when Lucy still thought that they were put on this earth to care for her and to love her, and because they were so good at those things, she would always feel their loss as the singularly worst moment of her life. Although losing her grandparents so many years later, and in exactly the same earth-shattering manner as far as she was concerned, had been a close second.

Lucy's grandparents swept her up in their love when her parents, and their only child, died in that terrible plane crash. Lucy's grandparents had always doted on their son. They used to joke that it had just been good luck that he'd become such a hard worker in spite of his spoiled upbringing. They had welcomed Lucy's mother, whose parents had already passed on when she married their son, as a daughter. After Lucy was born, they traveled to Manhattan every other month to see their granddaughter and attend the opera or Broadway shows. When her parents died, Lucy was her grandparents' only solace.

They had packed her up and taken her to Graceful Bay, South Carolina, where Lucy lived happily until she went off to college at NYU. Four years later, a degree in English Literature under her belt, she deferred graduate school to spend a year traveling around Europe. Her grandparents indulged her because they knew a year would not turn into two. Lucy had her father's work ethic and her mother's fascination with the world.

She had been leaving the Prado in Madrid when her cell phone jingled. An unfamiliar number with a United States country code came up. If she had thought before answering, it would have occurred to her that it was unusual to receive calls from unknown numbers from the States. Even with global technology, the call was expensive. But she didn't think, and so she was completely unprepared when the man on the other end of the phone identified himself as a police detective. He told her that her grandparents had been killed by a man so high on methamphetamine that he thought he was in a cops and robbers video game and her grandparents were simply another obstacle between him and freedom. He'd sideswiped their car and knocked them into a semi-truck. The truck driver was fine. The drug-addict was fine. Her grandparents were dead.

Lucy came home to Graceful Bay immediately. After the funeral she lived with Caroline's family for nearly a year, avoiding the sprawling beach house that was now hers, listlessly taking care of inheritance business. Her grandparents had taken steps to make the process as easy as possible. Their attorneys had instructions on how to advise their only grandchild and hefty retainers for incentive. The firm who handled the estate had been working with her family for years, and, she learned, had handled her parents' estate as well. Of course, back then her grandparents had been named trustees and had taken care of everything. Now, Lucy realized, she was going to have to take care of herself.

She asked questions, read far too much legalese, and after a year had a handle on what she had inherited and where it was. During the next month she realized that all of that toiling over finances and investments and inheritance law had served as a distraction from the absolute devastation she felt. Her friends and the citizens of Graceful Bay, who had become family to her, surrounded her with love and encouragement. Caroline never left her side. But Lucy couldn't live alone in that big old house on the sea.

Everyone said that police academy, and later her hard-earned promotion into vice, had been a way of dealing with the senseless way her grandparents had died. They were right. The man who had taken the last of her family from her had gone to prison for vehicular manslaughter, but Lucy wanted to play an active role in preventing men like him from being on the streets in the first place. It was only years later that she realized no amount of prevention could bring the people she loved back to her. By then, she was embroiled in what would be her last undercover assignment.

Now, sitting in the kitchen of the big house on the sea, now *her home* on the sea, hand perched over a little pad of paper, Lucy suddenly felt ready to once again fill this house with life. *Best place to start is with food*, she thought, and began her list.

By five-thirty that evening, she had finished writing her list, called to have internet and cable installed, and decided that she should give the place a few touches of her own.

LOVE LOST

AFTER LUCY HAD SHOWERED AND towel-dried her long, dark hair, she noticed a new text message on her phone. It was from Caroline and said simply, 'Daniel is joining us for dinner tonight. Hope that's OK.'

She wondered why Caroline hoped it was okay. Lucy had never liked Daniel particularly and the feeling was mutual, but they had also never spent much time together. Plus, she'd tried hard to mask her antipathy in front of Caroline. Maybe her friend wanted to let her know that it wouldn't be a girls-only night. *That's probably it*, she decided, and put it out of her mind.

Once she had scrunched some detangler into her hair, Lucy pulled her industrial strength blow dryer from the vanity drawer in the master bathroom and began drying while she finger combed it. As she did, she looked around the spacious bathroom in wonder and delight. It had been a very long time since she had been surrounded by such comfort. Her grandparents' house was not ostentatious, but it was well appointed with creature comforts and Lucy was ready to indulge a little. While under cover, her apartment in Miami hadn't been much more than a flophouse in a bad neighborhood. She had paid to have a deadbolt installed on the door, but a swift kick would have knocked the frame loose anyway. Fortunately, Lucy was known to all the local criminals as someone not to touch.

Now, here she was, fresh out of a steamy shower, wrapped in an Egyptian cotton bathrobe, her hairbrush resting on a pale marble countertop, a view of the ocean from the large window above the enormous bathtub, and all of it in her peaceful childhood home of Graceful Bay.

She let out a long, happy sigh and finished drying her hair and applying light makeup. Choosing jeans and a silk top with a seersucker blazer, she got her purse and headed out to her "hippie-mobile".

Five minutes later, Lucy pulled into the long, tree-lined driveway of Caroline and Daniel Lamont's antebellum mansion. When she got out of the car, the smell of dogwood and freshly cut grass transported her to a childhood of spring days spent in this precious Southern hamlet. She surveyed the rolling lawns and budding flowerbeds and then the house itself, which put Lucy's sprawling Cape Cod to shame. Not that she would trade it for Caroline's place, but this was old-world Southern architecture. She walked up the stairs, treading gently on her leg, and had no sooner put her hand to the bell than the door flew open and Caroline greeted her warmly.

"Right on time!" said Caroline as she ushered Lucy into the opulent foyer.

Lucy noticed that her friend looked pensive, so when they hugged each other she whispered, "Everything all right?" But before Caroline could respond, Daniel came down the grand staircase with a valise and a briefcase on his arm.

"Lucy. Very nice to see you again," he said without much enthusiasm, kissing Lucy on the cheek and then putting his free arm around Caroline. Even from a few feet away, Lucy could feel the tension between the two of them.

"Good to see you too, Daniel," she replied brightly. She could at least be pleasant for Caroline's sake.

What was it that rubbed her the wrong way about this guy?

Before she could even begin to contemplate the awkward dinner before her, Daniel announced, "Hope it's not too disappointing, ladies, but I got a call and have to go back to Atlanta tonight, so you'll be on your own for dinner."

Caroline looked up at him. "But you just came home last night, Daniel. I thought you didn't have to go back until tomorrow."

"Duty calls," he said and gave his wife a perfunctory kiss on the forehead. "I had to schedule a breakfast meeting with some out-of-town clients and I'd rather drive down tonight and get a good night's sleep than leave at three in the morning. You understand." He turned to Lucy and his mouth curved into a smile. "I should be back by the weekend. Perhaps we can all have dinner then?"

"Of course," she replied politely.

Caroline seemed to notice the cases on Daniel's arm for the first time. "Are you leaving right now? Can't you stay for a drink at least?"

"It's nearly seven already, Caroline. I'll be lucky to get to the apartment by eleven as it is."

Lucy looked away when she saw the expression of frustration on her friend's face.

"I'll call when I get in. Enjoy yourselves, girls." And then, Daniel was gone.

"Let me know when you'll be home," Caroline said as he walked out. Lucy turned back to Caroline, who was still looking at the closed door as if she thought it would open again and her husband would join them for a drink. Without turning, she said, "Well. That was very rude."

Without replying, Lucy put an arm around her friend and said, as cheerfully as she could, "Let's have some bubbly," and she lifted the cold bottle of champagne she had nicked from her grandparents' wine chiller.

"Yes, please! Good God, Lucy, I'm sorry about that. First I didn't think Daniel was coming home at all this weekend, then he surprised me by coming home last night and said that he would be staying until Tuesday, and now he's left again!" She let out a long sigh and looked directly into Lucy's eyes. "My marriage is in bad shape, Lucyfer."

Lucy hugged her. "I'm so sorry, Carolina. Do you want to talk about it?"

"I want a glass of champagne!" she replied and led the way to the den where there was a small, but well-stocked, carved mahogany bar. She took two crystal champagne flutes from a glass shelf while Lucy popped the cork. She poured, they clinked glasses, and Caroline said, "Bottoms up, baby!"

Caroline brought the bottle over to a grouping of club chairs and a deep leather sofa by an unlit fireplace.

"I feel like we should be smoking cigars," joked Lucy.

Caroline's voice was distant when she said, "We certainly can, if you like. Daniel keeps a supply of Cubans in the bar."

For a second, Lucy's mind flashed to smoking cigars with Cuban drug dealers in Miami. She pulled her mind away from those memories and asked, "Caroline, what's going on with you and Daniel?"

With a sigh her friend said, "It's a long story for such a young marriage. I honestly don't want to talk about it right now – I have to think through things a little. Daniel has done some things wrong. I've done some things that I'm not proud of too. Some things that I'm even ashamed of. And I don't feel like confessing my sins tonight." She refilled her empty glass and topped off Lucy's.

"Don't beat yourself up, Caroline. Everyone makes mistakes in marriage." She laughed, "As if I would know. But I've heard that it's true! The main thing is that you recognize your mistakes and work to fix them."

Caroline looked directly into Lucy's eyes. "I wish I could undo mine. And, I'm not convinced that Daniel wants to have anything different. Except, perhaps, that he would prefer that I was a happy princess locked up alone in her castle, instead of a restless, needy wife who has everything yet stills demands her husband's love and attention."

Lucy patted her friend on the knee. "You have never been needy. Wanting affection and attention does not make you desperate. It means you're human and want to be treated with love by the man who pledged to do just that."

"I don't know if I deserve it, Lucy."

"What on earth do you mean? Of course you do, Caroline. What aren't you telling me?"

Caroline looked at Lucy and wanted so badly to tell her everything that had happened in the last year, but she couldn't bring herself to do it right now.

"Tonight, let's talk about you, and the future, and the fact that my best friend has come home at last, and drink champagne and eat spaghetti."

"Spaghetti? When you invited me to dinner, I expected take-out. Have you taken up cooking in my absence?"

With a sheepish grin, Caroline said, "I stopped at Hoffman's Market and got deli food. Spaghettini with veal sausage and red pepper, butter lettuce salad with shaved cucumber and vinaigrette, one frosted chocolate brownie and one luscious Meyer lemon bar. Also frosted."

Lucy laughed, "I should have known! All right, tonight we talk about all things new and exciting, but soon, Caroline, or whenever you're ready, please tell me what's going on. I'll listen and tell you you're wonderful and give you whatever support you need."

Pouring more champagne, Caroline said, "It's a deal. Now, let's start warming our dinner before I get too drunk."

They walked through out of the den, through the formal living room, then across the foyer to the formal dining room, through a butler's pantry and finally into the kitchen.

"Good God, Caroline! I'd forgotten how big this place is."

Caroline smiled. "It does get lonely sometimes. I

don't know what we were thinking when we bought it. We would have to have five kids and a full staff, plus a couple of nannies, to fill it up. I guess I wanted something that felt like my childhood home."

"Well, you got it. This house is nearly as big as your parents' home."

"But my parents had three kids, a cook, a live-in housekeeper, a nanny, and my mother's parents living with them. I can practically hear my footsteps echoing here." She looked wistful.

"Let's eat at the kitchen table, Caroline. Our voices won't echo in here."

Lucy set the table with white plates, polished silverware and linen napkins while Caroline scooped the spaghetti into a pot to heat. She transferred the salad from its paper container to a glass bowl and set it on the kitchen table. Stirring the pasta, Caroline sipped the last of her champagne.

"Would you like some wine with dinner, Lucy?"

"I'd better not. I have to drive home later. But you go ahead."

"Honestly, I think I'm responsible for drinking most of that bottle and I'm a little tipsy! Just ice water."

Lucy got glasses of water and ice and brought them to the table while Caroline served hot spaghetti and sausages onto their plates.

"Now, onto more pleasant topics. Have you met your new neighbor, Lucy?"

"Maybe," said Lucy.

"You did! You're blushing! Isn't he a doll?"

"I am not blushing." But Lucy could feel the heat in her cheeks. She briefly recounted her encounter with Gabriel Black, leaving out her own nervous flirtation, and his easy flirtation, for that matter.

"Well, what's he like?" asked Caroline.

Lucy finished chewing a hunk of fresh bread before shrugging. "I hardly know! We only talked a minute or two. He knew about the Miami fiasco the minute I told him I'd been a cop there. He has a source in Miami, he said. He'd probably read the articles too but he didn't ask me anything about it. Not even about my injuries."

"You're almost smiling. Is that a good thing?" asked Caroline.

Lucy realized she was smiling a little. "Actually, it was kind of nice. He told me he'd been an MP and knew a little about undercover work. I didn't have to explain anything or assure him I was fine. But, it was more than that. It was as if he really cared."

Caroline jumped on that, "Of course he cares! He's interested in you." Lucy rolled her eyes. "So, he confirmed the MP rumor!" She looked triumphant. "What did he tell you about himself?"

"He has a security firm in New York and he has a cat named Baxter."

Caroline's eyes grew wide as plates. "And? Is that all? Is he divorced? Where is his family? Does he have kids?" When Lucy shrugged, she said impatiently, "Lucy, I know that you weren't born in Graceful Bay, but you were raised here! We ask questions so that we can gossip. My word, girl, you have gravely disappointed me."

"We just shot the breeze for a few minutes, Caroline. You are going to have to wait until the O'Connor sisters get to him."

In fact, Lucy had been very careful about what she asked Gabriel Black. She was anxious not to reveal that she already knew who he was and what he did for a living and that he was single. She didn't want to reveal that the whole town was talking about him. Talking to *Lucy* about him. And, she certainly wasn't going to start nosing around his relationship status. It would only be a matter of time before that was public knowledge anyway. She wouldn't have to ask him directly.

"At least tell me that you think he's as gorgeous as everyone else does!"

"Oh, yes!" Lucy finally let out the breathless giggle she had been suppressing. "I was afraid that if I accepted his offer of a beer, I might just loosen up and start gaping at him."

"He offered you a drink?" Caroline was incredulous. "You didn't mention that!"

"Only because he was having one. You are such a gossip, Caroline," Lucy chided her friend.

"I am only a gossip when it comes to my best friend and a handsome stranger." This was not strictly true, but Lucy let it go.

They ate and chatted about town gossip. Lorelei Davis had had a torrid affair with a college student while he was working at one of the nearby resorts during his summer break. Old Roger Wells had died and left his estate to his pit bull, Tiger Lily. His estranged children were contesting the will. The Bradleys' son, Marcus, was caught dealing drugs at his boarding school in Massachusetts and they had had to donate an entire library wing in order to clean up the mess and protect their son from expulsion.

"So, back to the most exciting thing to happen of late: are you going to go on a date with Mr. Black?"

Lucy rolled her eyes with exaggerated impatience. "I am not looking for a date, Caroline. Besides, I can't date my neighbor. What would happen if something went wrong? Every walk I took down the beach would be awkward. Plus, in this tiny town, where everybody knows who Lorelei Davis slept with last summer, even a single date would be big news, and if there wasn't a second date, that would be big news too!"

Caroline regarded her friend for a moment before observing, "So now you can't date Gabriel because of the gossip, but earlier it was because you didn't think anyone would date an injured former undercover cop. What do you reckon is the real reason?"

"Caroline! I'm not ready. I want to settle into my house and buy a new chair for the living room and fill my pantry and figure out what to do next with my life. A man, my *neighbor*, would complicate things. And who knows if he's even interested."

She knew that last sentence had been a mistake even before Caroline jumped on it. "If you're concerned about whether he's interested, then you must be interested yourself! And of course he's interested! You're beautiful and strong and smart. Now tell me the truth, Lucy, didn't he flirt at all?"

She blushed again and cursed herself for it. "A little. Okay? He flirted a little, I was totally awkward and he backed off like a gentleman." Caroline looked mortified, but Lucy went on before she could speak, "Then he figured out that I was the cop who'd been stabbed in Miami and there wasn't much to flirt about anyway. But before I left I threw him a little somethin' to seem nice, and I left it in a friendly, neighborly way that will never result in a date." Caroline raised her eyebrows. "He did offer the services of Baxter, the cat, as a companion until I get one of my own."

"It would have been a lot easier if you had told me all that in the first place, Lucyfer," said Caroline with a smile. "I want you to know that nothing in your past has put a limit on your life now. You can have happiness and love and even a cat!" Her eyes misted over a little.

"So can you, Carolina," Lucy said softly.

Later, at home, Lucy felt a profound sadness for her friend. Her marital problems were serious, but there seemed to be more to Caroline's troubles than she had let on. Lucy knew her, and she knew that sometimes it took time for Caroline to let everything out, and she was certain that there was more.

As she washed up for bed, Lucy's thoughts flickered back to Gabriel Black, his muscular arms and shoulders, his strong hands, and the warmth and mirth in his sparkling brown eyes... and then she remembered the oddly knowing look when he realized who she was. She decided to put him out of her mind. *Don't forget that he is your neighbor*, she chided herself as she undressed and stepped into the shower. *Even if I were fit for a fling, he would be the worst possible choice! Absolutely not an option!* With that, Lucy turned her mind, with limited success, to her to-do list for the next day.

BROKEN EGGS

THE NEXT MORNING, LUCY WOKE up feeling great. Her leg was a little stiff, but while she waited for her coffee to brew she did some stretches that her physical therapist in Miami had recommended.

Amazing what a day of South Carolina sea air can do for a girl. I guess the mid-Atlantic Ocean is my fountain of youth!

Lucy threw on a pair of well-fitting jeans and a dark green cashmere sweater, poured some coffee into a mug that said 'World's Best Grandma' and walked out to her car where she carefully balanced the coffee cup on the floor of the passenger side. *This might not be such a good idea*, she thought, but as she pulled out of the drive and onto the road, but the cup didn't tip over.

Fifteen minutes later she was parked at the local Piggly Wiggly, gulping down the lukewarm brew and searching for her grocery list in the overflowing black leather tote she called a purse.

The grocery store was not very busy on a Tuesday morning and Lucy took her time going through the aisles and adding things to her cart. It had been a long time since she'd had a real kitchen, and the time to cook in it. She decided on a pan-seared salmon filet, new potatoes, and a little salad for dinner. She was looking for Green Goddess salad dressing when she felt a pair of eyes on her. Turning, she broke into a grin in spite of herself when she saw Gabriel Black leaning on his cart near the croutons.

"Fancy meeting you here, neighbor," he drawled before looking into her shopping cart. He assessed its contents and said, "Restocking the pantry?"

"All I have is a half-pint of Ben and Jerry's, a block of cheddar and some coffee," Lucy replied easily, surprised at how pleased she was to see him.

"At least you have coffee. The first two mornings after I arrived, I woke up, went to start the pot and realized I'd forgotten to pick some up. The first day I wound up at a bakery in town and before I could even take a sip was halfway through a conversation with a couple of very charming, very nosy, sisters."

"The O'Connor sisters! You must have been at LaValle's. They wander in and out of that café all day, every day, and they love a handsome new face."

"Handsome, huh?"

"Well, that's how they described you. I think your arrival in town trumped my home-coming on the gossip mill."

"Far be it from me to steal your thunder." He gave her a self-deprecating grin.

"I give it freely. Now, let's see what's in your basket, Gabriel. Eggs, milk, spinach... some ham and you could make a great omelet."

"I only break out the omelet pan when I have company." He winked at her and Lucy thought she would melt.

Despite the warm tingling spreading all over her body from just being near him, Lucy hesitated,

"Gabriel, we're neighbors. We can't date." Suddenly she was flooded with uncertainty. He hadn't asked her on a date. Had he? Her cheeks were burning as she went on, "I know that you didn't actually ask me on a date, but...."

His smile softened as he interrupted her, "I was absolutely asking you on a date, Lucy, but let me make it totally clear: I would like to invite you to have a romantic dinner with me, either at my house or in a restaurant. I know that we're neighbors, and that could be awkward if it doesn't work out, but when you think about it, Graceful Bay is a small town and everyone in it is your neighbor in one way or another. Besides, I've only got the house until the spring. You would only be uncomfortable for a couple of months before you could feel free to chase me out of town with a pitchfork and a torch."

Lucy laughed. "I don't know, Gabriel, the O'Connor sisters already have you buying the house and living here forever." She rested her elbows on the handles of her shopping cart and looked up at him through a thick fringe of lashes. It was Gabriel's turn to melt. "But if you say it's only temporary, then that changes things, doesn't it?"

He reached over and gently brushed a lock of glossy hair over her shoulder. He managed to do it without touching her skin at all, but Lucy felt the gesture like a soft caress over her entire body. "My omelet has nothing on the sea bass at the St. George Hotel."

Lucy's eyes lit up at the suggestion. "Few things can top the restaurant in the St. George Hotel." She smiled coquettishly. "Are you trying to impress me, Mr. Black?"

"I am trying to avoid cooking for you until I know you like me."

Lucy laughed out loud. "Well, you've done both."

They walked companionably through the store, commenting on each other's purchases as they finished their shopping. While Gabriel hefted her bags into the back of her old Volvo, he arranged to pick Lucy up at seven for the short drive down the coast to the old hotel. They could have a drink in the bar before dinner at eight.

Lucy was halfway home when she realized that she was really excited.

It took three trips to carry all of her groceries inside, and her phone rang as she was putting the last of the dry goods into the pantry. Before she had even glanced at the caller ID on her mobile phone, the doorbell rang. With a box of baking soda in one hand, she answered the telephone and headed for the front door.

"Lucy! Something terrible has happened," Caroline nearly shouted into the phone just as Lucy opened the door onto a sheriff's deputy.

The coincidence of her friend's terrified phone call and the uniformed man on the doorstep made Lucy nervous. But if there was something to it, Lucy wasn't going to give anything away. She put a surprised smile on her face, a little drawl into her tone, and said into the phone, "Goodness gracious,

I just found a policeman on my doorstep. I'll have to call you back in a little bit."

Before she hung up, Caroline said, "Please don't mention my call, Lucy. Get back to me as soon as he leaves!"

"One little second, officer." Lucy made sure the call was disconnected before turning back to the deputy with a big smile. "Now, what can I do for you?"

He took his hat off and nodded at Lucy. "May I come in for a moment, ma'am?"

"Where are my manners? Of course! Please come in."

She ushered the young deputy into the foyer and sized him up as she closed the door behind him. He was probably in his mid-twenties, tall and lithe and a little uncertain. Lucy had no idea what was going on but she figured that if the sheriff's department thought she had anything to do with it, they would have sent someone with a little more experience to ask the questions.

As she led him into the kitchen she introduced herself. "Lucy Walker."

"Deputy John Lee Harper," he responded.

In the kitchen Lucy gestured to a stool at the breakfast bar and started a pot of coffee. She said, "I hope you're not here to tell me there's a fugitive on the loose, Deputy Harper."

"Well, not exactly Miz Walker. You see, there's been a murder just down the beach a pace and the sheriff sent me to ask you and your neighbors if you may have seen anything suspicious early this morning."

The shock on Lucy's face was genuine. "A murder?"

A murder couldn't possibly have anything to do with whatever had Caroline in a panic, thought Lucy, but the timing still made her uncomfortable.

Deputy Harper heard the surprise in Lucy's voice and mistook it for fear. "Now, there's no reason to think that you're in any danger, Miz Walker. I didn't mean to panic you..."

"Have you caught the killer?"

"Well, no, ma'am, but the man who was murdered doesn't seem to be local and Sheriff Grier said it looked personal, so we don't think there's a mass murderer..."

"A mass murderer!" A cop should never start mentioning serial killers or mass murderers when interviewing a witness lest they start making assumptions. Lucy was taking advantage of the deputy's inexperience to buy herself time to think.

"*Not* a mass murderer! Please don't worry, Miz Walker." The young deputy was a little flustered.

"Who is this poor man?"

"We haven't identified him, per se, but the sheriff said Sandy LaValle Senior from the restaurant doesn't know him, and if Sandy doesn't know him then he must not live in Graceful Bay."

Lucy thought that was probably true. Sheriff Grier must know Sandy well if he'd showed him a morgue photo, and it had to be a morgue photo because if the victim had had any ID on him, then the sheriff's department wouldn't be trying to identify him in the first place.

The coffee pot gurgled and spat a little, indicating

it was done brewing. Lucy noticed Deputy Harper's eyes move hopefully to the countertop, though whether it was desire for a beverage or hope for a little break in the conversation, she didn't know. Making him wait, she asked, "You found him on the beach?"

"Yes, ma'am, up by the Seaside Resort Hotel."

"That's barely a mile north of here! I walked past that hotel yesterday afternoon! Deputy, you are not convincing me that this man is not a crazy murderer on the loose, killing tourists and anyone else who gets in his way."

"No, Miz Walker, Sheriff Grier said it looked personal, like the perpetrator was real mad at this guy." John Lee Harper ran his hand through his curly brown hair and looked at Lucy imploringly.

"Goodness! Would you like some coffee, Deputy Harper?" When he nodded, she asked, "Cream and sugar?"

"Little of both, please."

Lucy removed two china cups from the cupboard and took a moment to fill the porcelain sugar bowl and creamer. Even in the face of death, Lucy couldn't ignore a little ceremony in her grandmother's house. Besides, it gave her a minute to collect her thoughts. Could Caroline possibly have something to do with a murder? Could it be that the two things were unrelated? Caroline hadn't sounded surprised when Lucy said there was a deputy at her door. But even if her friend knew the victim, he hadn't even been identified yet, so why would the Sheriff's department have even told Caroline that someone had been killed. Lucy's thoughts went to Daniel

Lamont and her stomach turned. Could Caroline's husband have something to do with this?

Lucy realized that the questions spinning around in her head simply couldn't be answered while she was filling a sugar bowl. She would have to be patient and get as much information as she could from Deputy Harper before he realized he wasn't dealing with a scared Southern belle, but a former cop who might be trying to gather more information than she was giving.

"Miz Walker, did you notice anything unusual early this morning? Hear anything? See anything?"

"What time are you talking about, Deputy?"

"It would have been early. Near dawn, is our guess."

"Five-thirty, six o'clock? I'm afraid I don't rise that early, and nothing woke me. But you said it happened a mile from here. What would I have heard? Was he shot?"

"No, ma'am. No. We're just covering all the bases."

"Didn't you find anything that could tell you who he is? Can't you take his fingerprints or something?"

Lucy was not treading cautiously. As soon as the Deputy found out that she had been a cop, he would know that she already knew you could take fingerprints from a dead body, and that might make the sheriff's department take a closer look at her, and then at Caroline. Playing dumb could backfire, but the cop and the friend in her wanted to get as much information as possible while she still could.

"We'll find out who he is, Miz Walker, and then we'll find out who killed him." He finished his coffee.

"In the meantime, if you think of anything that might be helpful, do let us know." Deputy Harper set a business card down on the breakfast bar and stood to leave.

As Lucy walked him to the door, she realized that her thoughts were only of Caroline, and not of the poor man who'd been murdered.

As soon as Deputy John Lee Harper had driven away, Lucy grabbed her cell phone and called Caroline.

"Lucy! What happened?"

"What do you mean 'what happened?' A deputy from the sheriff's department came asking if I had heard anything unusual around sun-up this morning because they found a man murdered down the beach from my house, and you are making me think that you know something about it! You tell me what happened, Caroline!"

"Oh, Lucy, it's terrible! When I called earlier, Sheriff Grier had just left my house. They found a scrap of paper with our home address written on the back in that man's pocket..."

"In his pocket?"

"Yes, his pocket! Mathew Wilson's pocket." Caroline began to wail. "It was Mathew! The sheriff showed me a picture."

Lucy was worried for her friend but this was no time to be gentle. "Caroline, who the hell is Mathew Wilson?"

In a voice barely above a whisper, Caroline said, "Last year I had an affair with Mathew Wilson. And now he's dead."

THE BOYFRIEND

WHEN HE FOUND OUT ABOUT Mathew Wilson, Daniel Lamont had spent ten full days and nights away from his wife. He always had someone watching over Caroline when she was away from Graceful Bay, and one day one of the watchers cautiously approached him and began to outline the time Caroline was spending in Charleston with a young student. When the man said that he was not absolutely certain that the nature of her relationship with the young man was romantic, Daniel had stood, taken a heavy crystal paperweight from his enormous oak desk and hurled it at the opposite wall. It shattered a picture frame, but Daniel didn't seem to notice.

Then he'd leaned across his desk, placing his fists on the ink blotter, and said through clenched teeth, "She's fucking him, not tutoring him in Math. Figure out who he is, where he's from. Go."

A few days later when he found out that Mathew Wilson was a law student with no money and a poor family, that Caroline wasn't giving him anything but companionship and sex, and vice versa, and that the two of them genuinely liked each other, he was even more furious. He flew from Atlanta to Mexico, and while he was there he talked to Rinaldo Santana about murdering Mathew Wilson.

"He's tall and young and looks strong, but he's not a fighter."

Santana replied that fighting didn't help against a bullet in the head.

"Beat him to death. Hands on, Santana. I want this kid to suffer. I want his family to bury him in a closed casket. Do it in Graceful Bay. Leave Caroline's address in his pocket. I want the cops to go straight to my wife. I want them to show her the crime scene photos, trying to ID him. I want her to see what she did."

Santana was a little taken aback. "Señor Lamont, it takes not just strength, but also great rage and determination to beat a healthy man to death. And it takes time."

"Get a couple of men, kidnap him, bring him to the beach, tie him up, and use a bat and brass knuckles. I don't care. Beat him so he has a while to think about what he did and so that my wife will have to face the consequences of being unfaithful to me."

Santana shrugged, "As you wish. When?"

"Couple of weeks. I have to think through a few details. In the meantime check him out." Daniel handed over an envelope containing Wilson's name, address, schedule, and a few eight by ten photos. A separate envelope contained twenty-five thousand US dollars in hundred-dollar bills. "Half now, half later."

Santana thumbed through the stack of bills. "For fifty thousand dollars you will get what you want, Señor."

When he returned to Atlanta he gave himself a

few days to think about the details. One of Caroline's watchers had called to update him and given him something else to consider. A woman, new to the team of followers, had sat next to Caroline and Mathew at their regular café and had overheard Caroline ending the relationship. She felt terrible, Caroline had said, about betraying her marriage and engaging Mathew in a relationship that would never go anywhere. *Bitch.*

It never occurred to Daniel to let the kid off the hook, or try and mend his relationship with Caroline. The marriage was over; the kid was as good as dead.

His concern was that if they were no longer in contact, and he would have to see if that really was the case, and Wilson died in Charleston, Caroline might not find out about it right away. A violent murder in a big city could easily be trumped quickly by other news. On the other hand, a murder in a sleepy town like Graceful Bay would be a big story, and town gossip would long outlive the murder's regional newsworthiness. Caroline would never stop hearing about her lover's gruesome death.

Still, Daniel didn't really want her to be considered a suspect. That would be embarrassing. He wanted Wilson identified quickly and blasted over the news. He wanted Caroline to find out about it immediately. And then Daniel Lamont wanted his dearly beloved to look into his eyes and know that she had fucked with the wrong man.

Next, he would figure out how to get rid of Caroline.

EX-COP TO EX-COP

F IVE MINUTES LATER, LUCY WAS off the phone with Caroline, and, despite the knot of anxiety in her stomach, gulping down another cup of coffee. What the hell was going on? She'd had absolutely no idea that her best friend in the world had ever had problems in her marriage until yesterday, let alone an affair! Then again, how would she have known? Two years ago, she had begun undercover work, pretending to be the ambitious girlfriend of an ambitious Cuban drug dealer who was also an undercover cop. She had been completely unavailable to her friend.

"What a mess!" she said to the ceiling fan.

Caroline had begged her to head straight over and that she would explain more in person, but as Lucy gathered her keys, purse and sweater, her mobile phone began to ring. She finally dug it out of the bottom of her substantial purse on the fourth ring and answered without looking at the caller ID.

"Hello?" she said a little breathily.

"Are you okay?" It was Gabriel.

It was the first time she'd heard his voice over the telephone and, despite her agitation, Lucy felt a little quiver of pleasure run up her spine. "Yes, I'm fine. I just had a troubling visit from the sheriff's department."

"So did I, that's why I'm calling."

It made sense that the sheriff's department would have talked to Gabriel since they were canvassing the whole beach and he actually lived closer to where the murder took place than Lucy did.

"Were you able to help them at all?" she asked, knowing that if he had any information she would use it to help Caroline, and feeling oddly uneasy about not confiding in him before she started asking questions.

"No, they think it happened early this morning and I was sound asleep."

"Did the deputy tell you anything?" *Why beat around the bush*, thought Lucy. Besides, it was natural to be curious when someone was murdered within spitting distance of your house.

"Sheriff Grier, actually. Tom and I go way back, so he stopped by personally." Lucy's pulse quickened at the revelation. "He told me that the victim was a white male, mid-twenties, beaten to a pulp and manually strangled, probably where he was found."

Lucy's breath caught. She wasn't expecting so much information. "Gracious," she half-whispered. "Do they know who he is or who killed him?"

"No wallet, but he had the address and phone number of a Graceful Bay resident on a scrap of paper in his pocket. The Lamonts. Any idea who they are?"

"I think I know everyone in town," Lucy replied evasively.

"Well, ex-cop to ex-cop, keep the intel quiet, okay? I don't know if Grier's been over there yet and we wouldn't want the Lamonts' neighbors asking them where they were between the hours of three and six a.m. before the sheriff gets to them."

There was no way Lucy could keep the details from her best friend and she was becoming really uncomfortable hiding the truth from Gabriel – not only because she was genuinely interested in him, but because 'ex-cop to ex-cop' meant trust. "Yeah, well, Caroline Lamont is my best friend in the world."

There was a long pause before he said levelly, "So the chances are slim that you'll keep this to yourself?"

"Closer to none, I'm afraid."

"Fair enough. I certainly opened my mouth without hesitation."

"Don't feel too bad. The only detail I didn't have was how he was killed."

"I bet you even know his name." Gabriel said this in a gravelly tone that made Lucy wish she was sitting in his lap.

"Are you trying to charm information out of me? I'll have you know, Gabriel Black, that I have been trained to stand firm against that particular tactic."

Gabriel laughed and said, "No matter. I'm sure Mrs. Lamont will share his name with the sheriff when he asks."

I hope she had the sense, thought Lucy, knowing that the sheriff had already been to see Caroline."

Even though she could understand the temptation to hope this whole mess was a terrible coincidence, there was no way Caroline was going to get away with lying about knowing the dead man. Not for long, anyway. Lucy had to get over there and convince her best friend to come clean with the sheriff before Caroline got herself in serious trouble. She still couldn't believe her friend had anything to do with the death, but she also couldn't believe that Caroline's lover happened to be brutally murdered in their sleepy town with her home address in his pocket and it was just bad luck.

"Look, Gabriel, about dinner tonight..."

"Rain check? I figured. Plus you should probably run over to Caroline's house and urge her to call Sheriff Grier if she *remembers* anything that might be helpful to his investigation. You know, like the name of the victim."

What a smartass, thought Lucy. "I might do."

"Call me if you girls need anything, Miss Walker. I might be able to help sort this out."

"Thank you, Mr. Black, but I fear we have a conflict of interest."

"The truth is my only interest. But, fair enough." They were both smiling into their respective cell phones when Gabriel said, "I can't wait to get to know you, Lucy Walker."

When they got off the phone, Lucy did a little dance around her kitchen before she remembered her friend's predicament and reality set in. Until she talked to Caroline and Daniel and got a handle on the situation, she had to watch her tongue around Gabriel. As a friend to the sheriff and an ex-cop, he would feel loyal to Tom Grier, and Lucy couldn't trust him with her friend's best interests.

On her way to Caroline's house, Lucy looped past the Seaside Resort where the man's body had been found. There were two highway patrol cars in the parking lot, but she couldn't see down to the beach where the body had been discovered and so didn't know whether it was still cordoned off as a crime scene. She thought maybe tomorrow she would go down and check it out. Little did she know that by the next day, the murder of Mathew Wilson would no longer be her primary concern.

INDISCRETION

L UCY PARKED ON THE STREET and crossed the hedge of hawthorn that opened to the long cobblestone path leading to Caroline's house. She breathed in the smell of spring. The foliage seemed alive with baby birds and bees fluttering and buzzing around the new blossoms and bright green leaves. Caroline and Daniel's antebellum home rose naturally and cheerfully out of the middle of the big yard that surrounded it, and the only indication that something was amiss was that all of the curtains were closed to the sunlight.

As soon as she stepped onto the porch the front door flew open, startling Lucy for a second before her instincts registered Caroline standing in the threshold looking pensive and disheveled.

"Lucy! I am so glad you're here!" Caroline wrapped her arms tightly around her friend. "Come in, come in. What a terrible day!"

"How are you holding up?" Lucy asked and took a good look at her friend. She looked tired and worried, but not panicked.

"I'm scared, Lucy. I'm really scared."

They walked through the darkened front rooms into the breakfast area off of the kitchen. The bay window overlooking the back garden wasn't curtained and the afternoon light flooding in made Lucy feel better immediately.

"I'm making tea," said Caroline. "Is there anything else I can get you?"

"Tea would be great, Caroline, but why don't you sit down and let me get it ready for us."

Caroline complied without a word of protest, which said more about her level of distress than the circles under her eyes. Normally, Caroline would never sit down until her guest had been fed and watered. She was a perfect Southern hostess.

While Lucy gathered the tea things and boiled water, Caroline began a rambling apology. "I am so sorry that I didn't tell you about this sooner, Lucy. It all began and ended so quickly and you were so far away and then in the hospital and I wanted to spill my guts the second you got home but I knew you needed to get settled and then lunch didn't seem like the right time and then of course dinner with Daniel was out of the question," Caroline stuttered a little when she said her husband's name. "And honestly, I didn't want you to think badly of me, and maybe I didn't want to think badly of myself either. I had never said it out loud before. That I had an affair, I mean. Today, on the phone with you, was the first time I admitted that that was what I'd done, and it made it seem very real all of a sudden..."

Lucy sat down by Caroline and put her arms around her. "You don't have to apologize for anything, Caroline! I have been feeling like a terrible friend all day for not being there for you! It's me who should be apologizing."

Caroline rested her head on Lucy's shoulder

and gave a rueful laugh. "I am so glad you're here, Lucille Walker."

"Me too." The kettle began to hiss and Lucy stood to turn it off before the piercing whistle began. "Why don't you begin at the beginning, Caroline? Who is Mathew Wilson?"

With a big grateful sigh, Caroline started her story.

About six months ago, Caroline had met Mathew in a café in Charleston. At the time Daniel was spending a lot of time in Atlanta. Normally she traveled with him, but these days he was so busy that they never spent any time together anyway, and she felt happier in her hometown or in the apartment they kept in Charleston. One day, Caroline drove to Charleston first thing in the morning to do a little shopping. She was meeting friends for dinner in the city that evening and decided to buy herself a new dress for the occasion. She stopped with her shopping bag at a café and ordered a salad for lunch when she noticed Mathew gazing at her from another table. He was younger, mid-twenties, and very handsome. Flattered by the attention, Caroline smiled at him. He said plainly, "You are the most beautiful woman I have ever seen." Before she knew what she was doing, Caroline assented when he asked to join her.

Her Niçoise salad arrived, along with a rare lunchtime glass of chilled white wine. Mathew ordered another cappuccino and they chatted for over an hour. Mathew was a charming law student with a curiosity and naiveté that Caroline found delightful. When he finally asked the question –

surely he had seen her wedding ring – "Are you married?" Caroline was forced to remember that she was, indeed, married. Happily, for a while, until sometime last year when Daniel had stopped paying attention to her, though she kept that to herself.

It wasn't that Daniel didn't dote on her as he always had, or tell her that he loved her, or ask about her days, it was more that it all seemed perfunctory. They didn't have wild disputes about the merits of the latest Hollywood action film, or the new politician on the scene. They didn't cook dinner together or go for walks before bed or feed each other ice cream. She felt like a trophy on a pedestal when they went to parties or work functions instead of a lover and ally and friend on his arm.

In short, Caroline was terribly lonely for her husband and also for simple male attention, and here was this utterly enchanting young man looking at her as though she was a goddess in the center of his universe.

"I was flattered, Lucy. And lonely. And I didn't let myself think about the consequences."

She told him she was married, but he had asked her to please join him at the same café at the same time the next day before she headed back to Graceful Bay, and Caroline had thought, *What's the harm in that?*

At dinner with her Charleston friends that evening everyone had remarked that she was positively glowing and she had blamed her radiance on the new peacock blue silk dress she'd purchased for the occasion. However, she knew it was because that afternoon, for the first time in too long, she had felt utterly beautiful and captivating.

"I swear, Lucy, I almost didn't go the next day, but after breakfast I packed up my purchases and wrote a few emails and before I knew it, I looked at the clock and realized that it was already quarter to one and Mathew would be waiting for me in a few minutes. I could either get in my car and drive home to Graceful Bay or I could go to lunch with that enchanting young man. It seemed like such an inconsequential choice and I really only had a few minutes to decide... and I went to lunch. I didn't even think about what would come next, Lucy, I really didn't."

Caroline had a faraway look in her eyes, and Lucy wasn't sure it held any regret.

"Caroline, you have to tell Sheriff Grier that you knew him." Her friend dropped her head into her hands and let out a long breath. "He's going to find out and it will look really bad that you weren't forthcoming. If you tell him now he may be able to rule you out and take another direction in his investigation without Daniel finding out about your relationship. But if he has to keep digging to uncover Mathew's identity, and your address and phone number in his pocket are the only clues, then Tom Grier is not going to stop looking at you until he gets some answers. One way or another."

"I know, I know you're right, Lucy."

"Where is Daniel?"

"He's still in Atlanta. I don't know exactly when he'll be home, but he said by the weekend."

"Then call the sheriff right now. Maybe he can

interview you while Daniel is away and you can get some of this sorted out."

Caroline nodded in agreement and finally crumpled down in tears and Lucy held her tight while her best friend in the world sobbed and shook.

Lucy was still disgusted with herself. She had trusted that Caroline's marriage was as picture perfect as she suggested whenever they had a rare telephone conversation. Thinking back, Caroline had never really said everything was going well, and Lucy had never asked. The few times she'd seen the couple together had been at times of celebration: their wedding, a couple of Christmases Lucy had spent with Caroline's family since her grandparents died, the Fourth of July a few years ago when Lucy had come home to celebrate the day with the whole town. The dinner last night would have been the first time she had ever spent any time alone with the couple, but Daniel had left. She had always assumed that Caroline would tell her if anything was wrong, but she'd never really given her friend the chance; she was always wrapped up in her all-consuming job and her grief and her fear of coming back to the empty house where her only family had once lived.

"Caroline, I am so sorry. No matter what, everything will work out and I won't leave your side until you kick me out the door."

Caroline chuckled through her tears and raised her head out of her hands.

"You look awful, Caroline." That elicited an actual giggle. "Why don't you wash up and I'll call Sheriff Grier?"

"All right. May as well bite the bullet, right?"

"Right."

Caroline stood slowly and headed for the narrow kitchen stairwell, a design detail common to these big old homes and once reserved for the help to move unseen from floor to floor. She turned back and said, "I may have to master the art of graceful tears in order to get through this." She gave a wry smile, but Lucy knew that her friend was rallying. Caroline was tough as they come.

After considering for a moment, Lucy called Gabriel. When he answered, she said, "Do you think you could round up the sheriff and head over to Caroline's house?"

"Is life with you always going to be filled with abrupt requests to bring in the law?"

Lucy stuttered, "Life with me? I..."

Gabriel laughed and said, "I don't mind darling, I just want to prepare myself."

Now that she had had a chance to catch her breath, Lucy replied coyly, "Don't be presumptuous, Buttercup, we'll start with dinner."

Now it was Gabriel's turn to stutter. "B-*buttercup*?"

"Is that a yes? Time is of the essence, you know."

"Is Mrs. Lamont going to change her mind?"

"No, she doesn't know when her husband might come home from Atlanta, and you can appreciate that it would be more difficult for her to be forthcoming if he is here."

"I see. Let me call you back in a couple of minutes."

A few minutes later, Caroline reemerged from the

stairwell looking less disheveled, but unquestionably like a woman who had been crying.

"I did my best."

"Much better, Carolina!"

"Have you talked to Sheriff Grier?"

"Actually, I called Gabriel Black. He and the sheriff are friends and I think he might be able to smooth things over a bit."

"Do you think Grier is going to come at me with both barrels for lying to him earlier?"

"I don't know him. Maybe." When Caroline groaned, she went on, "But Gabriel can probably mollify him. Plus, between the situation with your husband and the shock of hearing Mathew was murdered, I think Grier will understand why you were less than truthful, even if he pretends not to. Besides, you couldn't have killed him yourself. He could tell that just by looking at you."

Caroline blinked at her for a few seconds before asking, "What does that mean, Lucy?"

"Didn't the sheriff show you a picture of him this morning?"

"Yes. One. It looked like he'd been in a fistfight, but the photo was kind of blurry and didn't show much. I told him I didn't know the man." She looked horrified.

Lucy considered for a moment before deciding it was best that her friend learn the circumstances of her former lover's death from her and not when Sheriff Grier tossed a stack of death photos on her coffee table. Putting a hand on Caroline's arm, she said simply, "Mathew was beaten to death, Caroline. You are not strong enough to have done it. Plus, you don't have a mark on you, and there is no way that whoever killed him emerged unscathed."

Caroline paled and gaped for a moment before running to the downstairs powder room to vomit.

Lucy took a heavy glass from the cupboard and filled it with cold water. She went to the washroom and waited outside the half open door until the sound of retching had stopped. Pushing the door gently she stuck her head in and met Caroline's gaze in the mirror over the sink.

"Oh my God, Lucy. What have I done?"

Lucy left her in the powder room with a pat on the shoulder and a few minutes later, Caroline emerged, offered a weak smile, accepted the water glass and announced she was going upstairs to put herself together again.

"Is there anything I can do, Caroline?"

"Start some coffee for our guests. I wouldn't want them to think me inhospitable," she added with a grimace.

Just as the coffee started to drip in the kitchen, and Lucy had found and filled the sugar bowl and creamer, the doorbell rang. In a surprisingly strong voice, Caroline called out from somewhere in the front of the house that she would get the door and a minute later Gabriel Black, Tom Grier and Caroline entered the kitchen through the dining room.

COMING CLEAN

L UCY KEPT HER EYES ON the sheriff so that no one would notice the little thrill she got at the mere sight of Gabriel. The lawman didn't waste any time. He boomed, "Lucille Walker, I presume? I heard all about how you hoodwinked my young deputy."

Lucy held his gaze and replied, "I merely asked what any other citizen would when told there was a murder practically in her backyard."

"Except you are not just any ordinary citizen."

"I'm wearing my civvies these days, sir."

The sheriff harrumphed and his eyes twinkled in lieu of a smile. He stretched out one powerful arm, "Sheriff Thomas Grier. You can call me Sheriff."

They shook hands and Caroline offered everyone coffee. When they each had a mug, the four of them sat down at the ancient kitchen table. Even seated, Grier was an imposing man. Lucy thought he was probably six-three or four with broad shoulders and plenty of muscle. He was in his late fifties with a handsome, ruddy face, thick gunmetal hair and blue eyes beneath heavy brows. He kept his chair about a foot back from the table to make room for his long legs and leaned back, regarding Caroline with an unforgiving stare.

"You lied to me once, Mrs. Lamont. You'd damn well better tell me the truth now."

Caroline had known she was in trouble, but she was not used to being spoken to so gruffly. Still, the Southern belle in her came out only in the set of her jaw. She knew when to hold her tongue. "Nothing but, Sheriff Grier."

The big man looked at her for a few seconds before nodding. Evidently he had decided she was being sincere. He took a small stack of photos out of his back pocket and slapped one down on the table in front of Caroline. This one was of a man's face. It was the same photo he had shown her this morning. She slid the picture closer to her without picking it up. Silent tears began rolling down her cheeks. Before she could catch her breath, he placed another photo on the table and then another, until the horror of Mathew's last moments on earth was clear. Most of the damage had been to his torso. His entire chest, back and abdomen were purple and swollen. Some of his ribs were poking out through his skin. She picked up the last picture. It was of a slightly bruised and unnaturally pale left hand with a braided gold ring on the middle finger.

Caroline began weeping openly and turned away. Lucy put her arm around her friend and looked at the photos. The man had been beaten, but the shape and features of his face were recognizable. The bone structure of his face was intact, though his lips were split and one eye was swollen shut and blackened. She guessed that the injuries to his face and body had been made over the course of hours before he died because the swelling and bruising had had time to develop. His torso showed the most damage from the beating, but the young man's horribly bruised neck indicated that he'd probably died of strangulation. He'd been through hell first.

"Who is he, Mrs. Lamont?"

Caroline blew out a long breath and again looked down at the photo of the man's face.

"His name is Mathew Wilson. He is a second year law student in Charleston. Was..." Caroline put a hand to her face before going on. "He grew up outside of Richmond and his parents still live there. We were having an affair and I gave him that ring. I found it at an antique shop and had his name inscribed on the inside. He asked me why I hadn't put my own name there too and I told him it was because I wanted him to be able to wear it long after our affair had ended." Her head dropped into her hands and Caroline began to weep openly.

Lucy patted her friend's arm and Gabriel stood to retrieve a box of tissues from the countertop. Caroline took one silently and dabbed ineffectively at her eyes but continued to sob. Even Sheriff Grier averted his eyes from the obvious pain Caroline was feeling.

Finally, sucking in a ragged breath, she gathered herself up and said, "I can't believe he's dead. I wasn't in love with Mathew, not really. Infatuated, I suppose, and excited by the adventure, but I had a lot of love for him." She looked imploringly from the sheriff to Gabriel. "Does that make sense? I cared for him deeply as a man and a person and a friend, but I knew that our affair was transient, that we would have our time and then we would part and

I would always think fondly of him. I can't believe he's dead. Like *this*." She gestured angrily at the photographs on the table.

"Mrs. Lamont, I have to ask where you were last night."

Lucy piped in, "Sheriff, she obviously didn't do this! Even if she was anywhere near strong enough, she would be covered in bruises and you know it!"

"And as a former officer of the law, Miss Walker, you know I have to ask."

Lucy and Grier stared each other down for a second before Caroline said, "Lucy, it's okay. He has to ask." Turning back to the sheriff she said, "I was here. Lucy came over to have dinner with my husband and me. He decided to leave for Atlanta before dinner. Lucy left about ten, and I headed to bed."

"What time did your husband leave, Mrs. Lamont?"

"Six-thirty or seven. He said he had early meetings this morning and wanted to be fresh. So he spent the night in his apartment in Atlanta last night."

"Did your husband know about your affair with Mathew Wilson?"

"God, no!" Caroline was suddenly wide-eyed and shocked as if she had never even let herself consider the possibility that Daniel had known of her affair. Her body went rigid and even Lucy was surprised by her adamancy.

She kept her hand on Caroline's arm and said, "Carolina, are you sure Daniel didn't know?"

In a matter-of-fact tone she responded, "He

couldn't have, Lucy. I would have known. It would have been the end. The absolute end of everything."

But Lucy knew that nothing, especially infidelity, happened in a vacuum and she couldn't help but wonder if her friend's adamancy wasn't an indication of denial. She could see that Gabriel and Sheriff Grier were thinking the same thing. Everyone left it alone for now but she knew that Grier would be checking up on Daniel's whereabouts after he'd left home.

"When was the last time you saw Mr. Wilson?"

"Oh," Caroline looked rueful, "nearly four weeks ago. I met him for a drink in Charleston and told him it was over. No good explanation. I said it had been wonderful, but it was always meant to just be fun and it was time to say goodbye. He seemed shocked, but I didn't want him to think there was any possibility of continuing. Maybe I should have been gentler. I don't know." Tears started leaking out of the corner of Caroline's eyes once again.

Grier went on, "Why did you end the affair, Mrs. Lamont?"

Caroline paused and looked Grier straight in the eyes, "It was time, Sheriff. Any longer and our relationship would have been tainted by complications."

"Complications?" Grier's heavy eyebrows were raised. "Is that something you've learned from experience?"

"Certainly not!" Caroline's eye's flashed, "Mathew is young and naïve, and I'm married. I didn't want him to fall in love or do anything silly. As it was, I hoped I could leave our time together as a sweet memory for myself, and for Mathew too." She looked wistful. "*Was* young and naïve. Mathew was young and naïve. And I was very, very selfish." She began crying in earnest again.

"Mrs. Lamont, did Mathew have any problems that you knew of? Debts, enemies, jealous girlfriends? Had he had other affairs?"

Surprise seemed to stop the tears. It was becoming evident to Lucy that Caroline had not given a lot of thought to the possible complexities of Mathew Wilson's life. And perhaps there weren't any, but something had gotten him beaten to death in Graceful Bay with nothing but his former lover's address in his pocket.

Caroline looked up. "No. Of course not. Not that I know of." She looked away, "He told me he had never been with a married woman before and I believe that was the truth. The only time he seemed anxious about anything at all was when he was preparing for moot court. He took his studies very seriously. In fact, I used to tease him that he didn't have time for a real girlfriend while he was in law school so he was damn lucky he'd found me. As for debt or enemies, he never said anything. Maybe he had some student loans, but that's not what you're asking about, is it? He was a very kind young man. I can't imagine anyone not liking him."

Lucy read the unspoken words on Grier's mind: *Someone didn't like Mathew Wilson. Someone didn't like him enough to kill him.* She was grateful that he didn't say them out loud because Caroline looked like she was about at her wit's end.

C'MON IN

I T WAS NEARLY SEVEN O'CLOCK when Lucy left Caroline's house that evening and already getting dark. She had left Caroline reluctantly, but her friend had said she wanted some time alone to think and promised to call if she needed anything at all, even if it was only a hug or a cup of tea. Lucy took a different route home so that she could stop by Hoffman's Gourmet Market on the way and was delighted that it was still open. When she walked in, Mr. Hoffman was overseeing the restocking. Seeing him standing there with his bifocals on the tip of his nose, clipboard in hand, lips pursed in concentration, Lucy was taken back to her childhood, and, for a moment, her concerns for her friend were replaced by the absolute unconcern of being a kid. She half expected Mr. Hoffman to look up and hand her a lollipop.

When he did turn to face her, a huge smile spread across his lean face and he exclaimed with a slight German accent, "Lucy Walker, as I live and breathe! A little birdie told me that you were back in town and I have been waiting for you to walk in through that door!"

Then Joseph Hoffman did the most amazing thing: he pulled a lollipop out of his shirt pocket and handed it to her.

"Grape!" she said, delighted. Grape had always been her favorite flavor.

"Shirley, look who is here!"

Shirley, Mr. Hoffman's wife of over fifty years and clearly still the love of his life, came out of the stockroom in one of the ruffled aprons she was famous for, and, in spite of her age, nearly bounced over to Lucy and gave her a big hug and kiss on the cheek. "Welcome home, darlin'!" she said with the accent of a born and bred South Carolinian.

After chatting with Mr. and Mrs. Hoffman for a few minutes, Lucy headed home with two pounds of fresh strawberries, a pint of homemade vanilla ice cream, and warmth in her heart for her hometown and every single person in it.

Every person, except maybe Daniel Lamont.

It wasn't just the coincidence of Mathew Wilson's murder that had Lucy wondering about her friend's husband. Daniel was a CEO of a brokerage and banking firm in Atlanta whose name had come up when she was under cover. Granted, lots of firms came up in conversation once she had earned some trust in the upper echelons of the Miami drug trade: there was a lot of money to be laundered there. Lucy passed the information along to her superiors, and as far as she knew, there had never been an investigation. It was only later that Lucy realized why that particular firm's name had stuck out to her at the time. Daniel had apparently been working there since graduating from business school and during a phone conversation with Caroline, her friend told her that he had been promoted to CEO, and when she named the company, Lucy had remembered having included it in her reports. She never thought of the coincidence again.

Though she had only met him a few times, and certainly couldn't fault Daniel Lamont for his charm and charisma, Lucy had never really liked him. She chalked it up to not knowing him, and put her discomfort aside because Caroline was clearly in love. And Caroline had great taste.

But the tension between Daniel and Caroline when he left before dinner last night was disconcerting and made Lucy wonder about the state of their marriage. She had hoped Caroline would talk to her about it if they were having problems, but didn't want to make a mountain out of a molehill. After all, Lucy simply hadn't been around the two of them enough to worry about one uncomfortable instance, and Caroline clearly had not wanted to discuss it last night. Obviously the events of today had brought it all to the forefront.

As she pulled into her driveway, Lucy thought that maybe her instincts were right. A few minutes of marital friction were one thing, but follow it up with the revelation of Caroline's affair, and the murder of Mathew Wilson, and you had a mystery.

Lucy parked and gathered her groceries, but when she stepped out of the old Volvo, she sensed that she wasn't alone. She stood there for a second, feeling suddenly very vulnerable, when Gabriel's deep voice called out to her from the veranda.

"Hey, neighbor. Your timing is perfect, we just arrived."

Baxter let out a baleful meow as he came around the corner of the house.

Lucy tried to hide her relief as she walked over and gave the cat a big scratch, sending him into a fit of purring that sounded more like an out of tune car engine than a cat.

"To what do I owe the pleasure, Mr. Black?"

"Well, when I got home I told Bax about your friend's predicament and he thought we should walk over and check on you. I assured him that you were a strong, capable woman, but he would not be dissuaded. So, we had a little dinner and then headed over."

"What a considerate cat you are, Baxter!" she said as he rolled on his back and offered his belly for scratching. Lucy held up the paper bag from Hoffman's Market and said with a smile, "I can offer you dessert. Fresh strawberries and vanilla ice cream."

"We love ice cream!"

Gabriel took the bag as Lucy unlocked the door and flipped a light switch. Standing so close to him, inviting him into her home, made Lucy's skin tingle. She held the door open as Baxter carefully sniffed his way inside. As she turned to close the door behind the cat, Gabriel touched her bare arm.

"You have goose bumps. Won't ice cream make you colder?"

Turning back to face him, trying to keep her eyes off of the navy broadcloth shirt skimming his shoulders and chest, Lucy replied coyly, "I'm not cold at all, Gabriel."

They held each other's gaze for a moment until

Lucy winked and slid past Gabriel and into the kitchen.

After she put the ice cream away, Lucy offered Gabriel something to drink.

"A glass of water please."

Lucy took a bottle of water from the fridge. As she reached for a glass he said, "I'll take it just like that, Lucy."

She put some water on for tea and said, "Peppermint tea soothes me. Don't ask me why, but ever since I was wounded, I drink a cup when I need to sort out my thoughts. Or put the bad thoughts to rest."

"Today was quite a day. What a thing to come home to."

"I can't imagine what Caroline is going through. I offered to stay, but she said she wanted some time alone."

"At least there are no little ones running around. It's hard to hide things from kids – no matter how hard you try."

"Really? And where did you learn so much about kids?"

Gabriel put on a look of mock indignation, "I happen to have a lot of experience with children in the form of a gaggle of nieces and nephews. I am everyone's favorite uncle," he said proudly. "I'll show you the pictures to prove it when you come to my house."

"Why on earth would I come to your house, Mr. Black?" she teased.

"Why, Miss Walker, because you will hardly be

able to stay away once you have been disarmed by my charm and animal magnetism."

Lucy laughed out loud and then replied coyly, "I might come over to see Baxter."

Hearing his name, the giant cat leapt up onto the stool next to Gabriel and looked expectantly at Lucy. While she let the tea steep, Lucy found a can of tuna in the pantry.

"May I?" she asked Gabriel.

"He will love you forever if you do."

When Lucy opened the can Baxter jumped down, dashed around the breakfast bar, and commenced purring and rubbing against Lucy's leg until she set a small plate of the water-packed tuna on the floor in front of him.

Pouring herself a mug of tea, Lucy asked, "How about a tour before dessert?"

"I would love a tour."

DESSERT

THEY WENT THROUGH THE FORMAL dining room first and Lucy brought up the lights on the chandelier to give it an ambient sparkle.

"My grandparents used to have wonderful dinner parties in here. The table expands to seat sixteen people and they routinely filled it with friends. You know what? I think I might try to keep that tradition. I certainly know enough people in town. Though I'll have to wait until the scandal blows over."

"Scandal?"

"The murder of Mathew Wilson," she replied ominously. "Even if Caroline manages to keep her name out of it, it's going to be the talk of the town. I don't know what she's going to do." She suddenly looked sharply at Gabriel, "Please tell me Sheriff Grier doesn't suspect her."

"I don't think so. Even though it's too early, as you know, to rule anyone out, there's no way that a woman Mrs. Lamont's size could possibly inflict that kind of damage. And even if it was possible, she would have obvious injuries of her own." He thought for a moment. "She could have hired someone. Don't give me that look," he admonished with a gentle smile, "you know that I'm just running through the scenarios that Grier will have to tick off. If she did hire someone, it wouldn't make any sense to have it done in Graceful Bay. Charleston would have been a better choice."

"Gabriel, I can't talk about my friend like this!" Lucy was glad to know that the circumstances were pointing Sheriff Grier's suspicion away from Caroline, but she couldn't stand to hear the reasoning. As far as Lucy was concerned, the only reason anyone needed was that Caroline would never ever do something like that. Period.

Gabriel looked at her sympathetically, "I'm sorry, Lucy, that was the investigator in me talking. I don't think there is any reason to worry that Mrs. Lamont would be considered a suspect."

Lucy looked a little sheepish. "I know, I know, this is all such a shock."

She looked around the dining room again, at the white oak wainscoting and the square cut crystals hanging from the oblong chandelier over the huge oak table. "I once got into trouble when my grandmother found me standing on a stack of books I'd piled in the middle of this table, running my fingers through the crystals of her chandelier like it was fresh cut grass."

Gabriel laughed, "You must have been a dickens."

"I was!" she laughed too. "It wasn't that long after my parents died and I think my grandmother was terrified something would happen to me too. She had never scolded me like that. Later she found me crying upstairs in my room and told me that she just didn't want anything to ever happen to me, and she was sorry she'd been so harsh. Then she said that if she ever caught me climbing around about to break my neck again, she would lock me in my room and never let me out till I was eight feet tall."

Lucy's phone began ringing in the kitchen and she excused herself. Watching her walk away, Gabriel couldn't believe that a story of childhood mischief had made him want to peel her clothes off and ravage her. He wandered into the next room and was momentarily taken aback. The room – if it could even be called that, it was more of a gallery – extended the entire length of the house and had twelve-foot ceilings and a wall of windows. In spite of its size it managed to be a cozy, homey space. He spotted bookshelves and two fireplaces and a variety of seating areas that made the room feel intimate.

Setting down his water he walked over to the windows. The seascape was mesmerizing and the moon was making the room look magical. It had risen full that night and was literally lighting up the entire space. You could practically read by it. Gabriel felt like he was in another world.

Lucy found Gabriel standing in the center of a red Afghani rug, bathed in moonlight. He turned and said simply, "Wow!"

"It's incredible, isn't it? When the house was built in the early fifties this was two rooms, but when my grandparents bought it they took out the dividing wall and..."

Lucy didn't finish because Gabriel stepped toward her and wrapped one arm around her waist. With his other hand, he gently tipped her chin up toward him before parting her lips with a kiss that was anything but gentle. She felt her knees give a little as Gabriel's tongue found hers and though she felt his warmth, she could tell that her goose bumps were back. Lucy had never felt attraction this intense and she moaned as Gabriel pulled her hips against his body and she felt him hard against her. She heard herself whimper when he took a step away from her, but after slipping the mug of tea out of her hand and setting it down, Gabriel came right back to her.

Now that both of her arms were free, Lucy wrapped them around Gabriel's broad shoulders and pulled him into her. His body was powerful and lithe and his mouth was insistent. Gabriel slid his hands under her silk T-shirt and nuzzled the nape of her neck. He pulled back to look at her. The moonlight bounced off of Lucy's dark hair and blue eyes and made her pale skin glow.

"God, you are beautiful," he said gruffly as he kissed her again and his hand found her breast. Lucy felt his warmth through the delicate fabric and she felt wild with desire as he traced her nipple with his fingertips.

"I want to take this off," Gabriel growled as he leaned back and pulled the thin cashmere sweater over Lucy's head. Sliding it off of her raised arms with one hand, he had already unhooked her white lacy bra with the other and they both cascaded to the floor. Lucy's fingertips skimmed his chest as she slowly unbuttoned the soft cotton shirt and revealed Gabriel's chest. He looked carved from marble in the moonlight.

For a moment they simply admired one another until they found each other's eyes. Lucy gasped as he kissed her again and undid the zipper of her well-worn jeans. They fell to the floor and she stepped out of them revealing long legs and skimpy white lace panties. Gabriel took a step back so that he could see all of her. Then, he covered her bare breasts first with his hands and then his mouth as he slowly knelt in front of her and took her panties off. He held her as she stepped out of them and then sent shock waves through her as he moved his mouth between her legs. Softly at first, but with increasing intensity, he brought her through wave after wave of pleasure until she couldn't hold back. Grasping his shoulders as she climaxed, Lucy let out a breathless moan and her legs began to wobble.

Gabriel guided her down to the plush oriental carpet and kissed her stomach as Lucy continued to quiver with pleasure. He made his way to her breasts and then her neck and finally her lips, and she said, "Gabriel, I want you inside of me."

"Yes," came his husky reply as he sat up and unbuttoned his jeans. He barely had them off before Lucy parted her legs and drew him into her. She gasped as he filled her up and she felt herself throbbing around him.

"Yes," he said again as he pulled slowly out and then thrust into her. Again and again he drove into her, bringing her to the brink of ecstasy and then back down again. She clutched at his chest and moaned, clenching her legs around his back and pulling him in again.

This time he didn't stop but kept going until they both hit the peak at the same time. And then it was like flying. Gabriel shuddered against her and she throbbed against him until he collapsed onto

Lucy in utter bliss. They remained that way as their breathing went from panting to slow and steady. Gabriel gazed down at Lucy's closed eyes and half smile. The moonlight made her skin shine, and for a minute he felt like they were always meant to be together like this.

Suddenly Baxter's whiskers tickled Gabriel's arm and the cat let out a plaintive meow.

Lucy's eyes flew open and Baxter stuck his nose against hers and started sniffing gently. Laughing, she gave Gabriel another squeeze with her legs before he slowly rolled off of her.

"Baxter, did you finish your tuna fish?" She scratched the giant cat behind his ears and sat up. Gabriel was lying on the floor with his arms stretched out above his head. Lucy smiled at him and said, "Ice cream!"

When she got up and started for the kitchen, Gabriel yelled, "Nice ass!"

Lucy paused long enough to wiggle her butt and then grimaced and touched her leg. "Ouch!"

"Uh-oh, I forgot about your leg. Are you okay?"

Lucy found her panties and started putting them on. With a huge grin she said, "I am so much better than okay, Mr. Black, it doesn't bear description." Then she was off toward the kitchen.

Gabriel found her there a few minutes later, cleaning strawberries, framed by a single light above the sink and still clad only in her dainty white panties. He kissed the back of her neck and cupped her breasts in his hands. "I am so glad that Baxter insisted we come over tonight."

Lucy turned around to face him, smiled and

popped a berry in her mouth. He had put his jeans back on but had left the shirt off.

Giving him the once-over, she said, "Damn."

"Damn, yourself. I thought girls only ran around the house in their underwear in my teenage daydreams." They stood looking at each other, both of them suddenly a little uncertain. Their relationship had become intimate pretty quickly and it didn't feel like a passing fling to either one of them.

"Shall we dine on the patio?" Lucy asked tongue-in-cheek as she walked into the foyer and emerged with a thick, knee-length cardigan sweater that she deftly tied around her waist.

"If we eat inside, will you take that sweater back off?"

"I certainly will not. You'll never be able to eat ice cream if you are distracted by my perfectly formed bosom."

Gabriel laughed and wrapped his arms around her.

"You might need your shirt," Lucy said as she tucked a wool blanket under her arm. "Or I might be too distracted to eat my ice cream." He slipped his shirt back on, fastening a few of the buttons. They each carried a bowl of strawberries and ice cream out to the back porch and Gabriel and Baxter followed Lucy down a few steps to the patio. A hardwood trellis covered more than half of the expansive stone patio. Vines wound around the beams of the trellis and new leaves had sprouted throughout. By summer they would keep the patio in full shade, but now, moonlight dappled through.

STRAWBERRIES 'N' CREAM

T HERE WAS A SINGLE CHAISE longue on the uncovered portion of the patio and Lucy took a seat on the end of it. "Hope you don't mind sharing. I only brought one out. I wasn't expecting company so soon."

"I don't mind at all," Gabriel began with a smile, but veered off when he spotted the built-in barbeque under a stone portico in one corner of the patio. "Your grandparents must have had some fantastic parties out here too! Look at this!" He lifted a corner of the weather tarp and peaked at the stainless steel underneath. "I love barbeques." He turned to Lucy with raised eyebrows.

"You mean, as opposed to all other men who do not like barbeques?"

Baxter had settled into the oversized chair beside Lucy. "Move over, cat, that's my spot," Gabriel said as he eased himself into the chaise behind Lucy. She leaned back against him and they ate in silence for a few minutes, just listening to the ocean waves and Baxter's amplified purr.

After a while, Gabriel asked, "How old were you when your parents died?"

"Little. Five. I was staying with my grandparents for the weekend while they were away. It was the first time they'd left me for more than half a day and their plane went down in the Appalachians a few hours after they had said goodbye. I didn't know what had happened, of course, but I knew something was wrong. It was in the afternoon and my grandmother and I were swimming and playing in the sand when my grandfather came down from the house and called her. The next thing I knew, Grandma was yelling, "No, no!" and then she suddenly sat down in the sand. My grandfather picked me up in a bear hug and took me inside. We ate ice cream. In fact, the way I remember it, we ate *only* ice cream for the next few days. And cookies. Lots of cookies. The whole town seemed to stop in at one point or another, bringing piles of food and doting on me, but I don't think I understood why. My grandparents had told me that Mommy and Daddy had gone away for a lot longer than we expected and that it would be a long, long time before I saw them again and they would miss me, and it was okay if I missed them and felt sad...

"Anyway, at some point, there was a funeral. When I was older I learned that search and rescue had found the plane very quickly but had to carefully excavate it and investigate what went wrong before they could release my parents and the other passengers for burial. But at the time, I was so young. I missed my parents, but I didn't understand why they couldn't just come home. My grandparents took wonderful care of me from that day forward, and I grew up in this little town where everyone treated me like family.

"Caroline and I met that same summer. Our grandparents were very close friends and they got us together pretty quickly. We got along from first glance and eventually went to a girls' prep school outside of Charleston together. We spent the week boarded there and then came home to Graceful Bay on the weekends." She looked at Gabriel's bemused expression and said, "It was normal around here to send your kids off. And it wasn't a finishing school, in case that's what you're wondering."

Gabriel laughed, "I did wonder how you Southern girls all turned out to be so well behaved."

Giving him a little pinch, Lucy replied, "We are raised right, that's how."

Gabriel set his bowl down and Baxter didn't hesitate. He jumped off of Lucy's lap and headed straight for it. "So you and Caroline have known each other your whole lives?"

"Pretty much. And we're not just nostalgic schoolgirl friends. When we get together it's like no time has passed. We do some catch-up, of course, but it's mostly, 'Hey, what's going on right now in your life?' and I tell her, and she always gets it. And so do I." She paused and Gabriel felt her shrug. "At least, I thought I did."

"You didn't know about her affair?"

"No, but that's no real surprise. We haven't been in touch in a while and an affair is not something Caroline would discuss during a quick chat on the phone. Or with her hospitalized friend," she added. "The thing is, I feel like I should have sensed something. I never felt settled around Daniel but I thought it was because I didn't know him. Caroline and I have different taste in men but neither of us has ever leaned toward anyone who was scary or violent."

Gabriel turned Lucy to face him and asked very

seriously, "Do you think Daniel Lamont is scary or violent?"

For a split second, Lucy considered telling Gabriel that the bank where Daniel worked had come into question while she was under cover, but she wanted to talk more with Caroline first. Lucy didn't want to turn the investigation in a direction that would hurt her friend even more without being certain, and Gabriel's camaraderie with Sheriff Grier made it likely that he would feel compelled to tell the sheriff anything that might be pertinent to the investigation. It was this type of consideration that made Lucy a mediocre investigator. It was also exactly this type of consideration that had made her perfect for undercover work. She wanted to get the bad guy, but she used chess moves to do it.

"No, I have no reason to think that he's a bad guy, but obviously there were some big problems in their marriage."

Gabriel eyed her for a moment. He didn't think she was telling him everything, but decided to let it go for now. Lucy was a smart woman and this crime had hit close to home. Gabriel's investigative mind was already following each clue to its logical conclusion, but he would have to be patient with Lucy. *Not hard*, he thought, *when the object of patience is this gorgeous.*

The wool blanket had slipped off of Lucy's legs, revealing the ugly scar on her otherwise perfect thigh. When she noticed him looking, Lucy started to cover up but Gabriel stopped her, sliding a gentle hand from her knee up under her sweater to the hem of her delicate panties. She took a quick breath when he pulled her into him for a deep kiss. When they parted, Lucy stood and led Gabriel up the steps and back into the house. He picked up their ice cream dishes and took her hand. Baxter followed them inside and then she locked the French doors behind her.

With a very sexy wink, Lucy dropped her long cardigan on the floor as she headed for the stairs leading to the second floor. A large block of windows at the landing silhouetted her body as she untied her sweater and let it slip off of her shoulders.

"Coming to bed, Mr. Black?"

Gabriel stood at the base of the stairs, captivated, and had to untie his tongue before murmuring, "Yes, Lucy. Anywhere you go."

He followed her into the master bedroom. Inside, she turned to look at her new lover and, with a peal of laughter, eased the ice cream bowls out of Gabriel's hand.

"Oops," she said. "You must've forgotten to set these down."

"I think I forgot my middle name," he replied unabashedly and found her breasts with his hands.

Lucy arched her back and he bent to kiss her neck and then her mouth, slowly walking her backward toward the bed. When she felt the duvet touch her skin, Lucy sat down and began unbuttoning Gabriel's shirt, starting at the waist and slowly kissing his rock hard stomach. He shuddered with pleasure when he felt her fingers undo the top button of his jeans. She pulled them off, then his Calvin Klein boxer briefs. She stood and pushed him onto the bed, easing off her own panties.

Gabriel watched her from the bed but when he tried to sit up, Lucy pushed him back with the tips of her fingers. Starting at his broad chest, she slowly made her way, kissing and tickling, down his abdomen until she took his hardness into her mouth.

Gabriel let out a powerful groan and reached for Lucy's hand as she slowly eased herself up and down, flicking her tongue against the tip of his penis before taking him in again. When he knew he couldn't hold back, Gabriel lifted Lucy's slender body on top of his own. She straddled him and slowly took him inside of her.

For a moment he held her hips still against him and then pushed up into her. Lucy sighed and gasped in pleasure as she took over the pace and sped up. Gabriel pulled her toward him and filled his mouth with her breast until she was crying out in pleasure. Her orgasm was violent, and as she shuddered above him he let himself go and bucked and shook beneath her.

Lucy collapsed onto Gabriel, and when his strength came back he wrapped his arms around her panting body. A cool breeze came through the open windows and they rested there, entwined in each other's arms until their breathing became steady and regular and Lucy and Gabriel were asleep in a pile on the freshly made bed in Lucy's new room.

She stirred a little when the breeze made her shiver and slowly extricated herself. Lucy went to the bathroom and came back with a glass of water to find Gabriel tucked under the covers and Baxter cleaning himself at the end of the bed. In silence she petted the cat and offered Gabriel the glass of water and watched the moonlight dapple the ocean waves in the panoramic view from the bedroom.

Finally, Lucy said, "Wow!" They both laughed and she snuggled up against Gabriel's warm body. In moments they were asleep again.

They passed the night in and out of sleep, waking, making love, sleeping again. Finally, two things woke Gabriel for good: the morning sunlight streaming through every window in the room and Baxter sitting on his chest meowing for his breakfast. Despite his attempt to ease out from under the covers without waking Lucy, as soon as he untangled himself from her arms and legs, she rolled over sleepily and said, "Just five more minutes."

Gabriel laughed and mussed her hair.

"Stop it." She fluffed her wild mane. "It took me all night to get it this way."

"So, you're a comedian in the morning?"

"Right up until lunchtime. Then I become serious. What are you doing in my bed anyway?"

"You invited me, sunshine."

"I never! I am a lady, Mr. Black!" she lay back down. "What time is it?"

"Just past the crack of dawn," replied Gabriel on his way into the en suite bathroom. "This is quite a bathtub!" Leaning out the door, he added, "We should make use of it sometime."

From under the covers Lucy's hand shot out in a thumbs-up gesture.

Gabriel shook his head and smiled. "I'm going to rinse off..." but he trailed off because Lucy emitted a very lady-like snore.

DESPERATE HOUSEWIFE

S HORTLY AFTER CAROLINE ENDED HER relationship with Mathew Wilson, she found herself alone again on a Sunday night in the antebellum mansion in Graceful Bay. Daniel had been gone all week, and even though he had listed a dinner and an important cocktail party on Thursday as his reasons for staying in Atlanta the following week as well, he had not invited her to come along. When Caroline suggested she could join him in the city for a day or two and they could stay through the weekend, Daniel had shaken his head and said she would be bored. He would rather she stay home and then he would come back to spend the weekend in Graceful Bay.

These long stretches of time away from her husband had become a normal part of her marriage and she honestly didn't know what to do. Guilt and depression kept her from talking to Daniel about it. She felt as though she owed him something and she knew that she wasn't very good company just then. She missed Mathew's companionship, and the heartache that had been visible on his face when she told him their time together had to end made her very sad. But what she was feeling was more than sadness. She felt hopeless. Her doctor had recommended seeing a psychologist for a while to help her sort through the things that were making her feel hopeless, but Caroline hadn't made a decision about that yet. She wasn't sure she was ready to acknowledge the huge problems in her marriage, let alone admit to another person that she'd been unfaithful.

Even though she was the only one around to hear it, Caroline let out a big dramatic sigh and poured herself a glass of icy cold Riesling. She contemplated the small television in the kitchen, but started roaming around her big, empty house instead. It was a beautiful place to live, but it didn't feel like a home anymore. *Had it ever?* She and Daniel had purchased the house six months before their wedding, and then in true Southern tradition, had kept living in their own homes in Charleston until they returned from their honeymoon and moved into the big house in Graceful Bay. But it had quickly become clear that they would not be spending a lot of time here.

After they bought the house in Graceful Bay, Caroline gave up her apartment in Charleston. In the months after she and Daniel closed on the house, Caroline had picked out furniture and unpacked boxes, hung curtains and chosen new appliances. For a while she commuted to work, or stayed with Daniel at his apartment, but then she decided to resign from her executive accounting position in Charleston two months before she was to be married. She wanted the old mansion to feel like a home by the time they returned from their honeymoon so that she and Daniel could move in directly. She spent her weekends with Daniel in his Charleston condominium.

Caroline wondered for the thousandth time if it had been a big mistake to quit her job as a corporate accountant. Perhaps if she had kept working things wouldn't have changed so much between she and Daniel.

She loved numbers and, truth be told, she had loved being a bean counter. But when Daniel suggested they settle in Graceful Bay, Caroline had been over the moon. He would still commute to Charleston and they would keep his condo there, but Caroline looked forward to settling into her spacious antebellum home, getting another accounting job in the little town – God knew there was enough money floating around to support another CPA – and planning a family. It wasn't that she needed to work, but she liked to work. She liked the schedule; she liked being useful. She loved the accuracy and certainty of percentages and decimal places and plus and minus signs. And she liked earning her own money, more than she had realized. She had a trust fund and several assets in her name independent of Daniel, but being rich wasn't the same as being self-sufficient.

At any rate, after the wedding and the honeymoon and the move and getting settled into their new house, Daniel had been transferred to the bank's headquarters in Atlanta. He was pleased about the promotion, but it changed a relatively short commute to Charleston into a five-day week in Atlanta. Caroline was supportive but she was also disappointed. She and Daniel had finally moved in together but now, Monday to Friday, they would be living apart again. When Daniel suggested she put off getting an accounting job so that she could spend a few days a week with him in Atlanta it had seemed like a good idea.

For nearly a year and a half it had worked well enough. Caroline loved her days and nights in the big city followed by cozy quiet weekends in Graceful Bay. Apart from getting to and from Atlanta – which required either a four-hour drive or a short flight and a long time spent in the airport – it wasn't very taxing at all. Caroline knew they would have to make changes once they started having babies, but for the time being she was happy.

When Daniel's job began taking more and more of his time, Caroline started to realize how much she missed having a career of her own, and she missed the colleagues and friends that went along with having a job. Her friends were mostly in Charleston and Graceful Bay. The people she knew in Atlanta were all somehow affiliated with her husband. That was nice, she knew, but it was important to have your own people too. Caroline even considered finding a job in Atlanta and working there during the week. That way she and Daniel could still spend time together and she could develop her own network in the city. It was time to reestablish herself as an independent woman and not just the wife of Daniel Lamont. Besides, she was getting bored: a girl could only do so much shopping.

She smiled to herself again when she thought of the days when she would buy a sexy new dress for a dinner party and surprise Daniel with it when they went out, or the stunned expression on his face when she would greet him at the door in new La Perla lingerie.

It had been fun and she was in love, but over time she did not feel the deeper connection to Daniel that she had expected to feel with the man she married. It was almost the opposite. His workdays became longer and he was more distracted. He seemed less keen to discuss his days with her. Weeknight dinners and drinks were more frequently for business discussions and a means to extend the workday than a time to unwind with colleagues and their significant others. In Atlanta, Caroline found herself socializing more with the wives and girlfriends, and sometimes even the husbands and boyfriends, of Daniel's coworkers. More and more Daniel suggested she stay in Graceful Bay during the week since he wouldn't be much company anyway.

That was when she brought up the idea of working in Atlanta. One Saturday evening over a pasta dinner at their home in Graceful Bay, Caroline explained to Daniel that she was missing work, and now that he was so busy in Atlanta, she thought it might make sense for her to restart her career there instead of Graceful Bay.

Even as she had broached the conversation Caroline had been apprehensive. She told herself there was no reason to be, as Daniel had always been supportive of her career and praised her independence in the past. Shortly after they began dating, he'd even said that her natural independence was one of the things he loved about her. So, why did she feel nervous?

At the time she thought she was being silly, but when Caroline said that she had begun talking to a few of her old colleagues in Charleston about good Atlanta firms, the look of fury that flashed across her husband's face had been unmistakable. He recovered quickly but the smile that curved his lips was dismissive.

"I thought you wanted to start a family?"

The question surprised Caroline. "Now? With you in Atlanta so much? I thought we were going to wait until we were settled together somewhere."

"I thought we'd put this nonsense about you working as a bean counter to bed, Caroline. Besides, we'll wait forever to have children if you start a new career. I know how ambitious you are, and you're not going to be someone's part-time bookkeeper. You're too determined and I won't have you leaving our child in the corporate day-care while you work your way to the top."

Caroline was dumbfounded. Daniel had never even implied that he didn't want her to pursue her career after they married.

"I'm not going to be a childless hausfrau for the rest of my life, Daniel, and I don't want to start a family when you and I are basically living in different cities."

He looked at her sharply and, in a cold voice that made her skin crawl, asked, "What was the point of marrying a Southern belle if you are going to behave like a butch dyke on the corporate warpath?"

Caroline was stunned, but before she could reply, Daniel said with unmistakable bitterness, "Look, I just want to relax and enjoy this weekend together. Can we fight about this another time?"

Caroline thought about protesting, but she wasn't sure she wanted to have this conversation right now either. She hadn't expected Daniel's reaction and she didn't know what to do about it. She hoped it was simply that he was tired and irritable and they could talk sensibly another time.

Now, as she made her way through the empty guest rooms on the second floor, sipping her wine and feeling sorry for herself, Caroline realized that it wouldn't have made any difference if she'd kept her job when she'd married Daniel. He didn't want her to work and eventually, insidiously, he would have worn her down and she would have quit.

Good Lord, Carolina, when did you become so passive? she asked herself. It was time for a change and if Daniel Lamont didn't like it, he would simply have to adapt.

Half of her wine was gone when she opened the door to Daniel's office. She hardly ever went in here when he was away. Making her way to the desk by the light coming in from the hallway, Caroline pulled the chain on a table lamp. It bathed the nearly empty desk in a pool of light.

Daniel had this desk built when they bought the house. It was nine feet by four feet of solid dark-stained oak with elegant legs that seemed almost too narrow to hold its weight. Carefully camouflaged near the leather desk blotter was a little wood panel covering an internet and power station. They were wired through one desk leg and into a hidden floor outlet because Daniel hadn't wanted cords ruining the Roaring Twenties style of his office. He had taken his laptop and cell phone to Atlanta, so there was nothing attached to it now. On one side of the desk there were three shallow drawers, two narrow, with the widest directly in front of Daniel's leather desk chair. Caroline opened one of these now and fingered its contents. Two gold pens, a shallow bin of paperclips, stapler, stationery that he never used. Nothing unusual. The second drawer's contents were similar and the third drawer...

The third drawer was locked. Caroline tried again. It didn't open and she crouched down to inspect it. There didn't seem to be a lock mechanism, but the drawer would not open. She looked at it again. Perhaps it wasn't a drawer at all, but a false façade with the cables and power cords arranged inside the compartment. But Caroline could feel seams where it should slide out.

She went back to the office door and flipped on the overhead lights. Back at the desk she sat down on the floor and scrutinized it. The wood moved ever so slightly when she pushed on the bottom and she could feel the lines where the gliders would be hidden.

Caroline crossed her legs and leaned back on her arms. She knew the desk had not always been locked.

Standing up again, she perched on the edge of Daniel's chair and looked around at the oak cabinets where her husband kept papers and who knew what else. It had never occurred to her that there could be things in this room that Daniel was hiding from her. Even now, she wasn't sure why she felt compelled to open the mysterious desk drawer, but she knew would. She hadn't come in here with the notion of snooping around. She hadn't thought there was anything to snoop into. She looked at her now empty wine glass sitting on the floor, contemplated having another, looked around the room again, and decided not to. Her work here wasn't done and she wanted a clear head.

Caroline crouched down again and carefully ran her fingers along the underside of the locked drawer. On one of its corner edges, she felt a circle of ridged metal. That must be the lock. Picking up her glass, she dashed down to the kitchen in search of tools. In the pantry she rummaged around in a utility drawer until she found a flashlight. Then she went back upstairs to the office.

When she walked through the door, Caroline paused. In the brightly lit room she could see her reflection in the huge plate glass windows behind Daniel's desk. The room overlooked an expanse of side-yard that was lined with old hardwood trees. The next house was equally obscured in foliage and she knew that no one could see her, but she felt exposed. In fact, she suddenly felt like she was doing something wrong.

Caroline had always trusted her husband, perhaps because she had been distracted by her own infidelity. The last half-year, maybe nine months, now that she thought about it, had been particularly trying and lonely and she had discovered some serious discrepancies between the Daniel she thought she had married and the real life Daniel she talked to everyday. But didn't that happen in all marriages? Why was she searching though her husband's private office? He had never objected to her being in here whether he was home or not. Caroline slumped into a club chair and put her head in her hands. Suddenly, she felt terrible.

On the other hand, he wouldn't mind her coming in here if he had his secrets all safely locked up.

That was it. Caroline Lamont, née Dixon of the South Carolina Dixons thank you very much, banished her doubts and marched over to the windows. When the blinds were drawn she sat back down on the floor and using her Maglite, found the lock on the bottom corner of the drawer. It was a small stainless steel circle that would fit a very small key. The ridges didn't look very complicated. This was no deadbolt. Caroline undid the barrette that had been holding her long bangs back and gently tried to fit the metal clip. No good: it was too big. She examined the lock again and then took two paper clips out of one of the unlocked drawers.

As she unbent and reconfigured the clips, Caroline smiled to herself. She was not new to picking simple locks. As children, she and Lucy had been obsessed with books about child detectives. It had started with early edition collections of Nancy Drew and The Hardy Boys that Lucy's grandparents kept on the bookshelves in their great room. Lucy's grandma would only let them read the treasured books while sitting at the dining room table or by the soft chairs and small reading tables in the library. They usually sprawled on one of the thick rugs and occupied themselves reading, discussing, and planning their careers as detectives. They went through the collection on the bookshelves in no time and after that were amply supplied with as many books as they could read from Lucy's grandparents and Caroline's parents.

One of their imperatives was to learn how to pick locks with bobby pins. The powder room on the first floor of Lucy's grandparents' house had a push button lock and on several occasions the girls locked themselves out of the bathroom and had to ask Lucy's grandma to open it up. That was how they learned that credit cards also work to open locks.

By junior high school, Caroline and Lucy could easily open most simple locks. Just in time to turn boy crazy and forget all about Nancy Drew. Now, though it had been years since Caroline had picked a lock, she made quick work of the one on Daniel's desk drawer. With a deep breath, she opened the drawer and looked inside. There were three or four business cards, an errant paperclip, and a stray power cord. That was all.

Caroline sat heavily in Daniel's chair fingering the power cord and wondering if she was relieved or just embarrassed. She felt ridiculous, not to mention she had gotten really worked up over absolutely nothing. She really had to find something to do with her time.

Talk about a desperate housewife, she thought wearily.

Then and there she resolved to have a long talk with Daniel about how she was feeling and explain to him that she was serious about going back to work. At least then she could think clearly about their relationship from a place of empowerment instead of the sad, hopeless state she found herself in now. Caroline had been spending too much time feeling frustrated with her marriage. If she waited for Daniel to come to his senses and support her career decisions she'd wind up hating him.

She really needed a friend to talk to. *Damn*, she thought, *I can't wait until Lucy comes home.*

Her friend had been deep undercover in Miami for over a year, and now she was in the hospital recuperating from her injuries. Even before that she had been prepping for the assignment and busy all of the time. Although they had spoken a several times in the last few weeks, Caroline hadn't wanted to bug her with her marital troubles. Besides, she knew that Lucy would tell her it would all be okay one way or another and Caroline was afraid that the only way it would be okay was a divorce. And she wasn't ready to contemplate defeat yet. She could wait for that conversation until Lucy got home.

Lucy did not care for Daniel and vice versa, though Caroline had never understood why. The low-key animosity between them had been obvious to Caroline from the moment she had introduced her best friend to her then boyfriend.

Maybe Lucy had seen something that she hadn't, Caroline thought now. Because it had been a long time since Daniel had treated her with real love and respect. She glanced at the mangled paperclips sitting on top of the desk. This was it. They would talk, work it out, and be happy again. Or they would have to end it.

Even as she consoled herself, Caroline kept

playing with the power cord she'd found in the desk drawer and she began studying it now. It looked like a cable for a cheap cell phone. On the surface it was nothing. All of America was probably tangled in extra power cords they had no idea what to do with anymore. She had a drawer full of chargers in the pantry, most of them a mystery. The thing was that Daniel did not have a cheap phone. He was strictly, doggedly, a Mac kind of guy. He'd preordered the first iPhone when it came out, and every new version since. When he'd brought home the most recent version, he'd sat at this desk playing with it for an entire afternoon and evening.

Her husband did not have a generic phone or a generic anything else. So what was the cord for?

Caroline rolled the desk chair over to the waist-high set of oak filing cabinets and tried one of the handles. Locked. She tried the rest, just to be thorough, but they were all locked too. She had never tried to open the file cabinets before, so there was no way to know whether this was new or they were always locked. Her husband worked at an investment bank for goodness' sake, so there wouldn't be anything of interest to her in there anyway.

Desperate housewife, Caroline, she told herself again. *Desperately lonely and bored, and looking for a little scandal,* she thought.

MOTHERLY ADVICE

CAROLINE PICKED UP HER TANGLED paperclip lock pick and her flashlight. Then, with the phone charger still in her other hand, she left Daniel's office, turning off the lights and softly closing the door behind her. Back in the kitchen, she rummaged around in the refrigerator for some Swiss cheese and found a tomato in the fruit basket on the counter. A little sweet mustard and rye bread and she had her favorite sandwich. Just as she took her first bite her cell phone chirped.

"Hi, Momma!" she answered.

"Caroline, ladies do not answer the phone with food in their mouths."

Caroline laughed, nearly choked, swallowed her bite and said, "Since when have I been a lady, Mother?"

Though her voice remained stern, Caroline could hear the smile in her mother's voice, "Since I taught you how to fake it, little miss. How are you doing, dear? I thought we might see you for lunch last week, but you must have been in Atlanta with Daniel."

Caroline had not been in Atlanta last week, but she didn't want to tell her mother that. Susan and Robert Dixon had barely left each other's side in the thirty-six years they had been married, and if she heard that Caroline and Daniel were spending so much time apart she would suspect something was wrong between them. *And*, thought Caroline, *she would be right.*

The two women chatted for a few more minutes before Caroline's mother asked, "Honey, is something troubling you?" Caroline's hesitation was answer enough. "What is it, dear?"

"Oh Mom, I think I'm just a little bit lonely and a little bit idle. Daniel is spending so much time in Atlanta, and more and more he encourages me to stay here in Graceful Bay instead of joining him in his apartment in the city. I know he's probably busy, but I feel rejected."

"Don't be silly, Caroline! I'm sure that's not it. Daniel is probably trying to be considerate and doesn't want you to end up lonely in Atlanta. Honestly, your father and I could never stand to be apart for more than a day or two, and even then only if we had to, but your generation does everything long-distance. And why not? You can call whenever and wherever you want because everyone has a cell phone. You can email and instant message. You can even Skype."

For a second Caroline was surprised to hear the word 'Skype' come out of her mother's mouth, but then Mrs. Dixon had always been technologically savvy. "I know, Mom, but I like to be with him more than I like video chatting."

"I agree, dear. Perhaps you should remind Daniel that you're a hands-on wife and that it isn't more convenient at all for you to be away from him. You'll work it out if you are open and honest when you talk to each other. He probably wants you by his side, but thinks he'll be putting you out if you have to follow him to Atlanta every week."

Caroline actually thought keeping his wife in South Carolina while he was off working was more convenient for Daniel than for Caroline. She had loved spending time with him in Atlanta, and she would like it more if she started working there. To Caroline, it seemed that Daniel simply didn't want to be with her.

"Maybe," she replied.

"Of course that's it, dear. Now about feeling idle, you've been talking about going back to work for quite a while now. Why don't you do that? You've always been a hard worker, Caroline. You take after your father that way."

"You're a hard worker too, Mom."

"Yes, I suppose, but in a different way. Organizing charity balls and church events is my forte. You and your father are breadwinners, Caroline. You need more than a pat on the back from the Junior League to feel fulfilled."

Caroline knew her mother was being modest. She had raised funds and worked tirelessly to help children and struggling families in need. She had helped establish a fund specifically for young, unmarried mothers in need of prenatal care and help during the first few years of motherhood, in spite of opposition from some of the more conservative members of polite South Carolinian society. Her mother was a very strong-willed woman, and when she set out to do what she thought was right, not much could stop her.

"Momma! You are amazing and modest. No wonder Dad never wants to leave your side." Caroline sighed, "Maybe Daniel would prefer it if I was more like you."

"Whatever do you mean, Caroline? I can remember Daniel telling us that he marveled at your ambition. Besides, you are just the right amount like me. Mostly like your father, but I did pass on a few of my lady-like traits."

Caroline laughed a little. "Daniel doesn't seem very excited at the prospect of me going back to work. In fact, that's an understatement. He seems downright opposed to it."

Mrs. Dixon was surprised. "Really?"

"I think so, Mom."

"Well, Daniel has gotten used to having you around whenever he wants, so maybe he's just feeling a little selfish about your time. Sit him down and stand your ground and I'm sure everything will work out."

It pained her to know that her only daughter was having troubles in her marriage. She had seen the havoc that divorce had wrought on some of her friends, both emotionally and financially, and, God forbid that there were children involved.

"I'm sure you're right, Momma." Caroline didn't mention the nagging thought that if Daniel wanted her available to him, why was he insisting that she stay away?

"Come to think of it, Caroline, Daniel must be incredibly busy helping to set up this new hedge fund. Your father said that managing independent funds is a lot of work. Even though he still keeps his office at the bank, he doesn't have the same access to their personnel. Of course, your father always keeps half an eye out for Daniel. Now that I think of it, that must be why Daniel is being distant. He's just plain got a lot on his plate. Perhaps you should drive down to Atlanta and surprise him."

Caroline's stomach dropped to her toes. Daniel had never mentioned a private fund, a change in his position at the bank, or, for that matter, given any reason at all for his increased workload, despite the fact she had asked him about it. And for the life of her, she could not think why he wouldn't.

When Caroline didn't respond, her mother asked, "Dear, are you all right?"

Caroline shook her head, "Yes, Mom, I'm fine. Just worn out worrying. I might watch a little bad TV and tuck myself into bed early."

"Good idea. Get some rest and stop over-thinking everything. Sometimes it's hard to be married, but it's all part of the process. It will all work out."

Caroline didn't feel certain about that at all, but she thanked her mother and wished her goodnight. "Give Daddy a kiss for me."

When they were off the phone, Caroline's mind started racing. There was something fishy going on. She took another bite of her sandwich and tossed the rest, her appetite gone.

Caroline got a glass of water and stood by the kitchen sink sipping it. Then she picked up her paperclip lock pick and threw it in the trash. She eyed the wine bottle and decided to pour another glass and then she headed upstairs for another night alone in her big, empty bed.

The next time Caroline went into Daniel's office was the day after Mathew Wilson was murdered.

MORNING AFTER

WHEN SHE NEXT LOOKED AT the clock it said nine-twenty. Peering around the room Lucy saw no sign of Gabriel or Baxter. She stretched and realized that even though she hadn't slept very much, it had been the most thoroughly restful night she'd had in a long time. *Must be the sex*, she thought to herself.

Stopping in the bathroom to splash water on her face, Lucy made her way to the stairs and the aroma of coffee and toast wafted up to her. Gabriel was making breakfast. She quickly ran her hands through her hair and adjusted the robe she had tied on in the bathroom.

When she entered the kitchen, Gabriel turned to her. He was wearing fresh clothes and had shaved. He looked absolutely gorgeous.

"Good morning, sunshine! Baxter had to go home, but I came back so that you wouldn't wake up alone." He handed her a cup of steaming black coffee.

Lucy inhaled deeply over the piping hot liquid, "Hmmm! This smells amazing." Smiling up at him, she asked, "What time did you get up?"

"Shortly after the sun. It was bright and Baxter was ready for breakfast."

"I hope you don't mind me saying so, Gabriel, but your cat is a lot like a dog."

"I don't mind, but don't tell him. Your phone was ringing a few minutes before you came down. Want to check it while I make breakfast?"

Lucy felt herself melt. "You're going to make breakfast?" She swooned a little and put her hand to her chest, "Be still, my heart."

Gabriel held up her mobile phone and announced that she was going to have bread and water for breakfast if she didn't behave.

Lucy walked into the great room laughing and curled up in a leather chair the color and texture of butter. She felt a shiver of desire when she looked at the rug where she and Gabriel had first made love last night. *It's just sex*, she cautioned herself, but Lucy knew she was already in trouble. Where had this guy come from?

The moment she looked at her cell phone, however, all of her romantic anxieties fell away when she saw that Caroline had called her twice already that morning.

The homey smell of eggs and cheese emanated from the kitchen, but suddenly Lucy's appetite was gone. Caroline had only left one message and the tone in her friend's voice left Lucy cold.

"Lucy? I've been looking around Daniel's office, and.... Well, please call me when you get a chance."

Caroline sounded tense and resigned and Lucy didn't like it one bit. She hit the call back button on her cell phone and put it to her ear. Caroline answered on the second ring.

"Lucy?" Her voice was restrained.

"Caroline! I'm sorry I missed your calls. I slept in and didn't bring my phone to bed with me last night."

"I don't suppose you were sleeping in with a certain tall drink of water?"

Lucy had to laugh. Even though her friend was going through a lot, she was still matchmaking. "Caroline!" She paused, then said, "I can't tell you because he's in the next room! And I can't believe you're worried about my love life when you have your own troubles!"

Caroline sighed, "It's better than the alternative."

"What's going on?"

"Daniel called this morning to check in. He was cheerful, telling me about a new business deal. Meanwhile I was wound up like a spring. Then, before he got off the phone, Daniel said that he'd watched the late news last night and heard there had been a murder in Graceful Bay. Lucy, he asked if I knew anything about it!

"My stomach did a flip-flop, but then he explained that he was wondering if the victim was a local and when I said 'no', he said, 'well, keep the doors locked'.

"The thing is, everything he said was normal, but the way he said it wasn't. It was as if he was defying me to react. Does that make sense? As if he knew he was making me squirm and was daring me to say something. But he didn't really do or say anything out of the ordinary. Maybe I'm being paranoid. A guilty mind and all. But here's the other thing: why would a murder in Graceful Bay, South Carolina, be reported on the eleven o'clock headline news in Atlanta, Georgia?"

Caroline's voice drifted off and before she got lost in guilt and fear, Lucy spoke up. "It could very well be a little of both, but, Caroline, you said yesterday that you didn't think Daniel knew anything about Mathew Wilson. Are you sure?"

"I was sure, until I calmed down enough to let myself consider the awful possibility. You see, a couple of months ago I thought someone had been following me. Rather, a couple of someones taking turns, but I kept seeing the same faces everywhere I went. But as soon as I started looking for them, they disappeared, so I figured it was my guilty conscience. What if it wasn't, though? They would have seen me with Mathew. And if they worker for Daniel – if he'd been suspicious and had me followed –"

Lucy filled in, "Then Daniel would have known you had a relationship with Mathew. But, why would Daniel have you followed in the first place?"

Caroline sniffled and Lucy knew her friend was crying. "Lucy, I don't think Daniel is the man I thought he was. In business, in private, his past. I found some troubling things in his study."

When Caroline began to sob in earnest, Lucy announced that she was coming over and would leave in ten minutes. She had all but forgotten the gorgeous man cooking her breakfast, but when she hung up the phone the smell of food once again filled her nose and a warm feeling passed through her body. She went into the kitchen.

With a bittersweet smile Lucy said, "I have to go to Caroline's house and I told her I would be out the door in ten minutes. Daniel called and she's worried that he knows more than he's letting on." She decided not to mention that Caroline thought she'd found something incriminating until she knew what it was.

Gabriel's smile turned to concern. "Is she worried that he knows she had an affair, or is she worried that he will hurt her?"

"I don't know," she said, honestly. "But when I do, I'll tell you. I can't let anything happen to her, Gabriel, and if he had anything to do with this murder, then he's a scary, vengeful guy and Caroline will have to tread lightly."

Lucy went upstairs to shower and get dressed. Pulling on a knee-length pleated skirt and a short-sleeved blouse, she ran a hand through her wet hair, smoothed a few drops of make-up into her skin and contemplated herself in the mirror. Was it possible that Daniel had something to do with the murder? Caroline had said he hadn't known about the affair, but that's what most spouses thought, and, she supposed, they were occasionally right. However, a husband or wife generally knew when something was different in their relationship. Distance, anger, sadness, and resentment were much more apparent to those we slept with than most people wanted to believe. Caroline would not have had to say anything to Daniel for him to know that she was unhappy. How much more might she have revealed without realizing it?

The big question was whether Daniel had been checking up on her and why. Because if he had been, he would certainly known about Mathew.

It didn't sound like Caroline had gone to any real lengths to hide her affair. And if Daniel had found out that Caroline was sleeping with Mathew Wilson, what were the chances his murder in Graceful Bay was a coincidence? *Pretty slim*, thought Lucy, as she found her blush brushed some color on the apples of her cheeks.

Lucy was back downstairs in five minutes flat and Gabriel could not hide his surprise.

"That was incredibly fast for a woman."

Lucy gave him a teasing left right to the stomach and grinned, "That was incredibly fast for anyone, kid."

Gabriel caught her wrists and pulled her to him for a long deep kiss. "I'm off. Call me if you need anything at all." He gently kissed her forehead then pointed to a square of waxed paper. "Your egg sandwich is on the counter."

As she watched Gabriel walk out the door, Lucy could not keep the smile off her face. She got her phone and her sandwich and went to get her purse. Her leg was stiff and ached a little bit so she swallowed a few of the ibuprofen her doctor had recommended and put the bottle in her purse. Then she was out the door.

THE WHOLE TRUTH

I N THE CAR LUCY TOOK a few bites of her sandwich as she flipped through the radio stations for a news channel. She finally settled for a local station that promised a news brief after this commercial break. Then she buckled up and pulled out of the driveway.

The drive to the Lamont house was short, but the closer she got to her friend's home, the more trepidation Lucy felt. She was quickly losing her appetite and set the rest of her breakfast aside. Even a night of great sex and a clear blue sky couldn't stave off the dismay she felt for Caroline. What a mess! Lucy chastised herself once again for not taking a closer look at Daniel Lamont when Caroline told her they were getting married. At the very least she should've trusted her instincts and asked Caroline more about the man she was so in love with. Or maybe told Caroline that she didn't like her fiancé?

Right, because she was such an authority on men, having never had a relationship that lasted longer than a year. She hadn't even been much of an authority on her best friend since she started undercover work in Miami. Until then she and Caroline had gabbed on the phone several times a week, emailed constantly, and visited each other.

Caroline especially loved to come to Miami for weekends when she could. Two beautiful single women out salsa dancing in the clubs of South Beach into the wee hours of the night without a care in the world. It had been a blast!

When Lucy started her undercover mission there hadn't been as much free time, but she wasn't in deep cover for the first couple of years. She would pretend to be a prostitute for a couple of weeks until they caught the rich tax attorney who had it out for dark-haired hookers, or she would work as a teller by day until they caught the bank manager who was embezzling funds from cash accounts. Still, Lucy got caught up in it. Although she only had to be a different person during the day, or from ten at night until two in the morning, she became a different person all of the time. Being someone else, luring bad guys to confide in her, putting herself in danger, was a twenty-four seven affair for Lucy. It grew harder and harder to make the switch from cunning undercover cop posing as jaded street whore back to the girl who grew up happy. Sometimes she wanted nothing more in life than to be able to spend an hour each day down by the ocean, listening to the shorebirds calling and the waves crashing.

Caroline and Daniel became engaged around the same time that Lucy became consumed by the undercover narcotics world. It hadn't taken long before she was being primed for deep cover. She was given a name and a personality with an entire history that was completely different from her own. She had had to study endless details about her new self and act and respond unfailingly like a woman who'd grown up poor and desperate with a father in jail and a mother who would have sold her daughter on the streets, if she hadn't run away. She had to be a woman who'd survived all of that and learned there was only one way out, and it didn't have anything to do with what was right and what was wrong. Just survival.

She had emerged in the untrusting world of the Miami drug trade with a reputation as a badass and a rap sheet to prove it. Lucy couldn't afford to be herself anymore. Her life depended on it.

But Lucy couldn't blame deep cover for neglecting her friends. It had gotten worse with her first undercover job, but even before that she'd been distancing herself. Maybe even when her grandparents died and her life's goals changed so radically. She had wanted to avenge their deaths, to put away drug dealers and killers – all of them – but she understood now that she had really just wanted to undo what that one high-speed chase had done. She had wanted her grandparents back. She had wanted the closest thing she had to a mom and dad to be alive and well and ready to take care of her if she ever needed it. Even though she had technically been an adult when they died, and even though she was taken care of financially, Lucy knew better than most how hard it was to be an orphan.

And so Lucy had pulled away from her friends and from her hometown and the people who loved her most in the world because she was angry and wanted revenge. In Miami she had gotten justice, if not retribution. She had personally put away a lot of dangerous people and been instrumental in putting away many more. Now it was her time to find peace in her home in Graceful Bay and in herself. It was time to be a real friend to her best friend in the world.

Nothing Lucy ever suspected about Daniel Lamont came close to thinking he might be a murderer, and nothing she could've said to Caroline all those years ago, when she had announced their engagement, would have kept her from marrying him. Caroline had been head-over-heels in love. And she had been happy.

As she pulled into the drive, Lucy took a deep breath and willed herself to be strong for Caroline.

The smell of honeysuckle wafted over Lucy as she knocked on the door and she felt a burst of optimism course through her.

A few minutes later, when Caroline didn't answer her knock or the ringing doorbell, her trepidation started to return. Lucy tried the door and found it unlocked. She pulled her iPhone out of her purse and took a quiet step into the foyer and looked around before saying, "Caroline?" as loudly as she could without sounding panicked.

"Oh, sorry, I'm coming!" Caroline jogged around the corner of the second floor hall and started down the steps. "I was in Daniel's office and... Are you okay?"

"You scared the crap out of me, Caroline! Why didn't you answer the door?"

"I left it open. I figured you'd come right in. God, Lucy, I'm sorry! I wasn't thinking."

Lucy threw her arms around Caroline and let out a relieved laugh. "No, I'm sorry. I'm a little jumpy and I have to remember that I'm not in Miami where doors are locked unless someone is robbing you."

Caroline smiled, "Not many locked doors around Graceful Bay. If you're at home, your door is open to visitors. Come in Lucy. Do you want some coffee?"

"Love some!"

As they walked to the kitchen, Lucy assessed her friend. Caroline looked decidedly tougher today. Her perfect posture had never wavered, but yesterday she had lost her swagger. Now it was back.

When she had poured each of them a mug of coffee, Caroline said, "I have something I want to tell you, Lucy, and then I have a few things I want to show you."

Lucy nodded and inhaled the aroma of dark roast with a little chicory in it. "Anything, Caroline."

"First, I'm sorry I didn't tell you about my disastrous marriage right away. When we had lunch on Monday I wanted to give you a chance to settle in, for a day anyway, before I spilled my guts." She paused to gather her thoughts, "And then Mathew was found murdered."

Lucy took her hand. "Caroline, you have had an unbelievable couple of days. I wanted to tell you that I am so sorry I haven't been around to listen. I haven't been a very good friend to you over the last few years. I haven't been available if you wanted to talk or if you were having problems. Caroline, I want you to know that you are the best friend I could ever ask for and I am going to try to be that for you too, from now on. If you'll let me?"

Caroline looked stunned. "Lucy Walker, what are you talking about? You were working as an undercover cop in another state, risking your life to keep all the rest of us safe. Granted, I would have preferred that you had chosen a vocation that would keep you safe too, but you had to do what was right. It never occurred to me to feel upset or neglected because we couldn't talk on the phone every time I wanted to." She squeezed Lucy's shoulder. "Silly goose."

Lucy had a tear in her eye when she said, "Caroline, I never told you, and now I think maybe I should have, but..."

"You never liked Daniel. Lucy, you didn't have to tell me anything. I knew the moment you two met that you didn't care for him. My parents didn't like him either and they were much more obvious about it, but there wasn't anything they could point to and say, 'There, that's the reason you shouldn't marry that man.' Besides, we were making our home in Graceful Bay and they were pleased that we would be close by." She sighed, "I was in love, Lucy. I don't know why exactly or what had me so caught up in Daniel Lamont. It wasn't just because he's pretty." Caroline winked at Lucy and laughed ruefully. "It was more than a year after our wedding that I began to fear I'd made a mistake. Daniel was always generous with money and lavish vacations, but not with time or friendship. I felt lonely, and it was easy to identify a reason for my growing unhappiness, his work schedule or the amount of time we spent apart. What I didn't let myself admit was that he was becoming dismissive and sometimes mean."

"He was good on paper," Lucy stated.

"Exactly! And he still is, but in other ways, Daniel

is very distant. I don't need a husband to spoil me with stuff," she gestured around the room. "I *want* a man to love me. He used to call from Atlanta and ask whether there was anything I needed or wanted, send fresh flowers or other little presents. Before that, when he was working in Charleston I used stay with him and attend dinners and cocktail parties. Even when he first got the promotion in Atlanta, I would spend time with him there, but it wasn't long before I began to feel like an accessory, like a beautiful piece of jewelry occasionally taken out to be admired and then tucked back away in the safe. And then I just started to feel like a nuisance.

"Lucy, I know how this must sound, like I'm making excuses for my infidelity, but I'm not. I feel terrible that I had an affair. I don't know what got into me exactly. Mathew was fun and young and handsome and smart, and he talked to me and listened as though our conversation was the only thing of interest in the whole wide world. We were easy and attentive and genuine with one another. Lovemaking was spectacular. I know I was smitten, Lucy, but I wasn't in love.

"For months I didn't let myself consider what I was doing to Mathew and certainly not what I was doing to my husband, but when I finally did, I was disgusted. I ended it with Mathew and decided to try and talk to Daniel, maybe find a way to make it work, and if that failed..." Caroline's voice trailed off, but when she continued, it was firm, "If that failed, then I would consider divorce.

"The thing is, Lucy, Mathew had nothing to do with the state of my marriage. My affair was maybe a symptom of how unhappy I was, how frustrated and angry, but it was not the cause. I feel terrible that I was unfaithful to Daniel, but not that I have considered leaving him."

Lucy spoke. "Caroline, how long have you been thinking of separating?"

Tears spilled out of Caroline's eyes. "Longer than I would let myself admit it." Finally she whispered, "Lucy, there's more. There's more to Daniel than just how I feel in our marriage."

Lucy asked, "What do you mean?" but she was already thinking back to Daniel's name coming up during her undercover investigation.

"Let's get some more coffee and I'll show you."

COOKED BOOKS

THEY REFILLED THEIR CUPS AND Caroline turned off the pot. "Daniel keeps a home office upstairs."

Lucy noticed that Caroline had straightened her shoulders and looked very determined and a little angry as she led Lucy up one flight of stairs.

The room they entered on the second floor was paneled from floor to ceiling in oak with one wall covered in built-in bookshelves that were filled with leather bound volumes. Framed, beautifully detailed maps of the coast from the mid-Atlantic United States down to Mexico and Central America hung on one wall, and another had several large, windows shaded in spite of the early hour. The massive desk and leather club chairs completed the look of a traditional study. It looked like a place where men went to make deals and drink scotch.

Lucy had been in the room only once years before when Caroline had given her a tour of her new manor shortly after she and Daniel were married. "Impressive," was what she'd said then and she repeated it now.

Caroline regarded the space for a moment before saying, "Not a room meant to be shared with a woman." Then she looked at her friend, "And this, evidently, is where he keeps his secrets. Not many of them, but a few. Lucy, I think Daniel is involved with some very nefarious people. In fact, I'm afraid he's right at home with them."

"What did you find?" asked Lucy, crossing over to stand beside her friend at the enormous desk.

There was a landline on one side of the desk but no computer. Daniel must carry his laptop with him wherever he went.

Caroline had three neat, dark green folders sitting on the desk. She opened the first one, picked up a stack of papers and said, "These are ledgers, Lucy. There're in some kind of code, but I was in finance long enough to figure that much out."

Lucy wasn't looking at the papers. She was looking at the first in a small pile of photographs that remained in the folder. Picking it up she asked, "Caroline, when was this taken?"

In the photograph Daniel Lamont stood on one end of what had to be an enormous yacht. The water in the background was so blue that it must be the Caribbean. He was smiling broadly under a handsome Panama hat and was lifting a crystal low-ball glass to the camera. Three men stood with him.

Caroline set down the ledger when she saw the look on her friend's face. Taking the picture from her, she said, "These photographs are another thing that has me asking questions. I don't know these men, but in one of the other photographs the yacht is docked and there is obviously a party going on. A party with lots of bikini-clad beauties, one of whom is falling all over my husband, not that it's relevant." Lucy was now looking at the picture Caroline had indicated. "This was taken from the dock and you can see the name of the ship: *Cubanos Blancos*. I think the boat is somewhere in the Caribbean, but I can't be sure. The thing is, the linen shirt that Daniel is wearing is one that I bought for him on a trip to Manhattan last summer. That means that this picture was taken after that, and he's never mentioned a trip or a party on a yacht since then, let alone being anywhere near the Caribbean.

"If it was only the photos and not the ledger, I might suspect that he was having an affair, or simply doing fun things without me, and honestly, I think I've forfeited the right to complain about that." Caroline's expression was pained for a moment and Lucy put a hand on her shoulder encouraging her friend to go on. "But the ledger could be very bad, Lucy. There is a lot of money on those books." She pointed at the stack of papers. "And he's hanging out on that yacht.... I googled the name *Cubanos Blancos*."

"The boat belongs to the Havana Cartel out of Cuba, Mexico and Central America," said Lucy matter-of-factly.

When Caroline looked astonished, Lucy picked up the first photograph that had caught her attention. "Caroline, I know who these men are. I had to study them at length when I went into deep cover in Miami. They are very bad news, and if Daniel is doing any business with them, he's probably laundering their money so they can spend it in the United States and Europe."

Caroline went white and sat down abruptly in the leather desk chair. "That's not good. I know that. But exactly how bad is it?"

Lucy knelt down in front of Caroline and took her hands, "These are very scary men, Caroline, and if Daniel is involved with them and he has survived, then he is probably very scary or very devious. Now I need you to think very carefully. Is there any way that Daniel could have found out about your affair with Mathew?"

Caroline looked at Lucy like that was the last thing on her mind.

Lucy continued, "I don't know about your husband, but I can tell you this: these men believe in retribution, not forgiveness. If Daniel knows these men and wanted to have Mathew killed, he wouldn't have to go far to find someone who would do it for him. That doesn't mean that he did, but it's pretty incriminating. Tell me more about your suspicion that you were being followed."

Caroline shook her head. "I still don't understand why Daniel would have people watching me. I thought about it and it began long before I even met Mathew, so it wasn't because of that."

"If someone was following you, and was any good at it, he would have noticed that you had begun to notice him. Daniel may have switched him out."

"But why would he have me followed in the first place if it didn't have anything to do with the affair?"

When Caroline continued to stare at her, Lucy said, "I need you to think hard, Caroline. Did he leave anything around the house? Did he receive strange phone calls? Did he seem suspicious or scared of something happening to either one of you? Is there anything else that may have made him want to keep track of you?"

"No, I have racked my brain and I can't think of anything."

"I think that Mathew's murder should have us erring on the side of caution. Spouses are often aware of even subtle changes in the affections or moods of their husbands and wives. Daniel may have picked up on your dissatisfaction, or he may have noted that you were suddenly happier and wondered why. Another possibility is that he didn't have you followed because he suspected you were having an affair, but because he was negotiating with a drug cartel and wanted to make sure that you were safe." Lucy paused, "And another possibility is that someone was following Mathew."

"That's ridiculous, Lucy. I understand why you mention it, but it's more likely that my imagination has gotten away from me because I'm scared."

Lucy did not mention that the families of criminals were often used to ensure compliance if a deal went wrong. But she did say, "If you were being followed because Daniel is involved with the Havana Cartel, you could be in danger."

Caroline grabbed Lucy's hand, "In danger? From these people?" She pointed at the photograph of Daniel on the bow of the yacht with the three Hispanic men. "That never even occurred to me."

"I don't know what this is all about, Caroline, but these are scary guys. I know because they almost killed my partner and me. Maybe not exactly the same men, but the same kind of men." She looked at Caroline's stricken face, "I'm trying to figure out if Daniel may have anything to do with Mathew's murder."

"Oh God, what do I do now?"

"I think you should get out of the house for the time being."

"Maybe." She still looked skeptical. Gesturing at the papers and photographs on the desk, Caroline said, "If this is all true, then I will just leave him, but it would be easier to do if I knew for sure."

"It's hard to be certain, but I don't want you to take a chance." Lucy looked down at the stack of files on the desk. "Do you have a photocopier? It would be good to make a copy of the ledger before Daniel thinks to move it."

Caroline smile reached her eyes for the first time since Lucy arrived, "Already done."

Before they put everything away, the two women also photocopied the pictures. Then they tucked the files back into the cabinet where Lucy had found them and let themselves out of Daniel Lamont's office.

Back in the kitchen they sat in silence for a few minutes. Finally Lucy said, "Caroline, I think you should consider telling Sheriff Grier about Daniel's affiliations and the fact that he may very well have known about your affair."

Caroline looked exasperated. "I knew you would say that. At this point, I don't know anything for sure."

Lucy didn't mince words "What you found in those files upstairs is proof enough that Daniel is into something questionable or at least consorting with men who are. I understand your reluctance, but I'm worried about your safety. At least pack a bag and come stay with me."

But Caroline was adamant. "Not yet, Lucy. Soon, but not yet."

HE COOKS!

L UCY SPENT ANOTHER HALF AN hour trying to convince her friend to come home with her for a few nights. She was torn between wanting to get Caroline out of the home she shared with Daniel Lamont, and not wanting to terrify her best friend. In the end, Caroline promised to call her when she heard from Daniel again, but absolutely refused to leave her home without first speaking to her husband.

Lucy understood that, despite evidence to the contrary, it was hard for anybody to suddenly regard the one they had once loved as a danger, and especially so in Caroline's case because she felt guilty about her own infidelity. But she wished Caroline wouldn't take the chance. In fact, on the drive home, Lucy began to second-guess herself. She had recently been through years of lying and betrayal, living among dangerous and often cruel men, convincing them that she was one of them. She wasn't exactly objective. On the other hand, the fact was that Daniel was consorting with a corrupt group of people and had a set of cooked books in his home office. Lucy was also pretty sure that Caroline had been right about Daniel having her followed. Whether it was because he was suspicious or because he was having her protected, it was a dodgy thing to do.

Lucy's stomach was growling as she pulled into the driveway of her grandparents' home. *Her home*, she corrected herself and smiled at the thought. She mentally went through the contents of her refrigerator and couldn't think of a single thing she wanted to prepare. Mostly, because she was too hungry to cook. *Cheese and crackers*, she thought.

She had no sooner flipped on the kitchen light and opened the fridge when her cell phone began vibrating from inside of her purse. She pulled it out and answered without glancing at the caller ID.

"Hello, beautiful."

It was Gabriel. Lucy's heart did a little pitter-pat before she could tell it to stop. "Hello, yourself, handsome," she purred.

"Had dinner yet?"

"You read my mind! I just walked in the door and I'm starving!"

"I'm about to pull a lasagna out of the oven. A little salad, a little red wine..."

"On my way!" Lucy set the stack of photocopied files down on the dining room table, then, thinking better of it, she brought them into her grandfather's study and locked them in the safe. *Silly*, she thought, but felt better not leaving them out in the middle of everything.

The evening was getting chilly and she thought of changing out of her skirt but instead grabbed a light wool blazer and a linen scarf from the coat closet and slipped out of her shoes before locking up the house and skipping happily down the stairs to the beach. Lucy kept on skipping, shoes in one hand, purse in the other until her leg began to ache. "Darn it!" she said aloud. Being an invalid was getting tiresome. Still, she slowed her pace and in a quarter of an hour was letting herself in through the newly repaired gate at the back of Gabriel's house. She made her way up the cobblestoned walk, treading carefully in the dark. Suddenly the path lights came on and the back door opened.

"Lucy! I was about to call and see where you were when it occurred to me that you probably walked in spite of the fact that a man was killed on this beach just yesterday." He looked admonishingly at Lucy's rebellious smile and then down at her limp and said, "And don't you think you should go easy for a little while?"

Lucy continued smiling and shrugged. "We'll get along a lot better, Mr. Black, if you don't treat me like a wimpy little girl.

He looked sheepish, "Yeah, yeah. But I have a point about the dead body."

The kitchen was in the back of the house and she could smell mozzarella cheese and tomato sauce through the open door. Ignoring his last comment she announced, "I'm hungry!"

Gabriel took two steps toward Lucy and in one motion kissed her full on the lips and picked her up into his arms. He carried her over the threshold, past a sunroom and into the kitchen where he set her down at a little table in a bay window. Baxter rubbed up against her legs in greeting and then resumed his place on a wooden stool near the oven with his nose pointed toward the steaming casserole dish on the counter.

Gabriel carried two wine glasses and a big bowl of fresh greens tossed in a vinaigrette to the table. "Wine, my dear?"

"Yes, please," said Lucy. She felt positively giddy. How was it possible that this handsome man she had just met was making her dinner and serving her wine and generally spoiling her? "I must be the luckiest girl in the world," she said, and when he turned back to her she saw his eyes sparkle in delight.

Gabriel poured red wine and they toasted. "Thank you so much for having me over. When you called I was literally contemplating the things in my fridge that don't require cooking. It was dismal. I think I was falsely ambitious about my desire to actually have to cook food when I went to the grocery store the other day. I should've picked up a few frozen dinners just in case."

Gabriel grinned at her, "I'll cook for you whenever you like. All I expect in return is flattery and sex."

"Sex? I don't know about that, Mr. Black. I've been vulnerable to your charms the last twenty-four hours, but now that I've come to my senses..."

Before she could finish, Gabriel scooped her up in his arms and set her to the kitchen island. They locked in a kiss, and as she pulled at his jeans, he pushed her skirt up to her waist and slid his thumb under her panties. Lucy groaned and let go of his open zipper so that she could brace herself on her elbows. With his other hand Gabriel lifted Lucy's shirt over her breasts and undid her bra. He pushed himself against her, and with his thumb wet from her desire, gently rubbed circles over Lucy's hard nipples. Then he bent to take them in his mouth, first one and then the other. His mouth and tongue moved greedily down her stomach. Lucy lay all the way back on the granite countertop while Gabriel slid her panties down her legs and over her toes, his mouth never losing contact with her skin. When the lacy pair fell to the floor he began tracing slow circles around her pussy with his tongue. The circles got smaller and smaller while Lucy writhed in ecstasy until his mouth found her clit and remained there. With excruciatingly slow movements, Gabriel brought her to the edge, and when she couldn't stand another second, he sped up and took her over.

While Lucy caught her breath, Gabriel pulled his T-shirt off and pressed her body to his bare chest. She could feel him hard against her and desire swelled between them. He began kissing her neck as he fingered her. He pulled away and looked deep into Lucy's liquid blue eyes, opening his fly and sliding into her, gently at first and then insistently.

Lucy cried out in bliss as Gabriel thrust into her deeper and deeper. Her vision blurred with pleasure but she continued to hold his gaze. He grabbed hold of her hips and held himself as far in as he could go. Lucy nodded.

"Now. Gabriel, now."

And he pulled almost all the way out before burying himself over and over again. They came together, their eyes never parting as their bodies shuddered in rapture.

Gabriel buried his head in Lucy's breasts and

they stayed still for a minute. Then he slowly lifted his head and brushed Lucy's hair off of her cheeks and neck. He traced her mouth with his fingertips and then cupped her beautiful face in his hands.

"You are amazing, Lucy Walker."

"I am amazed, Gabriel Black."

They smiled stupidly at one another until the rustle of aluminum foil got their attention. Turning their heads at the same time, Lucy began laughing as Gabriel scolded his cat.

"Baxter, that's not for you!"

The cat looked up from the lasagna he was trying to get to with a piece of tin foil between his teeth. He seemed to sense that his master could not get to him right away because he slowly lowered his nose back to the pan. Gabriel sighed a little sadly as he gently untangled himself from Lucy's body and, with his pants around his ankles, chased the fat cat off of the stovetop.

Lucy started to sit up but she was laughing so hard that she couldn't quite manage it. Gabriel shot her an admonishing look and put the still-steaming lasagna back into the warm oven for protection. Then he waddled over and began tickling Lucy.

"You think it's funny that my cat is eating our dinner?" he asked through his own laughter while Lucy flailed around on the kitchen island. They wound up in a tight embrace, both shaking with laughter until they were exhausted.

"Is there time for a quick shower?" asked Lucy, glancing toward the oven. "I'm a little sticky, if you know what I mean," she raised her eyebrows suggestively.

"It'll stay hot," replied Gabriel in answer and finally stepped out of his pants.

He swung her up into his arms and carried her up the stairs, through a very masculine master bedroom and into an enormous bathroom. Catching a glimpse of the two of them in the mirror above gray granite sinks, Lucy marveled at how easily Gabriel carried her around. He followed her gaze and their eyes met in the mirror. Hipped her one way and then the other, bounced her a little as if he were weighing her and said, "I'm gonna have to keep you, Miss Walker." Then he set her down and left her to wonder while he turned on the shower.

It was a huge stone-tiled shower with five different nozzles and plenty of room for the two of them.

"I might have to start showering over here, Mr. Black."

"Anytime, Lucy," he replied with a silly grin. "The owners remodeled the master bathroom and the kitchen when they were thinking of selling the house, but apparently, with a few new amenities, they decided the house was too nice to sell and opted to rent it out during the winters. Lucky for me."

"Lucky for me too," said Lucy. "I heard the owners are a charming pair."

"Yep. Tom Westin and Darren Harrison."

"Explains why they remodeled it with no sign of a woman's touch."

Gabriel laughed. "Special Securities Provisions, my firm, did some security work for them in the Bahamas, and when it was all resolved we met for dinner in Manhattan, mid-January. I mentioned that I wanted a break from the city, and since I can run my business from just about anywhere as long as I can get to New York once a month, I was scouting a nice quiet place to spend the winter. Darren started spouting the virtues of the Bahamas in winter, but Tom interrupted and said, 'Gabriel doesn't want the islands, he wants quiet and charm and not cold.' And, Tom was right. As it happened, of course..."

"They happened to have a house."

"Exactly. So we traded a few precious hours of SSP's time for a couple of months in their summer home and I was down here by mid-February. I gotta tell you, Graceful Bay was just what the doctor ordered."

"Did you need some fixing?"

Gabriel looked at Lucy while he lathered shampoo through her hair. "I did. A little bit."

"Lucky for me," she repeated and twirled around in the water ducking her head under the rain shower spout. When she emerged, she asked, "How long do you have it?"

"The house? End of May."

"And then you'll go back to your apartment in New York?"

With a completely serious expression, Gabriel said, "No, of course not. Then I'll move in with you." He winked at her in the sexiest way and all she could do was laugh and roll her eyes and hide under the fountains of hot water while she took a second to wonder what that would be like.

Don't be silly, she admonished herself while she rubbed her soapy hands all over his muscular body.

When he was all rinsed off, Lucy pinched Gabriel's perfect butt and said, "Let's eat, already!"

Wrapping Lucy in a big beige towel, Gabriel went into the master bedroom and returned dressed in jeans and a WestPoint T-shirt. He must've run downstairs too because he handed Lucy the clothes he'd helped her out of a little while before.

Lucy grinned, slipped on her shirt and put her panties on with a snap of the band. "Thank you, Gabriel." Looking at his shirt, she asked, "Are you an alumni?"

"Yes, ma'am. It's why I have such good manners." He sighed as she finished dressing. "It's a shame to see you all covered up." Gabriel gave her the once-over and then picked her up again and carried her downstairs to the kitchen.

Laughing, Lucy exclaimed, "I can walk just fine, Mr. Black!"

"It's the soldier in me. Can't leave the wounded behind. And, your leg needs a little rest."

SLUMBER PARTY

Back in the kitchen, Gabriel set Lucy gently into a chair at the table and poured her more wine. The table was already set and he served salad while Lucy sipped her red wine and smiled up at him. Then he brought the lasagna over and placed it on a trivet and offered her a small basket of fresh baguette that he magically pulled out of one of the cupboards.

"Does Baxter like bread too?" asked Lucy.

"Baxter likes everything as soon as my back is turned. I sometimes forget which cupboard I've stashed my dinner in." He served Lucy a spatula full of lasagna, and then himself.

When she picked up a forkful of the hot pasta, a string of mozzarella cheese stretched from her mouth to the plate and she broke it with her fingers. "Mmmm!" she said when she was done chewing. "This is wonderful! So fresh and light. Did you make your own sauce?"

"I grew the tomatoes myself," replied Gabriel with a wink. "Well, no, I didn't, but yes, I did make my own sauce. I bought the tomatoes and mozzarella at a really nice little market I found in the center of town."

"Hoffman's Gourmet Market! I love that store! In

fact, that's where I bought the strawberries and ice cream we had for dessert last night."

"I had you for dessert, as I recall, and ice cream for fortification afterwards," interrupted Gabriel.

"You can have me again tonight," she replied with a wink and a smile.

"Cheers to that!" said Gabriel and they clinked glasses.

Lucy took her another bite of lasagna, blowing the steam away before she put it in her mouth. "This is so delicious!"

"I use fresh oregano." He looked at her thoughtfully for a moment. "When you're settled and Caroline's mess is over, let me take you to Manhattan."

Lucy thought for a second before replying, "I wouldn't say no, but where did that come from?"

"I won't be able to surprise you with anything new and fantastic in Graceful Bay. You already know where all the good stuff is. And," he added, "it's important to a man's ego to be able to surprise his girl."

"His girl?"

"Yep. My girl," Gabriel said matter-of-factly and smiled at Lucy.

She returned the smile and said, "This dinner is a fantastic surprise."

They ate and chatted about the small town, relatively new to Gabriel and so familiar to Lucy. Both of them were glad not to mention Caroline's troubles for an hour or so. When they were finished, Gabriel cleared the dishes and they carried their wine into a capacious and surprisingly modern living room with a gas fireplace and a lot of leather and glass furniture.

"Pretty modern for an old Georgian Court home," Lucy commented, "it's nice though."

"They did a good job remodeling." Gabriel studied the wall for a moment before saying, "Shall I build you a fire, milady?" He flipped one of the switches and a roaring fire sprung up in the stone fireplace. Lucy laughed. Ushering her to a plush leather sofa, he tucked a cashmere throw around her legs and handed her a wine glass. "How's Caroline?"

Lucy paused for a minute wondering how much she should tell Gabriel, but even though she had only known him a short time, she trusted him. She trusted him to do the right thing by Mathew Wilson and to help her protect her friend from the fallout of the affair and, if necessary, from Daniel Lamont. And Lucy was pretty sure it would prove to be necessary.

"When I went over to her house today, Caroline showed me some interesting documents she found in Daniel's office."

Lucy told him about how Caroline had discovered the documents and what she thought they were.

"So Daniel Lamont is committing tax fraud?"

"That and maybe a lot worse."

"I don't know enough about finance to know what the ledgers mean exactly, but they looked pretty damning. Caroline is sure that what she found is a second set of books and she's a really savvy accountant. Plus, she really doesn't *want* to believe that her husband is doing anything illegal but she still thinks those papers represent fraudulent accounting."

"She doesn't want to believe it, but she was looking through his file cabinet...." Gabriel left the rest unsaid. A lot of people who couldn't imagine that their spouses were up to no good went searching, for one reason or another, for evidence that their spouses were up to no good.

Lucy shrugged. "Love may be blind, but a troubled marriage leads to suspicion. Caroline isn't quite ready to accept what she found. She will, though, and her anger is going to outweigh her guilt. Then she'll start making decisions right quick. I've known Caroline all my life and she doesn't hesitate to act once she's made her mind up."

"If Daniel did kill her lover and suspects she's found those files, she might be in a lot of danger," said Gabriel carefully.

Lucy set down her wine glass and curled up closer to Gabriel. "I know. I can't imagine she would confront him before she has a plan of action. Caroline can be spontaneous and fickle when her emotions get her, but when it really counts, she knows how to strategize, and she knows how to protect herself. When I got there today, she had already made photocopies of Daniel's papers for me to take home..."

"You have copies of everything in your house?" Gabriel interrupted.

"Yes. They're tucked away in my Grandpa's office. My office," she corrected herself with an uncomfortable smile.

"Lucy, what if Caroline uses the photocopies to threaten Daniel?"

"Now that she suspects him of violence, she would never, not even in a fit of irrational anger, tell Daniel that she had made photocopies of his cooked books! Never. You're going to have to trust me on that. No one is going to find out that there's a bunch of evidence against Daniel Lamont in my house."

"Okay." He lifted her chin gently. "I trust you, Lucy. I just don't want anything to happen to you. You know, especially now that I've started to plan our future together."

Lucy laughed and nudged him in the side. He pulled her closer. "I know some forensic accountants in the army and the FBI if Caroline decides she wants to have those books looked at."

"She knows what they are. If she turns him in, the FBI will probably take them over anyway." Lucy looked uncertainly at Gabriel for a moment.

"Uh-oh. There's more."

"Well, yes. The thing is that the cooked books are dealing with an amount of money that's way beyond Daniel's personal wealth. Way beyond."

"Are you saying that the second set of books is not a record of Lamont's money? Whose money is it, Lucy?"

"I don't know for sure..."

Gabriel interrupted her. "Who do you suspect?"

"The Havana Cartel. They're a cartel out of..."

"I know who they are!" Gabriel looked completely exasperated. "Why do you suspect them?"

"In the files with the ledger there were photographs

of Daniel with several of the cartel leaders on a yacht somewhere in the Caribbean. At least, it looked like the Caribbean. Also, when I was an undercover cop in Miami, I heard the name of Daniel's bank bandied about a few times in not-so-polite society. I didn't think much of it then because those guys use real banks all the time after their money has been cleaned. But, now..." she trailed off. "I submitted the information to the task force along with all of the other info, but I never heard anything significant about Daniel's bank or anyone working for it being affiliated with the Havana Cartel."

Gabriel stared at her. "You can't have that kind of evidence lying around your house, Lucy." He ran his fingers through his hair. "This just got really scary."

"Daniel can't possibly suspect anything. He left the books locked in his file cabinet. He would have put them in a safe if he was concerned that Caroline would find them. We've got a little time."

"Maybe," Gabriel replied skeptically. "Either way, you are staying here tonight and tomorrow we're going to get those papers out of your house. Right after we get Caroline out of her house. Whether she likes it or not."

"What if she wants to wait until Daniel comes home to tell him she's leaving?"

He looked astounded. "She can't. She's got to get out of that house as soon as possible on the pretext of leaving her husband and then, in an unrelated matter, those papers have to be discovered by the Feds. If Caroline is linked to anything that might endanger the cartel, they will come after her. Then she'll either be dead or in witness protection. You have to trust *me* on this one, Lucy."

Lucy straightened. "I have thought this through a little, Mr. Black. I spent day in and day out with those guys when I was under cover. Remember? But I know Caroline, and this is going to take a minute to set in."

"Tonight is all she's getting. And she can't be the one to turn in the evidence."

"You seem to know a lot about it," said Lucy.

"I know a thing or two about protecting witnesses. And not just protecting them from the bad guys, but protecting them from the people prosecuting the bad guys too."

Baxter picked that moment to saunter into the room and break the tension with an ornery meow before jumping into Lucy's lap. "See, Baxter wants you to stay overnight."

"At least Baxter is asking and not ordering," Lucy replied a little hotly.

"I do apologize, Miz Walker," drawled Gabriel in a pretty good impression of a Southerner. "Forgive me if I was less than a gentleman. I've spent too many years in the armed forces, making decisions and kicking ass."

Lucy laughed, "Plus, you want to get in my pants again."

"You are correct, indeed," he said, brushing Baxter away as he leaned across Lucy's lap to kiss her.

"Well, if you play your cards right, Mr. Black, you just might get lucky."

"I've got three aces."

"You'll need some ice cream!"

Gabriel laughed and squeezed her tight. This time Baxter gave him a little bite on the arm to go with his irritated meow. "All right! All right! I see how you two are. Thick as thieves already." He got up and headed for the kitchen to find some dessert.

When Gabriel left the room, Lucy scratched the cat and considered calling Caroline and telling her they were coming to get her in the morning. Gabriel was right, of course, and Lucy would go over there tomorrow and drag her friend out herself if she had to, but she wanted to give Caroline a chance to catch her breath and come to the conclusion herself. She knew Caroline wouldn't want to stay in that house another night when all of the implications set in: Daniel Lamont had probably had his wife followed, found out about her affair, gone to his cartel buddies to put a hit on poor Mathew Wilson, and was figuring out how to further punish Caroline right this moment. It made Lucy shudder.

Meanwhile, Daniel was clearly involved with some very bad men, and though Lucy couldn't decipher the ledgers herself, Caroline was a veritable whiz with finances. If she said they were cooked books, they were cooked books. So, in a short time, Caroline had discovered that the man she married was probably a murderer, a money launderer, and had been spying on her.

If Daniel *was* going to hurt Caroline, he would have to wait until the heat was off from Mathew Wilson's murder, right? Unless he was just plain furious and wasn't thinking straight. Lucy padded into the kitchen and found her phone.

Gabriel looked over from the cupboard where he was pulling out two bowls.

"I'm going to call Caroline," she explained and hit the send button. With no answer by the third ring Lucy was about to start pacing when her friend picked up.

"Hey, Lucy," she said.

"Caroline! I'm so glad you answered! I was about to work myself into a frenzy of worry."

"Honestly, Lucy, that's exactly what I did about an hour ago. I'm scared. So, I started packing a few things and I was going to see if I could come over to your place tonight. I figure that Daniel won't know I'm gone anyway unless he comes home suddenly, and this way he won't be able to surprise me in the middle of the night. I'll have a chance to talk to him when he comes home."

Lucy sighed with relief. "I'm so glad to hear you say that. The more I thought about the whole thing, the more concerned I was. Better safe than sorry, right?"

Gabriel watched Lucy and held off on the ice cream until she was off the phone with Caroline. "What's up?"

"She's going to be at my house in an hour and stay with me for the foreseeable future. The more she thought about it, the less she wanted to stay alone in their house."

"I'm not sure your place is any safer, Lucy. When Lamont realizes she's left, your house is probably the first place he'll look."

"Gabriel, don't you think you're getting a little ahead of yourself? Even if he does come home and sees that Caroline has left, he's hardly going to charge all over the county looking for her and then drag her back by her hair."

"Probably not, but he might send some thugs after her. In fact, now that Caroline's affair is out in the open with the police, it is not inconceivable that the same guys who beat Mathew Wilson to death might come after his lover too. Looking for whatever they didn't find on Mathew Wilson." When Lucy looked skeptical, he went on, "All I'm saying is that if Caroline is killed or maimed in the same way as her lover, there is a plausible explanation for both deaths that eliminates Lamont as a suspect. If I was him, and I wanted to get rid of my cheating wife, I would probably take advantage of that."

"You're saying that because the police don't have a positive motive for Mathew's murder, Daniel could argue that Caroline's death was connected to her lover, and not to him?"

"That's exactly what I'm saying. I think that someone wants to tie Mathew Wilson to Caroline. Why else would a couple of guys beat the kid to death, and take everything out of his pockets except a piece of paper with her home address scrawled on it? Even more than that, I'm trying to stress the fact that if Daniel Lamont is as bad a guy as we think he is, and he does business with a gang of known sex and drug traffickers, he's capable of a lot more than being a shitty husband. Caroline should be taking every precaution. And, now that you're involved, so should you. And, now that you're my girl," he winked at Lucy, "I'm going to make sure that you do."

Lucy had about a hundred thoughts at once, including that she really liked this man. "Okay, will you feel better if you stay with us at my house tonight?"

"Not as good as if you two stayed here tonight, but it'll do."

Lucy had her own reasons for wanting to go home that night: two handguns locked up in her safe. Gabriel had convinced her of imminent danger, but she wasn't quite ready to admit it to him.

DESIRÉE

D ANIEL LAMONT STOOD IN FRONT of an infinity mirror straightening his tie in the bedroom of his luxury apartment in Atlanta. He deftly knotted the blue silk Hermès tie as he watched the reflection of a built-for-sex woman getting dressed by the bedside. She had huge fake breasts and a round bottom. Her waist was tiny and her legs were voluptuous and long. Her hair was dark brown and straight and long and she wore a lot of dark eye make-up around what had to be fake eyelashes and almond-shaped brown eyes. Over her red lace lingerie she wore a pale pink linen pantsuit and demure silk blouse that could hardly hide her figure, but camouflaged it enough so that she didn't look like a hooker. Which was exactly what she was, although the preferred term was escort. A very expensive escort.

Daniel Lamont was routinely *escorted* by several different women who all worked for a very discreet agency in Atlanta. They arrived anonymously, looking like businesswomen, carrying the modern woman's briefcase – a large purse and a laptop – wearing quiet clothes and Burberry glasses with clear lenses. They glanced at their smartphones for emails as they checked in at the desk in the lobby downstairs, and generally announced themselves like they owned the place. When the doorman called upstairs and confirmed with Daniel that he was expecting a guest, they headed confidently for the bank of elevators. All business.

Not that Daniel worried. He had chosen this building as much for its discretion as for the amenities. It was an extravagant high-rise, full of people who had at least a little too much money. It had twenty-four-hour room service, valet parking, a pool, a well-appointed gym and spa and even a crew of dog-walkers for the Pomeranians and tea-cup poodles that belonged to the ladies-that-lunch-crowd who came to stay with their husbands or boyfriends and do some shopping in the city. The permanent residents were all busy, rich men who liked their privacy. Having "company" from time to time when the women were away was neither unexpected, nor frowned upon. The staff was well trained to keep quiet about sex, marital disputes, drug overdoses, and anything else that might raise an eyebrow. The residents were not gossips.

When his tie was perfect, Daniel turned and watched the woman transform herself back into one of thousands of business men and women who walked on the streets of Atlanta every day. Her name was Desirée. *Of course it was*, he thought.

Daniel never talked to these women. He paid well for them and tipped extravagantly when they did a good job, but when they came to his door, he didn't engage in small talk. He wasn't interested in how they'd gotten into this line of work, or what their hobbies were, or if they had children, boyfriends, or how they lived outside of this hour or two in his apartment. He offered them bottled water, but no alcohol. No one needed a drunk hooker. And when he was finished, he let them dress and then whisked them out the door from whence they came.

When Desirée left it was nearly lunchtime and Daniel was meeting several colleagues at a seafood place two blocks away. The previous evening he had been pleased to hear that Mathew Wilson's body had been found with his home address in his pocket. Everything was going according to plan. A phone call from the county sheriff's department late Tuesday afternoon to confirm his alibi had also confirmed that the cops had already contacted Caroline.

When Daniel called his wife that night, however, to ask about the murder, she had not sounded nervous, afraid or guilty when she answered his questions and assured him that she was perfectly safe in their antebellum house, that Graceful Bay had not morphed overnight into a dangerous place to live. Daniel remained casual, but he was livid. He wanted her quaking in her boots, confessing her affair and begging his forgiveness. But from Daniel's point of view, Caroline was cool as a cucumber. The lying cunt.

In fact, last night Daniel was so angry that he had needed a different kind of escort. Chantelle was much more expensive than Desirée but she was utterly subservient. Blonde, with big doe eyes and rosy cheeks, narrow hips and small natural breasts, she reminded him of Caroline. Except that Caroline would never let him fuck her like Chantelle did. When she'd come through the door last night he had frowned at her while she undressed and then, as he unzipped his trousers and turned her around on the bed, he told her she had better be sorry.

And she was. Chantelle was always sorry, and always tried to make it up to him. Last night she had spent nearly three hours making up for Caroline's lies and infidelity. She'd left bruised and exhausted and significantly richer. For his part, Daniel felt calmed. Able to think clearly, regroup and adjust his plans. He considered driving home the next evening to surprise Caroline. *Maybe I will*, he thought, wondering how it would all play out.

His source in the sheriff's department had told him that Caroline had had two visits from Thomas Grier that day. She had requested the second one. *Probably spilling her guts about the affair*, and he took a few deep breaths to ease the thoughts from his head.

He wanted to watch Caroline suffer for a while. Suffer from guilt, from suspicion, and from fear. Daniel had chosen her to be his princess when he'd proposed to and married her. She would be the woman on the pedestal, who had his babies and lived in his home, his castle. He would protect her from harm and cherish her. His life away from her was his own, none of her business, but he had never let it affect her.

Daniel had known that his wife was dissatisfied with their marriage, but he thought it was only because he was spending so much time away. He was in the middle of strategizing a very delicate arrangement with some powerful men in Central America and, when it was settled, he had decided to take his wife on a trip to Europe, or Brazil, or wherever the hell she wanted to go. But he had been completely blindsided by her affair with Mathew Wilson. The men following Caroline were there to look after her, not to spy. Daniel had had someone tailing his wife since before they got married. It wasn't that she was in imminent danger, but in his line of work, at least the more lucrative part of it, you could never be too careful. Daniel was simply protecting what was his.

About a year ago when the crew who took turns checking in on his wife noticed that she seemed to have noticed them – not anything blatant, but they said she would look at them surreptitiously as if she'd begun to realize they were around a lot – Daniel had switched teams and varied the watchers more frequently. Having someone follow her in Graceful Bay was nearly impossible. Everyone in that town knew each other, and if a stranger started hanging around then those gossipy assholes would start asking questions. Besides that, it didn't seem necessary. The residents of Graceful Bay would notice anyone out of place – one of Daniel's babysitters or a guy sent by his enemies to threaten what was his. In this line of work bad guys were everywhere. They came from his rivals, of course, but also from the men he was allied with. When you had a guy laundering tens of millions of dollars a month for you, you checked out his weaknesses on the off chance you might need to make use of them one day.

Summertime was the exception. In summer the town was flooded by tourists and blending in, as long as you got a tan and wore flip-flops, was easy as pie. So, other than summer, Caroline had watchers on her frequent trips to Charleston, whenever she came to Atlanta, and anywhere else she might travel, but not at home.

His wife had never mentioned anything to him about thinking she was being followed and he assumed, correctly as it turned out, that when he had varied the watchers she had chalked it up to her imagination. Daniel had taken great care to keep his wife ignorant of the more questionable, more dangerous sides of his career.

But after all of his troubles that bitch had betrayed him with another man. He found himself taking a few more deep breaths as he finished a bottle of icy cold Evian. He didn't want to ruin the calming effects of Chantelle and Desirée. Besides, he had a new plan for his wife.

LEAD FOOT

LUCY AND GABRIEL ABANDONED THEIR ice cream and went upstairs to Gabriel's bedroom suite. She followed him into a very large walk-in closet that turned out to be more of a dressing room with seating. In addition to a center island with drawers for accessories and a broad top for folding clothes or, as Gabriel was doing, loading hand guns, the walls were also lined with enough shelves and drawers and hanging space for several indulgent wardrobes.

Lucy sat on a leather stool in front of a vanity mirror and spun herself around to face Gabriel. "I guess that's a good idea," she indicated the Heckler and Koch semi-automatic he was holding, "but it makes me a little more nervous."

"Better safe than sorry. We might be dealing with drug dealers." When Lucy nodded, he asked, "Where's yours?"

"Lock box in Grandpa's office, right next to Daniel's cooked books." Lucy had a 9mm Beretta and a Colt revolver with a bone handle that she was particularly fond of. She hadn't been to a shooting range in half a year and made a mental note to go in after this mess was resolved. *Even in Graceful Bay*, she thought a little ruefully, *a girl has to maintain her aim.* Hopefully she could still hold her own. Hopefully, she wouldn't have to.

"Honestly, Gabriel, I am still having a hard time believing this is happening. I never cared for Daniel, but I certainly didn't think my best friend was marrying a white collar criminal and a stone cold murderer."

Gabriel nodded at her. "If you had suspected he was that bad, you would have mentioned it to Caroline." He finished checking his weapons and placed the guns and extra ammunition in a small leather duffel bag, along with extra underwear, a T-shirt, and some socks.

"You moving in, buddy?"

"If I was moving in, I would pack my silk robe and jewelry case."

Lucy watched him as he wandered into the bathroom and came out with a dopp kit. "Let's go."

When they reached the front door, Lucy glanced into the living room where Baxter was preening himself on one of the chairs and asked, "Should we bring the cat?"

"Baxter is usually fine on his own." When he saw the look on her face, Gabriel said, "Actually, yeah, he would probably feel better if he's with us."

Lucy called the cat and Baxter sauntered into the foyer. She picked him up and walked out. Gabriel set the alarm and locked up behind them, then opened the passenger door of his Land Rover for Lucy and Baxter.

When he got in the other side he leaned over and kissed Lucy on the lips. "I never realized how easy it is to get the girl: I just have to show her my cat."

Patting him on the cheek and grinning, Lucy replied, "All there is to it, baby."

Both were quiet as they approached Lucy's house. The sprawling home was bathed in moonlight, but otherwise dark.

"As I'm sure you know, Former Officer Walker, it is a good idea to leave a light on."

"That must be why Miami Dade pushed my resignation, Former Warrant Officer Black," she smiled. "Besides, up until yesterday I thought I was safely back in the bosom of Graceful Bay, South Carolina, where we only lock up when the spring breakers and summer crowds are in town."

Gabriel put his hand on Lucy's leg before she could get out of the car. "Hey you, spring break came early this year. A little prevention goes a long way."

Lucy could feel Gabriel's exasperation when she unlocked the front door to her house and the alarm system didn't engage.

"What's your code?"

Lucy recited a pass code and Gabriel typed it into the keypad to set the alarm. "But I'll have to change it if we break up."

Gabriel took Baxter out of Lucy's arms and set the cat down on the floor. "Not gonna happen, lady."

She was about to protest when he picked her up, pressed her against the wall with his body and kissed her long and deep. When he released her Lucy said dizzily, "You're crazy, Mr. Black"

"Just certain, is all, Miss Walker. Now let's go get your gun."

They went upstairs to the study and Lucy flipped back a perfectly camouflaged wooden panel to reveal a wall safe. Gabriel smiled at the cliché. It was a digital safe, and when she had punched in the numbers, the thick steel door swung silently open. In it were the two guns, the photocopied ledger, several file-sized leather envelopes and two stacks of twenties with bank wrappers that said they were each worth ten grand.

"Are you concerned about the American banking system?"

Laughing, Lucy replied, "The cash was my Grandpa's. He was a kid during the depression and a few of his father's colleagues threw themselves out of New York skyscrapers on Black Monday when they lost it all. My grandmother told me he used to keep more in here until she convinced him to get a safety deposit box."

"That must be the key for said box," said Gabriel, indicating a numbered brass key on a leather and gold keychain.

"I guess so. Jesus, when this is all over, I'd better take a look at all of this stuff. I haven't really faced the responsibility of my grandparents' estate."

"It's in good hands, I'm sure, and you had your own life to figure out, Lucy. You were a kid when they died."

"What a luxury, to still be a kid at twenty-two."

"Hey, don't be hard on yourself. For one thing, you are an amazing woman, and for another, it's pretty indulgent to beat yourself up for having a little luxury when your grandparents died."

"Touché!" said Lucy and nudged Gabriel in the ribs. "All right, let's get these things locked, loaded and hidden away before Caroline gets here.

Lucy let Gabriel admire her well-oiled Colt while

she checked the Beretta. When the guns were ready for a firefight, and Gabriel had the ledgers in his hands, she flipped the safeties, closed the safe and they went downstairs to the kitchen. Baxter was waiting for them, rubbing against the refrigerator.

"Are you hungry, little kitty?" asked Lucy as she bent to scratch his ears.

"Little kitty? He weighs more than you do, sweetheart."

Ignoring him, Lucy pulled a can of tuna out of the pantry and opened it, putting half its contents into a porcelain bowl and setting it on the floor. Baxter commenced the half purring, half growling noise he made when he got something really yummy to eat, and tucked right into the tuna fish.

Lucy put on some water for tea and a moment later her phone chirped. It was a text message from Caroline saying that she had just left her house.

"She should be here in about ten minutes," Lucy told Gabriel, then corrected herself, "well, five, since it's Caroline driving."

"Lead foot?"

"Lead foot, speed demon, road hog, take your pick. Caroline's father gave her a sports car when she turned sixteen and six months later took it back because she had so many speeding tickets she was in danger of losing her license. In fact, all the money she earned from her first job clerking at her father's bank that summer went to paying her speeding tickets."

"Lesson learned?"

"Hardly. The next summer all the money she

earned clerking at a different bank went to buying another sports car."

"And the year after that?"

"Paying off speeding tickets." Lucy laughed, "Just kidding, the year after that, Caroline spent the summer in the Philippines building houses with Habitat for Humanity."

"Really?" He hated to admit it, but despite Lucy's reverence for her friend, Gabriel had figured she was a spoiled rich kid, grown up to be a spoiled housewife who had found herself in a mess of trouble she didn't know how to get out of.

"Yeah, Caroline likes to do things. With her brain, with her hands, to earn money or to help out, she has all kinds of interests. Her mom says she hasn't been still since she was in the womb."

"She worked even though she didn't have to?"

"Always. Caroline is very independent and no one can fault her work ethic. Sure, she could afford to take off for a summer of volunteer work because her family has money, but I think she would have found a way to do it if she didn't have a penny to spare. Caroline is tough as nails and incredibly capable, and she has always pushed herself to do more." Lucy grew thoughtful, "That was what was so strange about her marriage to Daniel. Suddenly Caroline quit her job to plan a wedding? To be a homemaker?" She shook her head. "Nothing wrong with that, but it's not Caroline. I guess I figured that love had changed her priorities, or that they were planning a family right away. But now I wonder if Daniel somehow coerced her."

ALARM BELLS

Just as Gabriel was reassessing his opinion of Lucy's best friend, the doorbell rang. Then the alarm went off when Lucy opened the door without first disabling it.

"Jesus Christ!" yelled Caroline. "I always expect a few fireworks to mark my arrival, but not an air raid siren!"

Gabriel punched in the code and the alarm went blissfully silent.

"My hero," said Caroline as she set down her small suitcase. "Hello, Mr. Black. I take it our Lucy explained my predicament?"

"She did," said Gabriel as he helped her out of her coat.

The three of them walked into the kitchen where Lucy gathered the tea things onto a tray and Baxter accosted Caroline's shins, purring and demanding attention.

"You look better, Carolina," she observed.

"I am better, now that I've taken action. Just don't let me brood or I'll fall apart." She noticed the stack of photocopies on the counter and riffled through them until she found the scanned prints of her husband on the boat. "I figured out why these men are familiar to me."

"Let's go into the living room. Baxter will follow

along," suggested Lucy and picked up the tea tray, which also held a plate of gingersnaps.

Gabriel picked one up and popped it into his mouth as they walked into the great room.

"Watch out, Gabriel," said Caroline. "Lucy has a sweet tooth and doesn't like to share!"

Lucy grinned and said, "I wouldn't eat anything else if I didn't have to!" She looked at Gabriel, "Except your lasagna, of course. Sweets and Gabriel's lasagna. That's all I need!"

Caroline gave Gabriel a mock look of wonder. "You cooked her dinner? Oh dear, you two are in deep."

Lucy rolled her eyes and left Gabriel and Caroline to pour tea as she went outside to gather logs from the cord of wood that had been delivered and stacked under the back steps while she'd been out that day. The alarm sounded as soon as she opened the door. "Ooooopsy!" she called out and Gabriel turned off the alarm. Lucy knew that she would keep the alarm enabled until this mess was sorted out, but she had to give Gabriel a hard time. She didn't need a hero. Although, she was beginning to think she might *want* one.

And, if a girl had to have a hero, he may as well be drop dead gorgeous, and charming, and smart, and a good cook, and... well, he may as well be Gabriel Black.

When she walked back through the door, Gabriel took the wood out of her arms and unloaded it next to the fire. "I'll get some more, tough girl."

As soon as he had pulled the door closed behind

him, Caroline pinched Lucy's arm and said, "He is fabulous!"

"Yeah," said Lucy with a big dumb grin on her face. "He is pretty good stuff." She looked at her friend and said, "Caroline, are you really feeling better?"

"I am. A little bit, anyway. It's good to be out of my house. I kept thinking that Daniel would come home in the middle of the night and surprise me in bed, and either want to have sex with me or kill me, depending on what he knows. Honestly, at this point both things are equally horrifying to me."

"Personally, I would rather have you alive, Carolina."

"Yeah, me too. I'll never be able to look at him the same way." Caroline looked a little lost for a second, and then there was a loud rumbling from her belly.

"Caroline! You're hungry! Let me make you a sandwich!"

"I guess I am hungry. Then I must be feeling better, because I haven't had an appetite all day."

Lucy went into the kitchen to make a sandwich. She pulled mustard, cheese, tomato and pickles out of the fridge and took a loaf of wholegrain bread from the breadbox. While she was making Caroline's sandwich, she decided to make an extra in case Gabriel wanted one. And then she made a third for good measure. She put the sandwiches on a platter with some salt and vinegar potato chips and the rest of the strawberries from the previous night. Lucy could hardly believe it was only last night that she and Gabriel had eaten ice cream and strawberries outside under the moonlight. And had made love for the first time. The thought of the two of them on the carpet in the great room made her toes tingle.

Lucy Walker, she scolded herself, *what are you doing*?

But she knew she was already beyond caring. Gabriel Black was something special. Even Lucy couldn't deny that.

When she carried the platter and a stack of linen napkins into the living room the fire was on its way to a blaze. Caroline was dipping a cookie into her tea and showing Gabriel something on one of the photocopies.

"Oh, yum!" said Caroline when she saw the plate of food. "Is that all for me?"

Lucy laughed, "As much as you want, Carolina. What are you looking at?"

"Two of these men looked familiar to me when I first saw these pictures, but I couldn't figure out where I had seen them. Then, after you left tonight, Lucy, I was sitting at the kitchen table, staring into space, when it hit me. And that's when I knew I had to get out of there." She held up a finger and took a bite of one of the sandwiches. Gabriel and Lucy each took a bite of theirs too while they waited for Caroline to finish chewing. She addressed Gabriel, "I am normally a little better mannered, but I am half dead from hunger. Honestly. Half dead!"

"I wouldn't have faulted you for talking with your mouth full, Caroline, being half dead and all."

Caroline looked affronted, "Please Mr. Black, I may be starving, but I am still a lady!" They all laughed. "Anyway, it came to me when I finally gave up trying to figure it out. Two of those men were at a fundraising gala I attended with Daniel about six months ago – last September, I think. I didn't realize it at first, because they were both in tuxedoes and looking a lot less mean and greasy than they do in this photograph, but it was them."

"What was the fundraiser for?" asked Gabriel.

"Brain cancer, I think. Is it important?"

"Could be important to the Feds if they start an audit of all this money, but I want you to lay low with the facts until we can figure out your role in any investigation into the cartel can be. The less you have to say, the better, Caroline."

She looked at Gabriel for a moment and then at Lucy. "You mean, the less I am a witness to, the better off I am?"

"That's it in a nutshell," replied Lucy.

Caroline looked thoughtfully at Baxter as he rolled himself into a ball by the fireplace. "Well, it was a big banquet, but their names would have been on a guest list and there were probably a couple hundred other attendees that night. Many of whom would have noticed two Latinos in that white bread crowd, so I don't suppose my testimony about the gala would be necessary. But let's talk about how scary this is another time, because right now I just want to lay some of the facts on the table before the consequences scare away my memories."

Gabriel was impressed with Caroline's bravery, but the effect only made him more determined to protect her as much as he could from having to testify as a witness.

"Anyway, they looked a little out of place in

that crowd, as I said, but I didn't talk to them and they may not have stood out so much to me except that Daniel clearly knew them and didn't introduce me. When I asked who they were, he was casually dismissive and I didn't think anything of it. Daniel had already cut down on 'sharing', if you know what I mean, and I was more concerned with the fact that I didn't feel like I knew my husband very well anymore than whether he introduced me to every Tom, Dick and Harry he had an acquaintanceship with."

She paused to take another bite of her sandwich, and Lucy asked, "But you saw Daniel talking to them?"

"I did. He went to get a scotch at the bar while I was chatting with a colleague of my dad's. He and his wife have known me since I was in the womb, and he mentioned a position opening at a Charleston bank. Daniel went for his scotch when I asked a few questions about it and I just figured he was pissed off because I was inquiring about a job – God forbid." She rolled her eyes so dramatically that Gabriel and Lucy laughed. "Honestly, I don't remember signing the pre-nup that promised I would sit on my ass for the rest of my marriage to Daniel Lamont." She looked exasperated. "Anyhow, I continued my conversation, and when I looked over to see where he'd gotten off to, Daniel was in a conversation with those two and looking very uncomfortable." She looked at Gabriel. "Uncomfortable is not on my husband's list of feelings, so I took notice."

When she didn't go on, Gabriel asked, "Did you hear any of their conversation?"

"Nope, sorry, I only noticed that he looked upset. And then, when he came back, I asked him who those men were and he said, 'Potential clients.' And that was it. We went back to hobnobbing and handshaking and he never acknowledged those men again. The only reason it stood out to me was because they looked a little out of place and Daniel was not happy to see them. Mostly, the entire evening stands out to me because Daniel was such an ass to me during and after the gala." She shook her head sadly. "It wasn't the first time by any means but it was the first time I looked at him and truly wondered who I had married. When we got back to the apartment that night he exploded. I was so stunned I didn't even stand up for myself. I had no idea he was capable of that kind of fury."

"What was he so angry about?" asked Lucy.

"He was furious that I would even discuss looking into a position at a bank without talking to him first. It was as if I had shamed him publicly, and then, even worse, that I had discussed it with my father's friend was like a slap in the face. Over the last year, Daniel has developed a lot of vitriol for my father and all of his associates. Anytime he crosses paths with them in Atlanta or Charleston, he describes their conversations as if they are nosey gossips only interested in him as far as my wellbeing is concerned. He calls them 'plantation people' and my 'father's gang of good ole boys'. He all but refuses to spend time with my parents anymore, even when he's in Graceful Bay, which has become rare in and of itself..." Caroline trailed off in dismay.

DEAR JOHN

"CAROLINE! I HAD NO IDEA it had gotten so bad between the two of you. I'm so sorry." Lucy felt like a terrible friend.

Caroline hugged Lucy. "First of all, you didn't know because I made a point of not telling you, or anyone else for that matter. Plenty of people were suspicious, but I kept quiet because I was embarrassed and didn't know how to explain that this successful man who gave me everything was not enough for me. The whole transformation was so gradual too that by the time I realized how bad it was, I felt defeated. And then," she sighed heavily, "then I had an affair and really didn't think I had any business complaining. What a mess.

"In hindsight, now that I know who those men are, I think part of his wrath that night after the gala was probably because he ran into them there. If Daniel was dealing with 'unsavory' elements, he certainly wouldn't want it known in good society. He's really preoccupied with social standing." Almost as an afterthought, she added, "Sometimes I wondered if that was part of my appeal to him – Southern debutante from an established family. It backfired, though. Even if my sniffer wasn't doing its job, the people who love me can smell a rat. I think I was the only one who didn't have any misgivings about marrying Daniel Lamont. And the more he tried, the more money he made and the more things he bought with it, it just seemed to make my people like him less. If only I had paid attention. My mother has always been diplomatic and supportive, but my father had a hard time hiding his dislike."

Caroline looked up at Lucy and Gabriel and set her jaw. "Here's the important thing: it's time to make a drastic change and I am finally ready to do it. So, what's our next move?" she asked as she took the last bite of her sandwich.

Gabriel smiled. Lucy was right: Caroline was a spitfire. "Sleep, I think. We can go over these documents in the morning, so I can get an idea of how much money and how many parties are involved. Then I'd like to make some discreet inquiries about your husband, Caroline. I'm hoping that someone is keeping an eye on him and we can figure out a way to steer that someone toward these papers without involving you. If there's enough money involved, and Daniel is anywhere near these guys," he indicated the photographs, "then someone is watching. I guarantee it. The trick will be to get the Feds into your house before Daniel makes his next move or destroys his books." Gabriel paused and looked at the two women. "But first, we get you safe, Caroline. And you too, Lucy. I don't want anyone looking in your direction as witnesses if this all goes down. That means the Feds, and that means the cartel. Otherwise, there's just too much danger."

"How do we avoid it?" asked Caroline.

Lucy spoke up. "We give Sheriff Grier enough evidence against Daniel for Mathew Wilson's murder that he can obtain a search warrant for your house and finds the cooked books. Daniel goes down for both."

Caroline winced and dropped her head into her hands, "Dammit. I used to love that man. I married him. I can't quite wrap my head around this whole thing."

"Caroline, you saw the pictures of Mathew. That is the man Daniel Lamont is. Maybe he wasn't that scary when you married him, but he is now, and if he's gunning for you then we have to do everything we can to stop him."

"He can't kill me now, can he? That would look too suspicious."

Lucy looked at Gabriel. "Not if it looked like the men who killed Mathew came after you for the same reason. You were having an affair, they attacked him in your neighborhood, and he had your address in his pocket. If the thugs who went after Mathew didn't get what they wanted, maybe they came looking for it from you."

Gabriel picked up the scenario. "If he's responsible, I'll bet Daniel has already planted some kind of contraband at Mathew's apartment. Drugs, guns, pornography, all of the above. The Havana Cartel have their hands in all of those pots, so Daniel wouldn't have a hard time getting access."

Caroline looked horrified. "I never thought of that."

"Well, that's what friends are for, Carolina," Lucy smiled ironically and gave her friend a reassuring pat on the shoulder.

The fire was dying down and Caroline put another

log on it while Lucy gathered the tea tray and plates. "Will you be able to sleep?" she asked Caroline.

"Maybe. I'm going to sit by the fire for a while. You two go ahead."

When Lucy took the dishes into the kitchen, Gabriel double-checked the alarm system and said to Caroline, "I don't want to worry you, but keep your eyes and ears open. If anything seems wrong, even if you're uncertain, come get me, or better yet, just start yelling."

Caroline looked at him gratefully. "Count on it."

Lucy came in and hugged her friend tightly. "Try to get some sleep. We'll get a start on..."

Lucy was interrupted by the sound of a cell phone pinging and the tension on Caroline's face told her it was her phone.

"That's mine. A text," said Caroline as she rose slowly and went to the kitchen to find her purse. She returned with her iPhone and read the message out loud to Lucy and Gabriel. "Daniel says, 'Darling, I am thinking of you. Let's have a romantic dinner when I get home. Just the two of us? Perhaps it will be a good time to make a fresh start. I do love you dearly.'"

Lucy and Gabriel weren't sure how to interpret the text. They waited for a reaction from Caroline. "I don't want to have dinner. Just the two of us. Very clever, Daniel," she said, still looking down at her phone with a curious look on her face.

When she didn't go on, Lucy asked, "What does that mean?"

Suddenly Caroline looked up, "Daniel is planning something."

Lucy let out an audible sigh of relief and Gabriel asked, "You don't think he is being sincere?"

"Nope. He is definitely not being sincere. It's funny how, as a wife and lover and woman who strove to know this man intimately, I've discovered a set of accounting books that are proof positive that my husband is laundering someone's money, and yet I still have doubt. I could, for half of our short marriage, endure his neglect and his ire, and still wonder what I was doing wrong. I could seek the love of another man and still believe that I just needed to fix things with my husband. And then, I could read one apparently sweet and innocuous text message from him and finally know, without a doubt in the world, that my husband is a liar and a conniver!" She hissed the last words.

"I don't know what his plans are, but that text sounds about five hundred miles away from anything my husband would ever have written to me. In a text message? Never. That sounds to me like he is creating proof that he gives a shit about our marriage. Whether it's for a divorce lawyer, or the cops after they find my bloodied body on the beach, I don't know."

Gabriel looked at Caroline and then at Lucy who was nodding sagely. "I don't doubt you, Caroline, but how can you reach such a definitive conclusion from one little text?"

"Woman's intuition," she replied matter-of-factly.

"All it takes is an odd word here and there," confirmed Lucy.

Gabriel looked from one woman to the other. "I'll keep that in mind."

Suddenly Caroline laughed ruefully, "Well, call it woman's intuition accompanied by a set of cooked books and a murdered lover. I mean, I'm not that intuitive."

"All right," said Lucy. "We've got until the weekend to come up with a plan."

"I'll have to tell him in person that I'm leaving him. I can't just leave a note. Maybe I should try to be home when he gets back into town. Sit him down and tell him that it's over."

"I'm not sure that's the best plan," said Gabriel cautiously. "Under normal circumstances, yes, face-to-face would be the honorable and kindest thing to do, but we know that Daniel is volatile, to say the least."

"Oh God!" Caroline threw her hands up in exasperation. "This whole situation is so backward! I can't even trust my instincts because trusting myself is what got me into this mess in the first place. If I had listened to my parents' instincts, or yours, Lucy, I wouldn't have married Daniel Lamont in the first place. Now I can't even end the marriage in a way that honors our relationship... or what I thought our relationship was. This is all so painful and exasperating!"

Gabriel took Caroline by the shoulders and looked at her squarely. "Listen carefully, Caroline. I don't know you well, but I've developed a lot of respect for your strength over the last few hours alone. I know that you're feeling guilty about having an affair, but you cannot let that guilt mitigate your certainty that in this relationship, your husband is the bad guy. Maybe you made a mistake, but maybe it was self-preservation that drove you to another, kinder man, and not because you are fickle or inconsiderate, but because some part of you knew that Daniel was bad for you.

"Right now, know this: Daniel Lamont is a very bad man who is associated with a lot of even worse men. Your duty is to protect yourself, your family and your friends by leaving him quickly and completely and distancing yourself from his business dealings. Once that is done, you can take a long look into your heart and figure out why you had an affair and why you won't do it again. Now, walk away from a bad man. The decision is that simple, even if carrying it out is a little complicated." Then Gabriel gave her shoulders another squeeze and said, "Stay strong and focused and we'll work everything out. Got it?"

"Got it," Caroline replied with as much confidence as she could muster.

SPEEDBALL

ANIEL LAMONT WAS STANDING IN front of the panel of windows that lined the living room of his apartment in Atlanta. Clad only in a pair of dark jeans, he looked at his own reflection superimposed on the glass over the striking view of the city at night. He ran a hand through his thick dark hair as he vaguely listened to the sound of the Chantelle getting dressed in the dining room. She had barely been in the door before he took her on the mahogany credenza by the dining room table. While he was fucking her he could hear the bone china rattling on the interior shelves. He had held the woman's buttock with one hand and held a fistful of her hair in the other, keeping her head turned to one side so that he could see her mouth clenched in pain and her jugular vein throbbing in her neck.

Chantelle knew to expect his violence. When he wanted a different kind of sex, he asked for a different whore.

When he was finished, Daniel turned around and walked to the bar cart to pour himself a very short scotch. Chantelle had pulled up her stockings and finally leveled her gaze at him.

"You can clean up in the guest bathroom," he'd said dismissively.

She knew where it was and limped in that direction with her purse in hand. He had hurt her this time. More than usual.

Daniel went to the open kitchen and added three more hundred-dollar bills to the envelope he had left there for her. Ten minutes later she came out of the hallway, looking neat and beautiful except for the pain in her gait, kissed him on the cheek and left, taking her envelope of cash with her.

When he heard the door click shut, Daniel walked over to throw the deadbolt and then back to the living room where he began pacing in front of the long leather sofa. For weeks he had been completely consumed with a growing rage at his wife, and since Mathew Wilson's brutal death it had become even clearer to him that Caroline would have to suffer a lot more before Daniel was going to feel any better.

The only thing that was keeping him from driving home tonight and torturing Caroline to death was that his revenge would not be so sweet if he was thrown in prison for it.

Abandoning his scotch glass, Daniel began pacing in front of the window. He wouldn't have to wait long before it was safe to get rid of Caroline. He would have his revenge. But the murder was going to require careful planning, and a little patience. And, unfortunately, if he was going to get away with it, Daniel couldn't do it himself. It had to seem like the same people who had killed Mathew Wilson had killed Caroline. Daniel would still be a suspect. At first, anyway – husbands are always suspects – but after the police found the drugs and money Santana had stashed in Mathew's pathetic apartment, and now that they knew about Caroline's affair with him, it would make sense that both murders were done by Mathew's unsavory colleagues.

He also had to consider that Caroline might have lied to the police about her affair with Wilson. It seemed unlikely, especially since their home address had been found in Wilson's pocket and the cops wouldn't rest until they knew why. Plus, his wife was so disgustingly honorable that she would probably risk her reputation to see that her lover's killer was found. That connection could work for and against him. On the one hand, it gave the police motive to suspect Daniel in Wilson's death. On the other hand, it connected the dead guy and his wife. Daniel needed that connection to be made if he wanted his wife out of the picture.

He thought again of Caroline and retrieved his drink. *That bitch,* he thought. Daniel had given her everything she could want. What woman didn't want to quit her job and shop her way through life with a charming husband who took her to nice places where she could wear all of the dresses she spent her days buying?

He never should have married a rich girl. Any woman who worked because she wanted to and not because she had to was trouble. Daniel remembered vaguely that Caroline's independence had appealed to him when they had met, but he assumed her work ethic was some kind of lure she had made up to catch a man. Not that she needed help. Caroline was gorgeous and smart and rich. Daniel pictured the first time he had watched her perfect, pink, Southern belle mouth take his cock. He had made love to her slowly that time, forcing himself to hold back every time she let out a little gasping breath. When she came he had been looking straight into her eyes as they lost focus and he had decided then and there that Caroline would be his. No one else would ever have her this way.

He was always considerate with Caroline, both in bed and out. When he didn't want to be considerate, he had other women who would take any level of his verbal and sexual abuse for a variable sum of money. Daniel put Caroline on a pedestal. She was to be treated like a princess. Never abashed or defiled. His ability to compartmentalize his romance with Caroline made it possible for Daniel Lamont never to consider the profound disparity between his life with her and his life when she was not around. He was satisfied in every way.

The courtship, engagement, and honeymoon phase had sustained Daniel. Caroline was his, there was no disputing that. When she had quit her job in order to finish planning the wedding and making the move into their big house in Graceful Bay – granted, with a great deal of persuasion by Daniel – he did not anticipate the resistance to his control that had followed.

It began when Caroline started making mewing sounds about going back to work. Actually, when he thought about it, it had started when she began spending more and more time in Atlanta because he was not spending enough time in Graceful Bay.

Daniel finished his scotch in one big swallow. He glared out the panel of windows thinking that the fastest way to make your wife unhappy is to give her everything she ever wanted.

"Bitch!" he yelled and threw his glass against the window. It bounced unharmed off of the tempered glass and then cracked into two pieces on the cement floor. Daniel looked at the broken crystal and then went back to the bar and poured another two fingers of scotch in a fresh glass. He paused for a moment and then reached behind the glasses and pulled out a stainless steel case about the size of a paperback crime novel.

Taking the box and the scotch to the dining room table, he carefully, almost reverently, opened it and began removing its contents from the velvet-lined interior. First, a small glassine bag full of brown powder and then another one full of white powder. Then came an antique silver spoon with an elaborately patterned handle, a gold Zippo and a glass syringe with a tiny thirty-one-gauge needle for the space between his toes. Daniel was always fastidious about his appearance and bruises from a needle were not an option.

First he mixed a vial of three parts coke and two parts smack and put it in his pocket. Then he called his driver and told him to pick him up in a quarter of an hour. He was going to a party tonight.

Daniel put some heroin in the spoon, added a few drops of scotch and cooked it with the lighter. He expertly drew the liquid into the syringe and injected it between the first two toes of his left foot. He felt his head loll back as the drug coursed into his nervous system and he quickly cut a short line of coke and snorted it just to mellow out. Daniel thought of himself as a recreational user, but he knew what kind of high he wanted and when. Tonight, only a speedball would do.

Ten minutes later, Daniel walked out his door in a black shirt loose around his jeans, and a pair of python Oxfords on his feet. He swung a black Tom Ford jacket over his shoulder and sauntered out to meet his driver.

In the backseat of the car, he typed a loving text message to his wife. Had to keep up appearances. And then he was off to the club.

Just like that, Daniel Lamont felt like a million bucks again.

SCARFACE

Lucy patted Gabriel on the butt and said, "I'll be up in a few."

Gabriel said goodnight to Caroline and was halfway across the great room when his mobile phone rang.

"Black," he answered and then listened for a minute. When he turned and looked back at Lucy and Caroline, they knew something was up.

"I see. Well, that explains everything if you let it." He came over and sat on the edge of the sofa. "I'd like to tread lightly here, Grier, but there's a lot to this case that might be happily overlooked if Mathew Wilson ends up being a drug dealer. Listen, I'm at Lucy Walker's house with Caroline Lamont and we're all still up." After a pause, Gabriel replied, "See you in a few."

Lucy and Caroline were looking at him with twin expressions of curiosity and apprehension. Caroline spoke first, "What's up and why is Sheriff Grier coming over here?"

"Charleston PD finished searching Mathew Wilson's apartment. They found a stash of crystal meth that is 'unreasonably large to consider for personal use'."

"Mathew was not a drug dealer!" snapped Caroline.

Gabriel looked at her sympathetically. "His murder makes a lot of sense if the police believe he was."

There were tears in Caroline's eyes when she said, "He *was not* a drug dealer! And I won't let him go down as one! He was a wonderful person." She looked imploringly from Lucy to Gabriel.

"That's what I figured," said Gabriel, "and that's why I think we should let Grier in on what's going on. He's a great cop and a stand-up guy and I think you can trust him with some info on what Daniel is involved in. He'll make sure you're protected without letting these assholes get away with anything."

Lucy looked sharply at Gabriel. "I hope you're right, because most cops would take those books and run with them. If Grier does that before Caroline extricates herself from Daniel, she'll be in a lot of danger."

Gabriel put his hands on Lucy's shoulders and looked her straight in the eye. "I'm asking you to trust me on this, Lucy," he turned, "and you too, Caroline. Tom Grier has some experience protecting witnesses because before he became sheriff here he was a fed, and he knows the best way to protect them is to keep them from being a witness at all if it's possible."

Lucy nodded. Even though they had just met, she did trust Gabriel. In fact, she would trust him with her life, but this was Caroline's life and it was up to her what she wanted to do. "Caroline?"

Caroline looked from Lucy to Gabriel and said, "Absolutely. I wouldn't be able to live with myself if I didn't defend Mathew, even though it's too late to protect his life." She looked like she was going to crumple in tears, but then she rallied with a weak smile. "I trusted Grier with the knowledge of my affair, so I may as well go all the way. Plus, a little extra fire power can't hurt."

Lucy went to make a pot of coffee and more tea before the sheriff arrived and she took the liberty of making Grier a sandwich too. She was always hungry after a long day of trying to catch bad guys and she figured he wasn't any different.

Just as she set a pickle on the plate next to the sandwich and chips, the doorbell rang.

"Got it," said Gabriel and she saw him whizz past the kitchen with a gun in one hand.

Lucy paused for a second and let the reality of the situation wash over her. Here she was, in a sleepy town, living in her childhood home where she had planned to take a permanent break from the madness and mayhem of Miami crime, and instead she was having a crazy affair with a tough guy she had only just met, who was, right this second, answering the door with a gun in hand and preparing for a fight to protect her best friend's life from the very drug cartel she had been trying to help take down in Florida! She smiled. Damn, it was good to be home.

Caroline came into the kitchen from the great room as Sheriff Grier and Gabriel walked in from the foyer. Grier surveyed Lucy and Caroline a little wearily until he saw the coffee and heaping sandwich. He grinned in spite of himself.

"For you," said Lucy, pointing at the plate of

food. She smiled coyly at the sheriff and Caroline winked at him.

"Well, Black, I can see why you're reduced to a bowl of jelly around these ladies. You just warmed my heart, Miss Walker."

They all laughed, enjoying a light moment, and carried everything into the living room. Grier took a swig of hot coffee and said, "All right, I feel like I'm looking straight at the cat who ate the canary, so before you lay it all on me and make my life complicated again, Mrs. Lamont, why don't I tell you what a neat little package your boyfriend's murder has turned into."

The lightness was gone. It was time to get down to business and Caroline felt her stomach tighten at what she was about to hear.

"First of all, we asked Richmond PD to notify Mathew's parents this evening. I know a guy on the force up there and he went himself. He waited until it looked like both parents were home from work and he and a lady cop went to the door. They've been offered victim counseling and I don't know yet if they'll take it, but they have a big family in the area and let my friend make some calls. Before he left, two of the Wilsons' other sons had arrived at the house." Caroline already had her head in her hands and Grier looked at her intensely before patting her knee and saying, "Mrs. Lamont, here's what you have to hold closest to you right now: mourn for Mathew and his family, but do not let guilt eat away at you. Bottom line? You did not kill Mathew Wilson, did you?"

"Of course not!" Caroline was a little surprised

by the gruff man's words of comfort and wisdom and she nodded for the sheriff to go on.

"Mr. and Mrs. Wilson gave written permission for Charleston PD to search Mathew's apartment. I drove to Charleston and joined the search. Wrapped up neat and tidy in a shoebox under his bed was a quarter pound of Mexican brown heroine plus single grams in baggies ready to sell. There was also a brick of cash in twenty-dollar bills wrapped in butcher paper in the freezer. We did not find a dope kit, which makes sense because there is no indication on Mathew's body that he used drugs himself."

Caroline looked appalled. "Mathew was not a drug dealer. And that's all there is to it."

"That's nice and neat, sheriff," said Gabriel.

"Maybe a little too neat, depending on what Charleston homicide finds out when they ask around the vice squad tomorrow. That's a lot of heroine for a dealer who is still off of their radar, even if it's a new enterprise for him. Anyway, like I said before, a nice little package. Not complicated. We got a big fat motive pointing at a dead scumbag drug dealer and probably a bigger scumbag drug dealer who got pissed and killed him. Based on that, we look for the guys who did this, but we don't kill ourselves over it." He looked at each one of them sternly with his piercing blue eyes and then said, "So, now I'm going to eat my sandwich while you all tell me what I'm missing." With that, he finished his coffee in one shot and picked up his dinner, adding, "This was very thoughtful of you, Miss Walker, thank you."

Caroline said nothing and Lucy turned to Gabriel who said, "We got a dead law student with a brick of dope who was having an affair with the wife of a guy who cooked the books for the Havana Cartel, the biggest smugglers on the Eastern Seaboard. The kid is not known to have dealt drugs. The husband maybe found out about the affair and rigged a murder to look like a pusher got himself killed over drugs or money, or both, when in fact it was all just revenge for sleeping with his wife."

Grier stared thoughtfully into the fire. He took another bite of his sandwich and took his time chewing it, washed the bite down with another swig from the coffee mug that Lucy had refilled. "Circumstantial," was his verdict.

Caroline was about to protest, but she saw that Lucy and Gabriel were calmly waiting for Grier to go on and she fell silent.

"Run that bit about the cooked books and the Cuban cartel by me again. I know I'm getting old, but Mrs. Lamont, when we spoke yesterday morning, you said that your husband was in investment banking. However, I don't remember you mentioning that his employer is Scarface!" The abrupt change in Grier's formerly moderate tone got Caroline's attention right quick, but she wasn't intimidated, she was irritated.

"Yesterday, Sheriff, I didn't know anything about laundering money, let alone drug cartels. I didn't find out until I spent today snooping through Daniel's office."

Gabriel was surprised by Caroline's quick retort, but Lucy had seen it coming. Grier seemed to take her outburst in stride. "Now, Mrs. Lamont, you can hardly blame me for wondering after your less-than-forthcoming interview yesterday. It took two interviews to find out you'd been having an affair with the victim. And three to divine that your husband works for a group of killers. I'm left wondering what revelations are coming in the fourth."

Caroline leveled her gaze at the big man. "Sarcasm won't get you anything but a swift kick in the ass, Sheriff."

Silence. Even Lucy gaped at her friend's response. The silence was broken by a huge guffaw. Sheriff Grier was laughing in spite of himself, and in a moment all four of them were laughing, even Caroline.

After a big sigh, Grier finally said, "I know one thing for sure, Mrs. Lamont: with that kind of spunk, you're going to make it through this ordeal just fine." Then with a frown, he added, "As long as we can keep you from going the way that Mathew Wilson did. I need to know more about your husband's dealings with this cartel, and call it due diligence but I need more assurance that you are not involved in this whole thing than my old friend Gabriel Black vouching for you." To Gabriel he said, "You understand."

"I do, Grier, but I'm afraid we might not have time to produce proof because we think Daniel Lamont might take Caroline out next." When Grier waited for him to go on, Gabriel continued, "He may have provided you with a built-in suspect and motive: whoever killed Wilson didn't get what he wanted and so he came after the lady whose address was in Mathew's pocket. Lamont would have to be quick about it so that there isn't much doubt about the sequence of events and he'd have to make sure there was no evidence pointing at him, but if he hires it out, there won't be any. Revenge, plain and simple: his wife has a day or two to suffer her loss and feel some real fear about what happened before she's dead too and he's home free. He has some henchmen from the Havana Cartel break into the house, kill Caroline in the same manner as they killed Wilson, ransack the place, pull the files and take off. It's not a bad plan for a confident guy with mob connections."

"Perfect one-two punch," said Grier. "Maybe, but maybe he doesn't want to take Caroline out, just teach her a lesson by killing the lover."

"No," Caroline spoke up, "he might not want me dead, but he doesn't want me anymore. I knew that before Mathew turned up murdered, before I found those accounting books, and before I started listening to my friends. Truth be told, I've known that for a while." She smiled wanly at Lucy.

"Caroline, I'm so sorry," she leaned over and put her hand on Caroline's shoulder. She could feel her friend's sadness and anguish in the tension she found there.

Grier finished another bite of his sandwich and opined, "Assuming you're innocent in all of this, and while I tend to believe you are, I'm not ready to presume. A fella would have to be crazy to let a livewire like you go, Mrs. Lamont."

Gabriel laughed and said to the two ladies, "If you ever meet Mrs. Sheriff Grier, you'll know that was a compliment, Caroline."

"Don't balk, Black, by all accounts you've got a spitfire on your hands too." He nodded at Lucy.

"Don't I know," said Gabriel with a dopey grin in Lucy's direction.

Caroline was smiling when she said, "All right, all spunky spitfires and livewires aside, can we get back to what I'm going to do if my husband does, in fact, try to kill me?"

"Black here told me that you're staying with Miss Walker for now," said Grier. "Did you tell your husband that you were leaving?"

"I left him a note saying that I was staying with a friend in case he comes home," Caroline replied. "I didn't want to call him, and honestly, after I found the ledgers and the photographs in his office, and Lucy sounded so horrified, and with images of poor Mathew broken and bruised, I finally got a little scared myself."

No one blamed Caroline for being afraid. In fact, Grier and Gabriel wondered that she wasn't terrified, but Lucy had known her forever and knew that Caroline was, but she was not the type to curl up in a ball and cry uncle. Lucy also knew firsthand what it was like to be in a dangerous situation and need a minute to figure out whether it was going to blow up in your face, or dissipate like nothing happened. During her years under cover, she had had more moments like that than she cared to count. And the danger had always faded until the last time, when she and her partner had both been made and both wound up in the hospital.

"A little scared is good, Mrs. Lamont."

"Please call me Caroline. What with the nature

of the situation I find myself in, Mrs. Lamont seems both too formal and carries a bit too much irony for my nerves right now."

Grier nodded. "What we're going to do now is wait, Caroline. There's nothing else to do unless you want to hand over those files you took from Mr. Lamont and get started with the Feds." Before anyone could protest, he went on, "And I know that's not in the cards till we can protect you. So, we wait."

KILL THEM ALL

D ANIEL LAMONT THREW HIS CELL phone across the room. It bounced off of the sofa and landed, unbroken, on the emerald green wool rug that covered most of the living area.

"That bitch!" he yelled into the empty apartment. He had just gotten home from the club in the wee hours of the morning when Rinaldo Santana called to let him know that there was a problem with his wife. Of course there was a problem with his wife. His wife had been nothing but a problem since she had become his wife!

The plan had been that Santana's brutes would go to Daniel's house in Graceful Bay, break in, torture and beat Caroline to death in the same fashion as they had tortured and beaten and murdered her lover. Then, they were supposed to toss the entire house, apart from Daniel's office on the second floor. The next day, he would drive home to Graceful Bay and take care of the office himself. After he had emptied his file cabinet of the ledgers for the Havana Cartel's money and replaced them with a stack of innocuous files that he had already prepared for the purpose. Then he would quickly trash the room, files and all. Next he would 'discover' his beloved wife's lifeless form and call the police. Without a scratch on him, and indications from the medical examiner that she had been dead for at least twelve hours, and his alibi in Atlanta for that time, he would not be charged with the crime. Eventually, after an acceptable period of mourning, he would sell the Graceful Bay house to somebody who had always dreamed of owning a plantation and had a pile of money burning a hole in his pocket – there were more men like that than anyone would imagine – and be done with the whole piece-of-shit town and piece-of-shit marriage.

Simple!

Or it would have been, except that his wife had fucked up the plan! Apparently, late tonight, Santana and his men had been watching Daniel's house, waiting for the lights to go out, when Caroline came out the front door with an overnight bag and jumped into her BMW. They followed her to a big, cedar shingle beach house a few minutes away.

Daniel didn't have to ask the address to know whose house it was. Lucy Walker!

She was another colossal problem. Daniel could not conceive of worse luck than that bitch coming back to roost in her family home just as he had begun to put his plan into play. But here she was, probably comforting her poor, dear friend Caroline for the loss of her fuck buddy. Daniel wondered how long Lucy had known that his wife was having an affair. Caroline had probably been sharing every detail with her best friend all along.

Daniel felt another wave of rage wash over him as humiliation struck him anew.

He hated Lucy Walker almost as much as he hated Caroline. When Caroline first told him she had a friend on the police force in Miami, he had briefly wondered if he would be able to use the relationship to his advantage. Perhaps his pillow talk with Caroline would yield some interesting information about upcoming drug busts. But it quickly became clear that Lucy didn't share classified information with her best friend, or, if she did, Caroline wasn't going to pass it along. He figured it was the former because God knew Caroline told him every other banal detail of her life and the lives of everyone she knew. Christ, she was boring.

Daniel had begun to pace. He stopped and poured himself a highball of vodka on the rocks. After a long drink he topped it off again, and added a shot of soda for good measure. This was no time to get wasted.

When Daniel had finally met Lucy for the first time, he knew right away that she was straight as an arrow. She politely thwarted all of his inquiries about her life in Miami, particularly about the job.

"I'm just a peacekeeper," she had said. "My patrol partner and I are on a pretty quiet beat in an upper middle-class neighborhood and not too much happens."

Daniel had asked his contacts in Miami about her and that seemed to be exactly what she was. A beat cop in a safe neighborhood. It was only after Lucy's cover had been blown, resulting in a shoot-out that left her and another undercover cop exposed, that Daniel ever knew she was in vice. That was another thing that Caroline had kept from him. When the news came out and his wife was in a panic about Lucy's wellbeing, she had admitted to Daniel that she had known all along that her friend was doing undercover work. Lucy had never told her directly, but she had laid out all the hints so that Caroline would understand the nature of her job, and her near radio silence during that time.

Daniel had been furious, but had kept his feelings to himself because he wouldn't have been able to explain exactly why he was so upset. It would have been priceless to have an undercover cop in the Havana Cartel organization. They would have been able to feed her false information and probably have saved tens of millions of dollars in profits lost to drug busts. That money would have translated directly into a hefty percentage for Daniel, and the knowledge would have made him a golden boy to the cartel's leaders.

All he had said to Caroline was that he understood her need to keep quiet.

But it had definitely not looked good to the cartel that his wife's best friend had turned out to be an undercover cop who had cost them millions and millions of dollars, and he had had no fucking idea!

He was lucky that they needed him to clean up their money trail or he probably would have been killed off as an example of supreme stupidity.

Now Lucy and Caroline would both have to die, and whatever asshole was holed up with them too. Santana said that he had seen a man open the door when Caroline arrived at Lucy's house and he was going to run the plates on the Land Rover in the driveway.

The more Daniel thought about it, the more he liked the idea of killing Lucy too.

He called Santana, and, when he heard Rinaldo's gruff Spanish-accented voice on voicemail, left a message. "I'll triple your fee. Just kill them all. Lucy and her friend can go out quickly, but once you have Caroline, knock her out, take her back home, tape up her big mouth and kill her slowly. I want her to know why she's dying. Then toss the house as planned."

Daniel hung up the phone and cut himself a line of coke.

A few minutes later, when Rinaldo Santana listened to Daniel's message, he rolled his eyes and hung up. Looking at the three men he had brought with him to do the job, he said, "Now he wants us to do them all. And he'll pay."

The others shrugged. They had left their post outside the Walker home when a commotion had driven the big guy out to look around. Retreating to the big black SUV, they'd parked on an abandoned side-road a quarter of a mile further up the beach road. The sun would be up soon and, in any event, proceeding as Lamont wanted them to would have to be postponed until the next night.

But Santana wasn't at all certain that Lamont's new plan was feasible. He was just the hired hand in charge of the other hired hands, and he didn't have many scruples, but he wasn't going to jail.

If they could get into the beach house and take the other two out with a silencer, he figured they could tape the wife's mouth shut and get her home in the middle of the night – there wasn't any night

208

traffic in this town – and take care of her and the house, no problem. Maybe she'd even go home on her own during the day, and they could take care of Lucy Walker and the other guy separately. The big question was, who the fuck was the other guy? Santana had made a call and was having his plates run. He was probably some rich asshole who happened to be sleeping with the lady of the house, but you could never be too careful. Either way, they would have to wait until nightfall.

BUMP IN THE NIGHT

AFTER SHERIFF GRIER LEFT, PROMISING to keep his cell phone next to him all night and check in first thing in the morning, Lucy got her friend tucked into the downstairs guestroom and went up to the master bedroom, where Gabriel was waiting for her in an overstuffed chair by the window. The moon was so bright that it cast shadows on the sand dunes and stone patio. The ocean sparkled in the eerie light.

"All settled in?"

"Yup," replied Lucy. "Looks like you are too."

Gabriel was barefoot with his long legs resting on the ottoman and a glass of water in his hand. His gun sat on a small table within reach.

"Yup," he said. "Now let's get you settled too, Miss Lucy."

He walked over and slid his hands under her shirt then up over her rib cage and her breasts to her neck, and pulled her toward him for a deep kiss. His tongue flitted against hers and then receded to her lips, before plunging deep inside of her mouth again. Lucy gasped even as she leaned into him for more. She raised her arms above her head and Gabriel leaned away long enough to slide her shirt up and over her head. He let it drop to the floor and unhooked her bra, gently pulling the straps down her arms. Lucy's nipples were rosy and hard and Gabriel took one and then the other into his mouth.

Arching her back, she unbuttoned his jeans and slipped her hands down and around his penis. It was Gabriel's turn to gasp when she cupped his balls and eased him closer.

Slowly kneeling on the floor she took his erection out of his jeans and eased it into her mouth. At first, she just took the tip and then, without warning, she widened her lips and took him further. Gabriel moaned and ran his fingers through her hair. Lucy reached around his waist and pulled his firm buttocks toward her to take him even deeper. She pulled his jeans and underwear down past his knees and leaned back to run her tongue along the length of his cock. Gabriel was swollen and hard as a rock when he lifted her onto the bed and yanked her skirt and panties off in one motion.

Lucy held his gaze as she stretched her arms above her head and spread her legs for him. Gabriel didn't hesitate. He knelt in front of her and licked her slowly and indulgently. Lucy could feel him in her toes as she grasped the pillows at the top of the bed and stretched her body until she climaxed in violent waves of pleasure. Her eyes were still closed when he picked her up and moved her further onto the bed, gently laying her back down and parting her legs with his warm, strong hands. Her eyes were still closed as he entered her slowly and deeply, and when he reached the ultimate place, she opened them and looked into her lover's liquid brown eyes.

As he pulsed in and out, Gabriel fingered her nipples and then wrapped his hands around her ass. Reaching until he touched the point of his entry, he opened her further to him and filled her more deeply, more completely, than she had ever felt before.

She wrapped her legs tightly around his lower back and his pulses became thrusts, harder and faster. Lucy's vision blurred as the ecstasy hit her, radiating from deep inside and flooding every part of her, from the tips of her fingers to the tips of her ears. She did not know where she was anymore when Gabriel thrust a final time and came inside of her with a lion's roar.

They lay there, panting and unmoving, for a long time afterwards, and Lucy did not realize she had fallen asleep until she surfaced briefly and felt Gabriel tucking the covers around her. She murmured and reached out to him, and he joined her in bed, but not in sleep.

"Sleep, beautiful Lucy. I'm going to do a little research on your iPad."

"Such a romantic," she muttered even as she curled her butt up against him and drifted off again.

Gabriel ran his hand along the length of Lucy's body and swept her hair back behind her. Then he opened Safari and started looking a little closer into Daniel Lamont's past.

This wasn't the first time Gabriel had looked the investment banker up. He had checked him out the first chance he'd gotten when he and Sheriff Grier had visited Caroline at her house after Mathew Wilson's murder. But it was the first time Gabriel had checked the guy out since he found out that he probably wasn't just an investment banker. Now there were a lot more avenues of inquiry to pursue, including his ties to the Caribbean drug cartels, which is where he began his search now.

Gabriel typed in the name of the yacht he had seen in the pictures of Daniel with the men Lucy had identified as the Havana Cartel. When he narrowed his search to a Mexican news blog, he found a few more photographs of the gleaming white hulk and a couple of quaint, boastful, and obviously well-edited stories about its prosperous, generous and clever owners. The articles were straight out of *Lifestyles of the Rich and Famous*. Daniel Lamont's name was mentioned in two of the Spanish articles. He was described as a "wealthy American businessman", but otherwise, Gabriel didn't find any connections between Lamont and the Havana Cartel.

Lucy stirred beside him and then jolted upright.

"Oh, goodness!" she exclaimed as Gabriel wrapped a strong arm around her waist. "I just had one of those terrible dreams where you suddenly fall into a random abyss at your feet. And then you jerk awake."

He kissed her forehead and said, "No psychoanalysis necessary."

She smiled and snuggled tighter against his chest. "Do you speak Spanish?" She had glanced at the iPad and realized Gabriel was perusing an article from a Mexican tabloid.

"I do."

"Curiouser and curiouser, Mr. Black. Have you learned anything new?"

"Not really, except that the photograph of Lamont on the yacht was not a singular incident. He has definitely spent some leisure time with these guys. I haven't found any business links, but if he's careful, I probably won't. At least, not on the internet."

"We have a pretty circumstantial case, so far."

"For murdering Wilson? Yes. For money laundering? Nope. That is pretty solid. For Daniel Lamont being a bad guy with scary friends and plenty of secrets? Again, solid. We have him beyond a reasonable doubt on that one."

"Hmmm." Lucy ran a hand across Gabriel's hard stomach and then pulled his face gently down onto her mouth. He slid his arms underneath her and pulled her close against him. The iPad went dark and the only light left in the room was from the moon. They held each other like that and kissed for a long time, and Lucy felt him growing hard against her still naked body.

Gabriel broke the kiss and stroked Lucy's cheek with his fingers. He looked deeply into her eyes and his breath became faster. She could feel his heart beating against her own and she wrapped her legs around his waist, her arms around his shoulders. He buried his face in her luxurious hair and inhaled the faint scent of citrus and sandalwood. He began kissing her neck, her ears, her cheeks and eyelids and finally found her mouth again. Lucy's lips parted and their tongues met, gently at first and then more insistently. She curled her toes around the waistband of Gabriel's boxer-briefs and tugged at them. He reached down and pulled them over his erection and between the two of them they got his underwear off without leaving each other's embrace.

Once their bodies were unencumbered by

clothing, Gabriel slid easily into Lucy's wetness. She moaned through his kiss, but their lips never parted. Gabriel ran his hands though her hair and lifted her face closer to him and they moved against each other in slow waves and soft circles. Lucy felt wetness on her cheek and realized that she was crying. It had been so long since she'd felt this close to a man. Before she could feel embarrassed, Gabriel kissed the tears away and looked into her eyes with adoration. Lucy didn't know what was happening between them, but for the next few moments in time she gave herself over to it completely.

Her orgasm was long and deep, like a warm river running through her body and across her mind, over her skin and between her fingers and toes. Lucy and Gabriel came simultaneously; his body shook and rocked on top of her and his eyes never left hers.

Finally, Gabriel rolled onto his side and curled Lucy tightly against him. Neither said a word as their breathing slowed and their bodies melted into one another. Gabriel brushed his lips against Lucy's cheek, neck and then her bare shoulder. Neither slept and neither spoke for a long time. Lucy felt too close to this man she had just met. She felt vulnerable and confused and utterly taken by him. But it was happening too soon. She was not prepared for this kind of connection and she did not know how to slow it down. She wasn't sure she wanted to.

Suddenly both Gabriel and Lucy were leaping out of bed. The sound of glass shattering followed immediately by the bleating of the security system tore Lucy out of her lover's embrace and pumped adrenalin into her bloodstream.

Lucy grabbed her gun from the nightstand and, naked but armed, threw open the bedroom door and ran for the stairs. As she turned on the landing she smacked right into Caroline and they knocked each other over. Gabriel was right behind Lucy, and in a harsh whisper he said, "Stay here," and passed the two women as he headed silently to the first floor.

After what seemed like an eternity, Lucy started for the first floor.

Caroline grabbed her and hissed, "Don't go down there!" A second later she said, "Are you naked?"

"Shush!" Lucy hissed back at her as the lights started coming on from the living room.

A moment later Gabriel came around the corner with a throw from the living room sofa wrapped neatly around his waist and his big stainless steel Heckler & Koch at his side. "No one's here."

Caroline had a sheepish grin on her face, mixed with a little guilt. "I was bringing the tea tray into the kitchen before bed and I thought I heard a noise on the veranda. I'm so jumpy that I dropped the whole thing on the hardwood floor and I was coming upstairs to tell the two of you that it was only me making all of that noise when you, well, ran downstairs buck naked with guns blazing. I'm so sorry!"

Lucy glanced down at herself. She was indeed standing on the landing with a gun and without a stitch of clothing.

"Excuse me a moment," she said and walked with as much dignity as she could muster up the stairs and into her bedroom where she found her cotton pajamas in a drawer and put them on. When she turned, Gabriel was standing by the bed getting back into his blue jeans and T-shirt. He looked at Lucy and laughed a little.

"We make a good team, little lady."

Scowling, she replied, "Don't ever tell me to stay put again. I am perfectly capable of taking care of myself, and my best friend. Even naked!"

Gabriel took her hand, "I know, Lucy. I'm just not used to having backup. And, I don't want anything to happen to you. Ever. Now, I'm going to go have a look at the porch and see if someone might have been out there. Caroline is pretty shaken up, so maybe you can figure out what she heard."

Dressed and still armed, they both went downstairs and found Caroline still sitting on the landing, but now she was huddled in the corner.

"I'm really sorry that I scared you," she said, her eyes still wide with fear.

"Hey," said Lucy, crouching down next to her friend, "no worries at all. That's why we're all here together."

Gabriel gave Caroline a pat on the shoulder and said, "Don't give it a second thought. You did exactly the right thing. I'm going to look around outside."

Lucy told him where to find the switches for the patio and driveway floodlights and he nodded, though she thought he probably already knew. He was the kind of guy who knew where all of the lights and alternative exits were the minute he walked into a building.

"Why don't we bring your things to the upstairs

guest bedroom? You might feel a little safer." When she saw the grateful look on Caroline's face, Lucy said, "Hell, we could make Gabriel sleep on the couch to protect us and bunk together in the big room."

Caroline smiled at Lucy's use of their childhood term for her grandparents' master bedroom. "Guest room upstairs is fine. Oh my God, Lucy, did I interrupt sex? Maybe for nothing? I am positively mortified!"

Even in terror, Caroline was concerned about her Southern propriety. Laughing, Lucy said, "Nope. Just the afterglow!"

"Good God, Lucyfer, I don't want to sound crass, but I got a look at his ass when he ran down the stairs, and I just about forgot that I was afraid for my life! He is yummy!"

Lucy giggled, "I know! And he's smart and funny and I like him."

"Careful, girl, them's lovin' words!" said Caroline with a wink and a grin.

Lucy left Caroline on the landing where she seemed comfortable and went down to check on Gabriel. She found him outside with a Maglite he must have found somewhere, crouched over something on the ground.

"What is it?" she asked.

Without turning his head, Gabriel said, "A cigarette butt. Marlboro. And a few rough footprints from the wet sand. Caroline doesn't smoke, does she?"

"Never has. So someone was out here."

"That's what it looks like. I'd better call Grier."

SHE'S GONE

FORTY-FIVE MINUTES LATER, GRIER WAS sending a deputy to patrol around the area through the night, Lucy had helped Caroline move her things upstairs and had tucked her in, and she was back in bed, but nowhere near sleep. Gabriel was seated on a chair near the window, looking out over the beach. He'd left the outdoor floodlights on and closed most of the curtains in the room. Except the one he was looking though.

"What do you think?" Lucy asked.

"I think sleep is not on the agenda. Grier will have a patrol rolling by through the night, but he doesn't have the manpower to keep constant watch. And a cigarette butt and a few vague footprints aren't enough to bring in state manpower. On the one hand, I have no doubts that Caroline is in danger. On the other hand, if we're right about Daniel's motive to hurt her, he would be crazy to try and attack us all in this house. But maybe it's worth it to him. Maybe he is crazy."

Lucy shook her head. "I don't know him well at all. And I don't know what kind of thugs he's having do his dirty work, but if they know that she's here, then Daniel will suspect that I know why she's afraid. I wouldn't be surprised if he's added me to his hit list."

"And me, if they've run my plates."

Lucy had forgotten that Gabriel's car was parked in the driveway. "I'm sorry to have gotten you into this mess, Gabriel."

He looked at her for a moment and then came over to the bed and sat beside her. "You didn't get me into anything. In fact, you couldn't have kept me away if I knew it would mean protecting you from harm." Lucy began to protest but Gabriel placed his palm gently on her cheek. "I know that you can take care of yourself, Miss Walker. But I am going to do everything to ensure that I keep you in my life for as long as I can. And that's that."

She looked at him thoughtfully and then smiled. "We only just met."

"We did only just meet," Gabriel agreed stoically.

"Look, Gabriel, the last time I even had a boyfriend was while I was in the police academy in Miami, and that ended as soon as I graduated and became a cop. Since then, I've dated plenty, sowed some wild oats and never ever taken anything seriously. Then, when I was under cover, the closest relationship I had with a man was with my undercover partner – who, by the way, almost got killed."

"You blew cover to save him."

Lucy looked curiously at Gabriel. He went on, "I have a friend in Dade County Sheriff's Office. After you and I met, and I recognized you from the stories in the news, I found that I was curious about the details that weren't in the paper."

"You checked me out?"

"Absolutely, Lucy," he said seriously. "Mostly, I wanted to know why you were a cop on the Miami vice squad in the first place. But that information wasn't readily available and I didn't want to violate your privacy." He took her hand. "Lucy, how did a Southern debutante with an Ivy League education in arts and literature, and what I imagine is a substantial inheritance," he gestured around the sprawling beach home, "decide to become an undercover cop working with some of the worst low-lifes on the planet?" He observed Lucy's look of increasing indignation. "And before you get too upset, all I asked for was the skinny on what happened in Miami. My friend added that you had been a liberal arts grad when you entered the police academy because it was unusual, and because everyone had been so surprised at how well you took to becoming a coarse, hardened drug Moll for the cartels. I did not do a full background check."

"I bet you could have, though."

"I could've found out what color underwear you wore to your first day of high school, young lady, but I didn't. I wanted to hear those details from your own beautiful mouth, on your own time."

"Don't excuse your invasion of my privacy by telling me that you could have been more invasive."

"It usually works."

"Not with me," replied Lucy, but then she gave him a coy smile and said, "They would have been white and one hundred percent cotton. I was not introduced to the wonders of color and shapes that could be my bras and panties until I was sixteen and Caroline and I went shopping on our own at a Victoria's Secret in Charleston. We came home with pink bags full of demi-bras and thongs and pieces of satin and lace that took two of us to figure out." Smiling, for a moment Lucy forgot why she was telling Gabriel any of this in the first place.

She looked at him hard. "I guess, if I'd recognized you from a sensational newspaper story I would have checked into it as well."

"Probably," said Gabriel. "But getting back to the original topic: Lucy, you are in a relationship with me. We are having a romantic relationship, and I want to pursue it as long as you'll let me." He put his hand up when he saw Lucy begin to protest. "And, yes, I know that intimacy is scary for you. You've made that clear. But, sweetheart, I'm not afraid. So let me be the tough guy for now, and you just go with your gut instead of your head and we'll be fine."

"But sometimes people become intimate without meaning it and..."

He stopped her. "I do though. I mean it. And I want to be with you in this long life ahead of us, Lucy Walker." He leaned down and kissed her gently. "Now, shut up and try to get some sleep."

He sat next to Lucy, caressing her cheeks and hair until her breathing became soft and even.

Eventually, they both dozed off, Gabriel, back in the armchair by the window, Lucy, a little more comfortably, in the big bed.

When the sun came up over the horizon, Gabriel headed downstairs.

He was looking through the cupboards for the coffee. Finding it on his second try, he put a pot on to brew and then headed toward the front door where Baxter was mewing to be let out. When he reached up to disable the alarm, he realized that it had already been turned off.

Caroline had awoken at the crack of dawn on Thursday morning. She'd showered, dressed, paced. She'd awoken feeling significantly less certain about the plan than she had the previous night. She was positive that she wanted a divorce, but she couldn't quite get her head around the idea that she and Daniel couldn't end their marriage like civilized people. Caroline believed in universal justice, or karma, or that what goes around comes around, or whatever you wanted to call it. If Daniel was doing wrong, he would be caught and punished, but their divorce was separate from that crime. She didn't want anything from him. She had her own money and wanted to start working again anyway, and she didn't think she wanted to continue to live in the big old house in which she'd spent so many lonely days and nights. If Daniel was amenable – and she couldn't imagine that he cared too much about their marriage – they could have a relatively simple parting.

Gabriel and Lucy were still asleep and Caroline felt restless with no one to talk to. It hurt her in the pit of her stomach to think that she had been married to a man who might have killed her lover and laundered money for a drug cartel and she had not even suspected. She felt like such an idiot! And, there was a part of her that knew if she tried really hard, she could almost believe that it wasn't true. But deep down, she knew that it was. Her suspicions of Daniel had been lingering in the back of her mind for a long time, even before she went looking through his office for signs of betrayal, though she'd never imagined the scope of his crimes.

She felt tired but jittery.

Caroline began to pace and finally typed in the alarm code and let herself out onto the porch where she paced from one side of the house to the other in her bare feet. She walked down to the stone patio and looked around for more evidence that her husband's henchmen had been here the previous night, but saw nothing. Finally, she sat on the singular lounge chair and closed her eyes to the morning sun so that she could listen to the roar of the ocean and think.

Rinaldo Santana picked up his cell phone and answered, "*Que?*"

In Spanish, with a heavy accent, the man on the other end of the line responded, "She's sitting alone outside of the house."

Santana paused. "Where?"

"Between the house and the beach. She's sitting there on a chair, not moving. She might even be asleep; I can't see her face from my position."

The man was tucked into a thick copse of beach grass and trees about five hundred feet away from the property with a powerful set of binoculars. He was perplexed by the woman's behavior, but also wondered if this might be their chance to snatch her.

Santana asked, "Where is the other lady and the guy?"

"Can't see 'em, boss."

During the night he had learned that the guy was a former army cop with a thriving private security business and the lady was a former Miami vice cop with a fucked-up leg and maybe something to prove. The situation was about as bad as it could get, and Santana was seriously considering telling Daniel Lamont to fuck himself. Or to demand more money. He was on the fence about which course of action was better, but one thing was certain: he wasn't going to move on Caroline Lamont in broad daylight when two ex-cops could be standing just inside the door watching her.

Still, he was pretty sure that Caroline had snuck out there on her own because her friends, if they were worth anything, would never let her sit outside in the open waiting to get picked off by a sniper rifle. *This whole thing is going to shit,* he thought, and once again he considered bailing on the job. Lamont was a white-bred pansy anyway, but he was important to the Havana Cartel and that made him important to the men who worked for the Havana Cartel. Namely, Rinaldo Santana.

Just as Santana was considering calling someone in the crime syndicate and alerting them that Lamont was about to have his wife killed, his burn phone rang again.

"*Si?*"

"The big guy just came out the door, and when he saw the Lamont lady he looked like he was going to blow. They're inside now, with the curtains closed and I can't see 'em no more."

"Fine. Stay where you are and watch."

Santana hung up and thought a moment. This made more sense to him. The ex-cops were protecting the wife and the wife was just a dumbass who didn't think she was really in danger. The latter would make it easier to kill her and the former might make it impossible. At least, impossible to kill her the way that Lamont wanted him to. If the three of them bunkered down in the house, the only way to get at them would be a full-on offensive and Santana's men would be at a serious disadvantage. They were going to have to get the lady out of the house somehow and forget about the friends. Lamont would just have to hope that they didn't suspect he was behind the whole thing.

He would feel a lot better if the crime bosses had sanctioned this job, but Lamont was freelancing this one out. Killing the lover had been fine. Expected even. Killing the wife would have been fine too, but for some reason Lamont had come straight to Santana for this; he hadn't wanted to mention it to the bosses. At the time it sounded reasonable, since most of the guys Santana worked for did not go crying to the bosses for help getting a hit man to take care of their cheating wives, but Lamont had asked Santana not to mention it to anyone. *So what?* he had originally thought, but now he was wondering what the fuck was really going on here.

Caroline was standing by the fireplace in the living room, just inside the door leading to the porch, which Gabriel had closed loudly and locked before setting the alarm.

He turned on her suddenly and Caroline felt like a disobedient child who was about to be punished.

"What the hell were you thinking, Caroline?" he barked at her.

"What's going on?" Lucy had come down the stairs in jeans and a T-shirt and heard the frustration in Gabriel's tone.

Caroline colored, but before she could speak, Gabriel said, "Your friend here, whose life is in danger, thought it was a good idea to wander out to the patio alone and take a little cat nap."

He was clearly disgusted and Caroline felt her head bowing in embarrassment. When she looked up, Lucy was looking at her with irritation.

"I'm sorry! I know it was dumb. I wasn't thinking." Lucy and Gabriel continued to frown at her like parents who had agreed to maintain a united front. Suddenly Caroline felt ridiculous. "Mom, Dad, I was wrong and I know it. Ground me for as long as you like."

Gabriel rolled his eyes, but Lucy laughed and headed to the kitchen saying, "Coffee first, naughty children second."

It was barely seven in the morning and all three of them were tired from a fitful night's sleep, but wide-awake from anticipation, fear, and anxiety. They congregated in the kitchen around a fresh pot of coffee. Gabriel stood behind the breakfast bar and poured everyone a cup. Caroline liberally added sugar to hers. When she caught Gabriel watching her add teaspoon after teaspoon from the china sugar pot with one eyebrow raised, she said tartly, "Breakfast of champions, Mr. Black. It got me through college."

He shrugged. "Well, I'm going to make us a real breakfast." Opening the refrigerator door he began pulling out eggs, milk, and feta cheese. When he looked like he was going to sniff the cheese, Lucy called out from her seat at the counter.

"Are you impugning my housekeeping? You were with me when I bought that."

He smiled at her. "You two are tough to please in the morning."

Caroline interjected sardonically, "And you two have been grocery shopping together? You only met two days ago! Next you'll be moving in and having babies. Cocktails at five, dinner at six, put the twins to bed and finish the crossword together. What's a four-letter word for sweet?"

Lucy regarded her friend. "What's up your butt this morning?"

Caroline ran a hand through her loose blonde hair. "Everything! My husband is a very bad man, so I have to divorce him, but first I have to make sure he doesn't kill me. An innocent young guy was beaten to death because he went to bed with me. I'm too terrified to sleep. The sun was barely up when you," she looked at Gabriel, "scolded me like a child, and I feel so lost in this nightmare that I don't even know which way is out. That's what's up my butt." Silence. "And, I know you guys are helping me and I'm being a jerk. So I feel badly about that too."

Lucy put her arm around her friend. "I know, babe. It's okay to feel like shit, but I promise you there is a way out and we are headed for it today."

Gabriel chimed in, "I've been up against crabbier women than you," he said with a wink. "And as long as you don't put yourself in harm's way, I won't yell at you. Plus crosswords and cocktails with Lucy sounds good to me any way you put it."

Lucy smiled, turned pink, rolled her eyes, and turned back to Caroline.

"Sheriff Grier is going to be here in an hour and we'll figure out a way to get the cops into your house to do a search and find Daniel's files without implicating you. Then you can worry about the divorce while Daniel is being held for tax fraud. In the meantime, we'll keep you safe. The Havana Cartel will eventually find out that Daniel was keeping copies of the books, but they won't blame you."

"How can we get the police to search my house without me informing them that there is proof of illegal activity there? How can they come up with probable cause without me first handing over the files to provide them with probable cause? It feels like a catch twenty-two, Lucyfer."

"I've been thinking," Lucy replied slyly, "and this is when Mathew Wilson comes to the rescue." Caroline winced, but Lucy continued, "We give Grier a strand of your hair, or something with your DNA, to plant in the evidence box on Wilson. He takes it to the DA, and they issue a search warrant, which your attorney does not protest too much. They search the house, find no indication that you killed

Wilson, but do find the files. The local DA realizes this is a bigger fish than he can handle, gives the evidence to the Feds. Daniel is encouraged to turn State's evidence against the cartel, but whether he does or not, you are out of it."

Gabriel grinned at Lucy. "Smart lady."

She smiled and batted her eyes with false modesty. "Oh, you flatterer!"

Caroline laughed and then sighed. "Daniel and I used to flirt like that. I wonder if anything he ever did was genuine. I wonder if he ever loved me at all." She wiped a tear from the corner of her eyes, straightened her spine and asked, "It sounds complicated. Do you really think it'll work?"

"I think it might."

When Caroline frowned at her friend's words, Gabriel said, "I think it will work. I'm pretty sure that Tom Grier will be on board, even though he'll protest at first. And, it would get Daniel out of your hair sooner rather than later. When he finds out that the Feds have his cooked books, he's going to be too scared for his own life to worry about killing you. My guess is that the reason he kept the books in the first place was in case he ever had to save himself from being prosecuted along with the cartel if they got caught up in a legal mess. They're his insurance policy. On the other hand, they're a death sentence if the Havana Cartel ever found out he was holding onto that kind of evidence. All the more reason to give himself up and get into witness protection as soon as he can."

Lucy added, "If I wasn't a cop at heart, and if it wouldn't mean that you would become a liability to the cartel, I might even suggest that we just let the Havana Cartel know that Daniel was keeping records and wait for them to get rid of him. But, like I said, they would probably kill you just for good measure. And me. And Gabriel. And, I really want them to pay for what they're doing. Even if it doesn't stop the cartel, a federal racketeering indictment would slow them down."

Caroline looked sick. "Are they going to kill Daniel? It's not that I feel sorry for him, but he is my husband."

Gabriel said, "They are definitely going to try. That's why I think he'll flip and cooperate with the Feds. It's a dismal prospect to be moved into witness protection, but it's better than being dead."

Meanwhile, Daniel Lamont was considering that going out in a ball of flames might be worth it just to murder Caroline with his own bare hands. He had received another phone call from Rinaldo Santana and the prick seemed to be wavering on the job. And, he wanted more money. Of course he wanted more money. He wanted more money, didn't want to deal with Lucy and her new boyfriend, and wanted Daniel to get Caroline out of Lucy's house himself. When Daniel had asked him how he suggested this be accomplished, Santana had said vaguely, "I don't know, man. You're her husband, make something up. Offer to take her to dinner and then we'll grab her on the way."

That might work, depending on how much Caroline suspected. But the fact that she was staying with Lucy Walker made him think that something was wrong in paradise. Was the bitch planning on leaving him? Did she know that he was responsible for her lover's death? He could tell her he was coming home and hoped they would have dinner together. Of course, if she told Lucy that she was going home to meet him, then he would be suspect number one when she was found dead, supposing she even agreed to meet him at all. He thought about his wife for a moment. Even if Caroline was planning to leave him, he knew her, and she would feel obliged to tell him face to face.

Daniel ran his hands through his hair. He had a moment of doubt. Was any of this even worth the potential consequences? Maybe he should scrap the plan to kill Caroline. Divorce her. Go on with his life. Let her go on with hers.

But it was imagining Caroline going forward with her own charmed, Southern comfort life that revived his rage. *That bitch doesn't deserve it*, he thought. He couldn't stand to let it happen.

How to do it, though? There were so many complications at this point and he would be a suspect no matter what, simply by virtue of being her husband. But if she were killed when she had planned to be with him, he would be under a lot of scrutiny. Which could be dangerous.

Unless...

Just like that, Daniel Lamont had a new plan. He called Santana on his most recent burn phone and told him to be ready to go ahead with the hit tonight, details to follow, and then he took a hot shower and got ready to be in the office all day and into the evening.

PLANTING EVIDENCE

SHERIFF THOMAS GRIER ARRIVED AT Lucy Walker's shaker home at eight o'clock Wednesday morning. Seeing the house under cover of night had not done it justice. It was sprawling, but still homey and beautiful. The kind of house that sheltered a big happy family. Grier hadn't told Lucy, but he'd met her grandparents a few times at town hall functions and around town. They'd chatted at LaValle's one night during his first election, when the crowd of diners swarmed around him and his wife to put in their two cents about what a wonderful community they had and what they wanted in a sheriff. The Walkers had stopped by their table once the crowd dwindled and reintroduced themselves. The four of them started chatting and wound up having coffee and dessert together.

Lucy's grandparents had told a brief story about their beloved granddaughter, now traveling through Europe, after Tom's wife asked whether they had any children. In that brief encounter, Grier had gotten to know them well enough to know they were good people with more than their share of hurt, but they had never let it make them mean or pessimistic, and they considered Lucy a gift straight from God.

Two months later, Grier was elected sheriff. Shortly before he began his term, the Walkers were killed by a tweeker in a fast car. He had read about it in the local paper.

Now, looking at the Walker home in the light of day, he could just about feel the happiness their family had had here. As if the shaker tiles had been made out of it. Of course, Grier knew better than most that appearances could be deceiving; that a family of alcoholic serial killers could just as easily live in a house like this. But, despite the tragedies in Lucy Walker's life, he also knew she had had a good, strong family. He hoped she could fill this home with that kind of love and strength again, maybe even with his friend Gabriel Black. God knew he deserved it. The trouble was that there was one glaring thing that might keep her from doing that: her pig-headed involvement in this mess with Daniel Lamont and the Havana Cartel.

He understood perfectly why Caroline Lamont didn't want to end up a witness in a case against a powerful drug cartel, and he was willing to help keep her out of it, but he wished there was some way to protect Lucy Walker. Black could take care of himself. SSP, his security firm, was one of the best and most elite in the country, primarily because Black had a sixth sense for what the bad guys might take advantage of and where the good guys' weaknesses lay. But Grier wasn't sure that Black could see that his feelings for Lucy were his own weakness.

He shook his head and shut the door of his cruiser. His wife was right: he was getting sentimental in his old age. He wanted a happy ending for everyone.

There was only one thing to do. He had to do his

best to protect his friend, Gabriel Black, and this young lady Black was so obviously smitten with, and for whom Grier had a sense of responsibility because he had met and liked her grandparents. And their friend, Caroline, because she was a spunky lady who deserved another chance at happiness.

With purpose, Grier marched up the steps to the veranda and rang the doorbell just as Gabriel Black opened it.

"Sheriff," Gabriel said and nodded for him to come inside.

Baxter was the first to say hello when the sheriff came into the kitchen. "Damn cat," he said even as he reached down to vigorously rub the orange tabby.

He greeted Caroline and Lucy, and, after wrapping his big hands around a mug of fresh, hot coffee, said, "I say we get the Feds in on this right away." He paused to let that sink in, and then went on, "Mrs. Lamont, I know what that will probably mean for you. You'll either end up in witness protection or spend the rest of your life hiding from the Cuban mob, and that sucks. But," and now he looked directly into Caroline's eyes and spoke slowly and deliberately, "as a member of a United States law enforcement agency, as a patriotic believer in the law and the judicial system, I must suggest first and foremost that you trust in the law and follow protocol."

When Caroline began to protest, Lucy put a hand on her arm and, with her eyes, urged her friend to listen. Lucy thought she knew where Grier was going.

After a moment's silence and a nod at Gabriel, he continued. "However, I have no access to the evidence you have alleged against Daniel Lamont, and you cannot be compelled to testify against your husband in a court of law. So, without your cooperation, I will continue with the investigation before me: the murder of your lover, Mathew Wilson. I will continue to pursue the most likely suspects, namely you and your husband, while Charleston police continue to pursue the drug angle. If I find just cause, I will take it to the county prosecutor and request a warrant to search your home."

Caroline got it. Sheriff Grier had come up with the same idea that Lucy had. Give Grier enough evidence against her to get a search warrant for her home and let him find the cooked books on his own. Hopefully the cartel wouldn't seek retribution against Caroline.

Lucy picked up a paper envelope and handed it to Sheriff Grier. Inside were two glassine bags, one containing several strands of Caroline's hair, pulled from the root, and the other a generous sample of her saliva.

When he looked up, Caroline said with as much jocularity as she could muster, "These two had to convince me that this was one time when I should set aside my Southern gentility and spit like a man."

He smiled, and Lucy laughed out loud. "It wasn't easy, Sheriff. Caroline has never spit, drooled, burped or farted in her entire life."

"Neither have you, Miss Lucy," Caroline shot back with false indignation.

"That's absolutely true," Lucy conceded, and this time everyone laughed genuinely.

Gabriel asked, "Do you need anything else, Tom?"

Grier eyed the envelope of spit once more and said, "Nope, this is plenty."

He grinned at Caroline and she blushed. "Would you like some breakfast, Sheriff? Gabriel makes a mean scrambled egg."

"Nope. I've got evidence to plant," he replied grimly. "Plus, my dear wife has me on a muesli and yogurt breakfast diet. It's not as good as eggs, but those nuts and oats stick with you all day." He patted his flat belly and picked up his hat.

"Watch out for the juice cleanse," said Gabriel. "It's a slippery slope."

Grier chuckled, "That little lady could talk me into anything." Picking up the envelope with Caroline's DNA samples, he said, "I'm off."

After the Sheriff left, Caroline listlessly began rinsing dishes and putting them into the dishwasher. Gabriel checked his gun and went outside to make a phone call to his firm. He had his techies running a check on Daniel Lamont and wanted to see what they had turned up.

Lucy poured the last of the coffee and sat down at the breakfast bar.

"Everything is going to be fine, Carolina," she said with more conviction than she felt.

Lucy thought their plan had a good chance, but she was far from certain. The Havana Cartel, evil as they were, were careful and predictable. It was why they were so successful at evading the law. They wouldn't go after Caroline unless they had reason. If the blame for providing evidence of money laundering rested on Daniel, they would take care of him and that would be it. The farther away from him Caroline could get in the meantime, the better, but the cartel was not in the habit of wantonly targeting family members of their enemies.

Lucy's main concern was Daniel Lamont. He seemed like a free radical. His involvement in this mess wasn't solely financial. He'd had Mathew killed out of rage and that made him unpredictable. If he wanted Caroline dead it was because he was furious with her, even hated her. And, his pride had been hurt, which made men like Daniel crazy.

Caroline finished scrubbing the cast iron pan and put it on the burner to dry. As if reading Lucy's mind, Caroline turned and said, "Call me crazy, but I'm a lot more afraid of Daniel than I am of a big scary drug cartel."

"I get it. What Daniel did to Mathew is scary."

"It's not just that, Lucy. I have a soft spot when it comes to Daniel." When she saw Lucy's eyes widen she hurried on, "Not because I have any doubt anymore that he is not the man I thought he was and that he's a bad guy. But because I don't want to believe it, Lucy! I don't want to believe that I was that blind."

"You weren't blind, Caroline. You were unhappy. You had an affair. You felt compelled to look through Daniel's documents because you knew that something was not right. You have not been walking around like June Cleaver on cloud nine. You just didn't expect Daniel to be as corrupt as he is."

"If it was just money-laundering, I think I could

forgive myself for not knowing, but the level of violence he demonstrated with Mathew..." She shook her head. "I saw him angry, but I never would have guessed that he would have a man beaten like that."

Lucy had seen it all, but she had been surprised too.

"I would do anything for a reasonable explanation right now. Some new fact that I haven't considered that makes this less horrible, and makes me less of an idiot."

Lucy stood up and hugged her friend. "Even Ted Bundy had a fiancé."

Caroline began giggling and then laughing outright. "Lucille Walker, you always know how to make a girl feel better!"

Just then Gabriel walked in and regarded the two women who were now laughing so hard they had tears in their eyes. "What did I miss?" he asked.

"Lucy just told me to stop feeling sorry for myself," Caroline managed through her gasps.

Gabriel looked from one woman to the other and said, "Good, because Daniel Lamont has a long history of fooling people savvier than you, Caroline. Plus, he's what shrinks call an organized psychopath."

They went to the living room and sat down before Gabriel told them what his team of hackers and investigators had discovered about Daniel Lamont.

"First of all, his name isn't Daniel Lamont. It's Freddy Selvers. He was born Frederick Allen Selvers to a single mom in Omaha, Nebraska, who died at the hands of her boyfriend – who may or may not have been Freddy's father – when he was three and a half years old. The guy went to prison, and Freddy went into the system. He was in and out of foster homes until he was fifteen, when he basically disappeared for a couple of years. During that time, he assaulted three other foster children badly enough for them to end up in the hospital and he went after his last foster mom with a knife. After that, the state of Nebraska elected to keep him in a special home for troubled boys, where he stayed until the day he went out into the yard and never came back. Even though the boys' home was out in the sticks, there was a highway nearby and it wasn't so unusual to lose a kid now and then. So, the custodians at the home put his name on a runaway list with the Nebraska cops and figured he'd be picked up and returned before too long."

Caroline looked sick and Lucy went to get her a glass of water.

When she came back, Gabriel went on. He figured it would be easier to pull this bandage off quickly. Patting Caroline on the shoulder, he said, "It took my guys two days to dig all this stuff up and they're the best. And, they're willing to bend the rules of legality. You never would have discovered any of this even if you had been looking."

Caroline merely nodded and said, "What else?"

"He never popped up in Nebraska again, but two years later he was arrested for burglary in Upstate New York. He had allegedly stolen several pieces of jewelry from a wealthy older woman, but the charges were dropped and the police suspected it was because she'd been having a little fling with the handsome, but much younger Frederick Allen, as he was calling himself then."

Caroline felt like she was falling down a hole. "I can't believe this!"

"After that, Frederick Allen seemed to mix with the right crowd. He became very adept at passing himself off as one of the 'right people' and hobnobbed with the wealth and good breeding of Syracuse, and then Long Island and Manhattan. People who knew him then thought he was part of so-and-so's family, or a friend of someone-or-another, and he was certainly always charming company. He was smart and people liked him so nobody asked too many questions. He seemed to have enough money to justify the crowds he was moving in.

"My investigators found him later on Long Island because his fingerprint showed up in another jewelry theft investigation there. Again, the victim of the robbery decided not to pursue charges."

As Gabriel went on, Caroline began to feel something new growing inside of her. It was a calm, cold fury. Caroline's blood ran hot and so did her anger, but this new feeling was pure and quiet and she kept it to herself as she continued listening to the real history of the man she'd thought she knew.

AKA FREDDY SELVERS

A S GABRIEL WENT ON, TELLING the sordid history of Freddy Selvers, Lucy studied her friend. Caroline's expression was unreadable and Lucy couldn't remember a time when she couldn't tell what her best friend was thinking by the look on her face, but now there was no discernable emotion.

She put her hand on Caroline's shoulder and gave it a squeeze, which prompted a moment's smile in her direction but neither assured nor convinced Lucy that her friend was simply taking in all of this new information about her husband in stride.

"A couple of years later, one month before he was to matriculate at Yale University, a young man named Daniel Lamont from Houston, Texas was killed along with his mother and father in a house fire. In their grief, the surviving family members never thought to contact the school, and they never heard from Yale because Daniel Lamont aka Freddy Selvers, showed up at the beginning of September as expected. He was a brilliant student and his tuition was always paid in full and on time, though my team hasn't found his resources yet."

"What happened to Freddy Selvers?" Lucy asked.

"The name disappeared as soon as he took Daniel's identity. The change was seamless because he didn't have to legally change his name. He simply took over where the real Daniel Lamont left off. He probably ordered birth certificates, and the Lamonts were all in Texas, so there was no one on the east coast who would have known Daniel or how he died. Freddy didn't try to take their money or use their credit to make purchases that he didn't make good on. In short, he did nothing to engender suspicion, and from the moment he began school at Yale University, he never wavered from being Daniel Lamont, Ivy League student, only child of a deceased Texas businessman and his wife."

"Jesus," said Lucy.

Baxter meowed plaintively as though affronted by this turn of events. Caroline reached down to pick him up but remained otherwise silent and inscrutable.

"After that, he stuck with his new identity. After graduate school, he continued to rise in the world of investment banking and earned a high, legitimate income from that. I suspect that his ties to the cartels began when he was in his twenties and it was through them that he managed to amass most of his money, masking it as inheritance and tucking some of it away in banking countries in the Caribbean."

"So, apart from who he was and where he was born and where his personal wealth came from, he basically told me the truth?" Caroline rolled her eyes and ran her fingers through her thick, blonde hair. "I can guarantee that my father checked him out when we got engaged, even though he never told me so."

"Even with a solid background check, your father wouldn't have turned anything up. My team didn't find anything until they ran his fingerprints through the national database, and we were specifically looking for a criminal history. Daniel Lamont was a perfect alias: a real person, with a real past and present. Unless you or your family was really suspicious of wrongdoing, you never would have discovered the truth."

"I should have felt it!" shouted Caroline in exasperation. "I should have known somewhere in my being that the man I was in love with was a liar!" She gently moved Baxter off of her lap, got up and began pacing the length of the great room. Finally she turned to Lucy and Gabriel, "I'm going to my room. I need some time to process. Or sleep, or cry. I don't know."

Lucy gave her friend a hug. "Take all the time you need. I'll bring you some tea in a little while."

Caroline tried to smile and shook her head. "No thanks, I'd like to be alone for a bit."

Watching her walk away, Lucy took Gabriel's hand. When she heard the door to Caroline's room close she turned to him, "This is bad. Caroline usually deals with anger and anxiety by talking, or shouting, or crying and stomping her feet until the worst of it is over, not by beating a silent retreat."

Gabriel nodded, but added, "She's never had to deal with this kind of anger and betrayal and sadness before. Caroline is probably in shock right now and the flood of emotions will come later."

Lucy nodded thoughtfully. She hoped Gabriel was right, but something was not sitting well with her. She decided to dismiss her concerns for the moment. Her friend was in a safe place with people who cared for her and she would let Lucy know if she needed anything.

While Caroline had been pacing the living, she'd felt her iPhone vibrate in her back pocket. A text message had come through and when she escaped to the guest room she read it.

"We need to talk. Please meet me at the St. George Hotel. I'll drive up at eight. Daniel."

"You're goddam right we need to talk!" Caroline growled at the phone. She wanted to strangle Daniel, or Freddy, or whoever the fuck he was.

She sat there for a few minutes, thinking. Lucy would not want her to meet Daniel. She would try to stop her. Caroline felt like she was spinning in circles of unreality. She wanted to punch Daniel or Freddie or whoever right in the eye.

She went into the attached guest bathroom and peered closely at herself in the large mirror behind the sink. She had circles under her eyes and her normally rosy cheeks were pale and hollow from lack of sleep and tension. Her lips were drawn with rage against her pearly white teeth. Caroline was breathing too fast and she suddenly heaved into the porcelain toilet. Eggs, coffee and bile came out, but her body kept retching until there was nothing left. When the convulsions stopped, she sat on the floor and caught her breath, and then she rinsed her mouth out in the sink and crawled under the covers of the downy queen-sized bed.

When she woke, the light was changing. She'd been asleep for several hours.

Caroline sent her husband a text. "See you there," was all it said.

DINNER AT EIGHT

D ANIEL WAS NEARING GRACEFUL BAY. He had left his cell phone in Atlanta so that records would show that any calls to it would ping off of cell towers in Georgia and not in South Carolina. He was going to get out of this clean.

Steering with his knees, he squeezed his left nostril shut and inhaled from a coke spoon then performed the same exercise on the other side. He felt invincible. Glancing at his burn phone on the passenger seat he thought of Santana's skepticism.

"Why do you want to bring her to your own house?" he had asked when Daniel had told him the new plan.

It was simple. He had asked Caroline to meet him at the St. George Hotel at eight so that they could talk. Santana and his goons would snatch her along the way. Then they would take the old plantation service road through the wooded area behind their house. It hadn't been maintained in years, but would provide complete cover for them to sneak up to the old mansion without any neighbors noticing. Then they could park their SUV and sedan, along with Caroline's BMW, in the enormous carriage house they had converted to a garage, and no one would be any the wiser. The house was completely obscured from their neighbors' homes and from the street, both by distance and by ancient oak and sugar maple trees. And if they were quiet and used only the lights at the back with the curtains closed, it would appear as if no one was home, even if someone showed up and rang the doorbell.

Daniel laughed a little hysterically. He had known this wretched house would come in handy. Of course, he'd thought it would serve its purpose as a castle in which to keep his Southern belle wife happy, but that hadn't been the case. It had turned into a happy little irony for Daniel that she would be beaten to death in it. He was looking forward to watching and his only regret was that he couldn't participate. He had to remain unmarked. Scratches, bruises and bloody knuckles would land him in jail.

Santana would pull off the snatch with no problem. Daniel hadn't been surprised when Caroline had agreed to meet him. He had known Caroline would fall for it. She thought she was above harm. Stuck-up bitch.

She would have no doubt told Lucy that she was meeting Daniel at the St. George, so if Lucy and her new fuck buddy got worried, that's where they would be looking.

Lucy fucking Walker. When she had come home to Graceful Bay, Daniel thought she might pose a problem, but she had turned into a guilt-ridden gimp after her stint as an undercover cop. Santana seemed most concerned about Lucy's boyfriend. He said he was former military something or another and now owned a ridiculously successful corporate security firm, but why should he care about Caroline?

Why would anyone care?

AMBUSHED

S ANTANA HAD PLANNED THE KIDNAPPING well. Lamont had told him that Caroline had agreed to meet him at the St. George Hotel restaurant at eight. Santana had approximated the time she would need to leave Lucy Walker's house in order to get there on time, but he had also put a lookout at the end of the driveway and he had called the minute Caroline passed him in her car. The scenic road along the waterfront properties outside of Graceful Bay was a two-lane highway running parallel to the Interstate, and was relatively quiet outside of tourist season.

Less than half of a mile down from the Walker house, Santana and his men tucked themselves and their Range Rover on a dirt patch behind an overhanging copse of sugar maple and Spanish moss. Another lookout down the road sent Santana a text when Carline passed him and Santana backed the SUV straight out across the middle of the highway. It was a plan that depended a little on Caroline's reflexes and the BMWs' reliable brake system, but he wasn't worried. He'd done the same thing a dozen times in the past and everyone managed to stop. Every time.

He had stationed Roberto, a very cold and precise member of his team, on the other side of the copse with a stun gun so that when Caroline slammed on the brakes, he could step out from behind the car and take her by surprise before anything got messy.

The next few minutes were quick and professional, and, for Caroline Lamont, terrifying.

A strong, broad Hispanic man was at the driver's side door and had it open before she had even turned from the black SUV that was obstructing her path, and certainly before it occurred to her that the doors of her car were unlocked. In shock, she didn't even have time to fight, or, blessedly, to think the regretful thought: if only...

The man opened the door with his left hand, reached up with his right and shot her with a Taser. She felt pain and was vaguely aware of convulsions before she lost consciousness.

The strategy had worked perfectly, and before the lady even knew what hit her she was tied up, wrapped in a blanket and stuffed in the back of the Range Rover. Roberto followed them in Caroline's car, and when the lookout who'd been stationed at Lucy Walker's driveway caught up to them a few seconds later, they all drove in a caravan until they could loop around onto the Interstate. They had a couple of hours to kill until they would take the old service road that led to the Lamont house.

At half past seven, Lucy's tummy began to rumble. She looked up from her laptop and realized that the living room had grown dark around her. An hour earlier, feeling a little chill in the air, she'd built a fire and moved herself to a club chair by the fireplace. The sun had been setting then, but now the eastern sky had grown dark. With the only other light in the room coming from the dying fire, the bright computer screen was straining Lucy's eyes. She had spent the last few hours staring at it, reading as much as she could about the Havana Cartel and everything she found on about Daniel Lamont.

Career-wise, Lamont had flown mostly under the wings of the successful investment banking company where he was a junior partner, but she found mentions of him in a few international investment deals and hedge funds. She was mainly interested in his past, and had looked him up on the Yale alumni website and checked out his now dormant Facebook page. She didn't learn much, and she certainly didn't find any indication that, underneath it all, Daniel Lamont was a murdering money-launderer.

Now Lucy was tired and hungry. Caroline hadn't come out of her room since three o'clock when she'd made a cup of tea and some toast, and Gabriel had left around the same time to spend a few hours at home on his secure phone, checking in with his band of security geniuses. He had called an hour earlier and said he'd be back around eight.

After turning on a few lights and adding logs to the fire, Lucy wandered into the kitchen to find something to make for dinner. She had chicken breasts, new potatoes and fresh green beans from her trip to the Piggly Wiggly. She also had plenty for sandwiches and a salad, if they weren't all going to eat together. She decided to check on Caroline and see what she felt like having. She hoped her friend would eat something for dinner. She knew that Caroline must be sad and anxious and angry, but a little sustenance kept you going through these times.

As she walked to the other end of the house and into the downstairs guest room where Caroline had left her things when she'd moved upstairs the previous night, and where she had gone to rest earlier today, Lucy heard the front door open. She turned around and went to greet Gabriel and Baxter.

He stood there in faded blue jeans, James Bond Oxfords and a light wool sweater, carrying a shopping bag from Hoffman's Gourmet Market that was full of deli food he had picked up for dinner. He had even brought three pieces of chocolate pie for dessert. After Lucy had told him Shirley and Joseph Hoffman's love story, he had wanted to go introduce himself to the couple and pick up some things they would all like to eat for supper. Plus, he knew that Lucy was worried about Caroline and would like to see her eat and maybe put a smile on her face. After the revelations about Daniel Lamont this morning, Caroline had turned an unhealthy shade of white and then hidden herself away for most of the day.

Gabriel closed the door behind him and reset the alarm before kissing Lucy on the forehead and scratching his cat. "The alarm wasn't set."

Lucy saw the concern in Gabriel's face. "I went out to the patio for a bit of sun earlier, but I'm certain I reset it when I came back in," she frowned.

Gabriel looked at Lucy for a moment. Quickly, he went back to the foyer and looked out the window to the now empty spot on the far side of the garage "Lucy, Caroline's car is gone."

Lucy's face went blank. "Where is it?"

"I assume she took it, Lucy."

"She hasn't left her room all day."

Gabriel looked at her as realization dawned. The alarm wasn't set. The car was gone. Lucy had been occupied in the living room for hours and Caroline had just walked out.

Lucy turned and went back to the guest room, opening the door without hesitation – but she knew Caroline wouldn't be there.

The room was empty, a scribbled note at the end of the bed read, "L, G, sorry I snuck out. Daniel wants to meet at the St. George. I'm going to go slap him silly. I just gotta, Lucy. You know."

"Oh, Caroline." Lucy turned and looked at Gabriel, handing him the note.

He read it and said, "She went to meet him and smack him?"

"Yep," she nodded. "Classic Caroline. He must have called her or sent a text and asked to meet and talk, and she was so outraged that she agreed. She knew I would make a fuss and so she snuck out. She did stuff like this all of the time in high school, though it was usually to meet a boy and it was her parents she was evading."

Gabriel ran a hand through his brown hair. "This isn't high school, for God's sake."

Lucy took the letter back and walked out to the living room and then the kitchen. She picked up her mobile phone and called Caroline. There was no answer, but she left a message. "Caroline, I need to know you're okay." After hanging up she looked at Gabriel, "What should we do? Maybe Daniel really did want to talk. Try to smooth things over? He doesn't know that we've discovered all of his lies."

Already shaking his head no, Gabriel replied, "He might not know all that we've found out, but by having Mathew Wilson murdered practically on her doorstep, Daniel wanted to scare Caroline. At the very least, he knows she's scared and suspicious, and if he's waiting for her at the St. George – and that's a big if – and Caroline walks in and starts screaming and slapping him around, he's going to know everything pretty quick."

"But you don't think he's meeting her there?"

When Gabriel shook his head again, Lucy lifted her iPhone and asked Siri to find the phone number for the St. George Hotel in Graceful Bay, South Carolina. When the reassuring, computerized voice announced it had found the number, Lucy tapped it to make the call and raised the phone to her ear.

A moment later, Gabriel heard Lucy inquire, "Henri, it's Lucy Walker. I wonder if Mr. and Mrs. Lamont are dining with you tonight? No? Could they be in the bar?" After a pause during which the maître d' must have been fruitlessly checking the bar, Lucy thanked him and said that, no, she didn't care to leave a message in case they came in later.

"Where is she?"

"I'm going to call Sheriff Grier and tell him she's gone. He won't be able to do much, but at least he can have his troops look out for her car."

When Gabriel went into the other room to make the call, Lucy began to pace. Then she opened the refrigerator and took out the milk. Pouring herself a tall glass, she began to breathe deeply. It was time to be sharp. No panicking allowed. She drank half of the milk in a few long swallows and put the carton back in the fridge, already feeling her hunger and fatigue lessening. By the time Gabriel came back into the kitchen, she was feeling steadfast and determined. Caroline was in trouble and Lucy was going to find her and bring her home safely.

"She's in trouble," Lucy stated.

"I agree," said Gabriel, and then, "are you drinking milk?"

"Milk makes me a champion," she replied seriously and then, in spite of everything, she smiled at her lover.

"What do you think happened?"

Without hesitation, Gabriel replied, "Ambush. Daniel got her out of the house and he or his men ambushed Caroline and took her somewhere. I guarantee he knew she was here, which means that he's been having her watched. Any hit man worth his salt would have avoided coming in here with you and I around. Even if Daniel wants us all dead, it would be a mistake to attack us at the house. So he got Caroline out of here, and somewhere between this house and the St. George Hotel, someone stopped Caroline and took her away to kill her."

Lucy clenched her jaw, "That shit! He can't possibly think he can get away with this."

"I don't know what he thinks, but Daniel is wrapped up in a world that makes killing your wife and her lover possible, and he's mad enough to do it."

"What did Sheriff Grier say?"

"He's putting the word out to call in if anyone spots her car, and he's sending an officer to check her house, but other than that, there's nothing he can do. He wants me to update him if we find Caroline or discover anything new. Right now, I think we should drive to the hotel and look around. They may have stopped her car along the way, or gotten to her in the parking lot when she was going into the restaurant."

"Then let's go," said Lucy, already heading for the office. She'd left her shoulder and ankle holsters there after getting them out of the safe the previous day. Gabriel was already armed.

Pulling a canvas coat off of a hook in the entryway, Lucy followed Gabriel out the door, dutifully engaging the alarm system before pulling the door firmly shut. They got into Gabriel's Land Rover and pulled out of the drive, turning right down the scenic highway toward the iconic St. George Hotel, and hopefully, toward Lucy's best friend in the world.

Gabriel drove slowly with his high beams on. It was dark in spite of the periodic lights along the old highway. After a minute, he said, "There's a Maglite in the glove box. Maybe it'll help."

Lucy found the powerful flashlight and rolled down the window, aiming it out along the roadside.

"Damn," she said. "Unless they crashed right into her car and left glass all over the road, we're never going to see anything in this dark. And even if we do, all it'll tell us is where she was snatched, not where they've taken her." She felt suddenly helpless and frustrated.

Behind the wheel, Gabriel sighed and squeezed Lucy's knee. He had been thinking the same thing, but at least they were doing something while he thought about what to do next.

Just then, something caught his eye and he stopped.

"What is it?" asked Lucy, craning her neck and unbuckling her seatbelt so that she could turn around in her seat. "What did you see?"

"Maybe nothing," he replied as he backed up. He stopped again and said, "If I were going to ambush a woman who was driving a car on this road, I would pull my own vehicle – something big like a truck or an SUV – out into the road to make her stop. And, I would do it on a blind curve in the road, so that if she were at all suspicious, she wouldn't have time to stop early and turn around. And," he said pointing to the copse of trees he had just pulled up next to, "I would do it right here."

Lucy studied the curve in the road and dense grouping of trees and foliage.

"How would they know it was Caroline coming down the road? What if another car came? From either direction?"

"I would install a lookout for Caroline. We're only

a half-mile from your driveway, so I would probably put someone there. The timing would be about right to relay a message and then block the road. The highway is completely dead at this time of the year. Everyone is driving on the main road. So they could probably count on privacy." Gabriel got out of the vehicle and Lucy did the same, bringing the flashlight with her.

"What's to stop her turning around anyway? Or backing up?"

"She would have been driving the speed limit at least. Maybe more if she's still a lead foot. She would have stopped fast, just in front of the roadblock. They could have pulled another vehicle out behind her except that it would be harder to hide a truck over there." He pointed beyond the trees to a stretch of road bordered by short bushes and grasses so dense it would have been impossible to pull a car into the brush. "They probably went in fast and subdued her before she could react. Maybe a man walked up behind her car when she stopped and got in with a gun."

"Caroline would have fought," said Lucy, her skepticism waning. "They would have had to knock her out somehow."

As they scanned the road, the light from the torch caught on something dark and shiny. Lucy bent to pick it up, and when she again shone the light on the object, they could see that it was a women's size eight Gucci loafer, black leather buffed to a high shine.

GLASS SLIPPER

"IT'S HER SHOE."

Lucy felt sick. She had been secretly hoping that Caroline would call and say she was fine, or, maybe less likely, that they would discover her car and find that Caroline had somehow scratched the names and license plate numbers of her captors along with a map of where they were taking her into the dashboard. The shoe said it all. They had her.

The rising moonlight caught the tears in Lucy's eyes and Gabriel wrapped his arms around her. He kissed her head and told her it would be okay, but Lucy wasn't sure. She couldn't lose another person she loved. She just couldn't.

Finally, she leaned back and looked into Gabriel's eyes. "We have to find her. We have to."

"We will, Lucy."

They scoured the ground and the roadside, and apart from some broken branches and tracks in the dirt that seemed to confirm Gabriel's theory of where they had hidden their truck, found no clues that would tell them where Caroline had been taken.

They got back into Gabriel's Land Rover and he called Sheriff Grier, putting him on speaker so that Lucy could be part of the conversation.

"Found her yet?" asked the sheriff after Gabriel said hello and told him Lucy was on the phone too.

"Not her, but we found her shoe in the middle of the road."

"That damn stupid girl!" said Grier angrily. "What was she thinking? Which road? How do you know it's her shoe?"

Lucy said, "We found it on the scenic highway less than half a mile down the road from my house. Towards the St. George. And I know it's her shoe because it's one of a pair of six-hundred-dollar loafers she was wearing this morning."

"Six hundred dollars? Well, whatever. Where do you think she is, Miss Walker?"

"I don't know."

"You're the only person who can make an educated guess. Where would Daniel Lamont take his wife to kill her? Think. I'm going to put an APB out on Mrs. Lamont and send another cruiser past her house. Call me if you get any ideas," and he was gone.

Gabriel reached over and took Lucy's hand. "What do you think?"

When Lucy just looked at him blankly, he said, "We need food and we need to brainstorm," and he turned around and headed back to Lucy's house. She didn't even protest, though hunger at a moment like this seemed selfish, she knew she would be able to think more clearly in her own kitchen with something in her stomach.

Three minutes later, they walked through the door and into the kitchen. While Gabriel started a pot of coffee and pulled cheese and ham out of the refrigerator for sandwiches, Lucy went to her bedroom for a sweater to wear over her short-sleeved shirt. When she came down again she could smell the hot dark brew.

"You take good care of me, Mr. Black."

"It is my pleasure."

She sat at the breakfast bar and watched him slice tomatoes and pickles. Gabriel handed her a sandwich and poured a cup of strong coffee for each of them. He finished half of his own sandwich in three big bites and washed it down with a swig of java.

"Eat," he instructed when Lucy just stared at her plate. She did, but only because she knew he was right. Lucy was running on empty and her last bit of adrenaline had burned out when she found Caroline's shoe.

As she gulped the last of her coffee, feeling human again, something occurred to Lucy. Setting down her cup, she said, "For all we know, Daniel thinks Caroline came over here for consoling after her lover was killed, not because she was scared of her crazy, murdering husband."

"But he has to know she would be freaked out that Mathew was killed. Killed in her hometown, no less."

"I'm sure he does, but he wouldn't know that Caroline thinks he did it. He surely doesn't suspect that we know that he works for the Havana Cartel."

"How does that help us?" Gabriel asked, but he was already following her train of thought. "If he could, Daniel would want to be there when Caroline realized he was the one who'd had Mathew beaten to death. And if he doesn't think we know he did it, there's no reason for him to worry about being there. All he needs is a plausible alibi and he's home free."

"And," Lucy went on, "if he's vengeful enough to have a man killed, he's vengeful enough to want to watch Caroline die."

"Where?"

Lucy didn't have to think. "At home."

"Really?" asked Gabriel. "It would take a lot of nerve to kidnap his wife and bring her to their own house."

"Why? He doesn't know that we're on to him. Plus, Daniel is arrogant enough to do it there. Caroline loves that house. Or she did, anyway. She once mentioned that at first, Daniel had seemed to like that she was a Southern belle living in a plantation house, but after a while he resented it. He would want to hurt her where it hurt him, so to speak." Lucy was already strapping her shoulder holster back on. "It has a nice irony. Call the sheriff for a welfare check or something. Let's go."

Gabriel thought she could be right, but either way, they may as well start looking there. Still, if Daniel Lamont had had his wife snatched from her car on the highway, brought her back to their home, and intended to kill her right there in Graceful Bay, right under their noses, then he was more than arrogant. He was a little stupid too. Or, maybe he'd been partaking in some of the drugs the cartel smuggled into the country.

Gabriel called Sheriff Grier while Lucy rooted through a drawer in the kitchen island that seemed to be full of junk.

The sheriff answered on the third ring. "What's up, Black?"

Gabriel could hear sirens and people shouting in the background over his mobile phone. Lucy could obviously hear them too, because she paled and looked questioningly at Gabriel. He had a sinking feeling when he asked, "What's going on?"

"Some tweekers were cooking meth in a little house on the north side of the county. They blew the whole friggin' place to bits and at least one of them is dead. What a mess."

Gabriel was relieved, at least, to know that the sirens and chaos didn't have anything to do with Caroline Lamont. He gave Lucy a reassuring squeeze and said to the sheriff, "We think Daniel might have taken Caroline to their house in Graceful Bay. Lucy and I are going over there now."

"I sent a car over there to knock on the door, but he said that no one answered and it didn't look like anyone was home or anything was amiss. But I had to call him up here to help out. The house next door caught fire. Neighbors are all over the place in a panic. I don't have the manpower to handle more than one crime at a time," he said wryly. "I couldn't keep my officer down there."

"I understand, but we're still going to check. The house and the grounds are big enough so that a lot could be happening there and you wouldn't know by just knocking on the door."

There was a long pause before Grier said, "Shit. If the cartel is involved they could have an army in that house. But why do you think Lamont would take his wife back there? Seems like a guarantee for getting caught."

Gabriel explained his reasoning and the sheriff responded, "Criminals always get caught – most often because they miss something. I guess Lamont could assume no one suspects him. Still, it takes a lot of nerve to do it in his own home."

"We've got nothing else right now, Sheriff."

"Wait until I get back with some manpower to head in there."

"Can't wait. If they've got her there then we have to move now. You won't be done there for hours."

Grier sighed. "All right. Keep me posted. As soon as things start clearing up here I'll be able to send someone down, maybe even come myself. But be careful. If Lucy is right, you could be walking into a shit storm."

They disconnected and Gabriel went in search of Lucy. She had finished rifling through the drawer and then run off somewhere. He called her name and got no response. Finding the front door open, he headed outside and saw a light on in the garage.

It was a sizeable garage. Probably three plus cars, and styled like the house, with a high roof, cedar shingles and whitewashed walls. The side door was open and he walked into a workroom with another door on the other side that must to parking spots. It was full of carefully organized professional toolboxes and solid worktables. All on castors. Every wall was covered in pegboard with different configurations of tools hanging from hooks. There were two eight-by-two -foot skylights that couldn't be seen from outside and must offer a really pleasant natural working light during the day.

And there was Lucy. Standing in front of an open weapons cabinet.

It was about seven feet tall and just as wide, made of grey powder-coated steel and set against the far wall and into the concrete floor. It had an interior light and double doors and both of them were swung wide open. Lucy stood framed by the cabinet. She had turned to him and she was holding a high powered .223 Winchester in one hand and a sawed-off shotgun in the other.

"Which one do you want?"

"What is this?" asked Gabriel as Lucy stepped aside to let him look.

"Both my father and grandfather were sharpshooter and handgun champs. When my father died my grandfather added his guns to his own collection. Locked them all up in this vault, and when I was old enough, he started training me." She paused and then added, "I'm a really good shot with a small caliber handgun."

"Curiouser and curiouser," Gabriel replied. "I guess you were prepared for the police academy then." He was talking to her but studying the impressive selection of firearms in the cabinet. It wasn't an enormous collection by any means, but it was quality.

Gabriel looked at the sawed-off shotgun in Lucy's hand. "That doesn't fit with these," he indicated the selection of small and large caliber handguns, high-powered rifles, and classic hunting guns carefully hung in the vault.

Lucy smiled, patted the shotgun and winked at her lover. "I acquired this little darling while I was doing my undercover stint in Miami. I kept it by the front door of my apartment and never answered a knock without it in hand. A sawed-off is considered a necessary accessory for those in the drug trade."

Gabriel laughed wryly. "And you saw fit to keep yours?"

"Souvenir," said Lucy without mirth. "Besides, now it's coming in handy."

She opened a drawer and pulled out a second shoulder holster and began strapping it on opposite the one she had put on in the house. "There's a spare belt holster in there too, if you'd like."

"You seem pretty certain that we're going to meet with a lot of fire power."

"Look," Lucy said, turning to Gabriel with clear eyes. "Caroline being held captive in her own home is not only plausible, given what we know about Daniel, but it is the only scenario that I have any control over. If she isn't there, I won't know what to do. If she is there, and she will be, and Daniel's thugs are there, we will need to be well armed and smart about how we handle them. They will go out in a firefight. It's how these guys are trained."

Gabriel knew what she meant. This simply had to work. They had to save Caroline. He pulled the belt holster out of the drawer and put in on opposite the one holding his H&K. Lucy was checking the ammunition on a Sig Sauer semi-automatic.

Reaching for a Glock 20 and doing the same,

Gabriel said, "I don't suppose you've got another one of those?" He pointed at the sawed-off.

"No, but you can carry it, because if I have to fire standing with this thing, I'll launch myself about fifteen feet in the wrong direction."

When she locked up the gun safe once again, Lucy was carrying a Glock, with two semi-automatics holstered and a revolver on her ankle. Gabriel had two holstered semis and the shotgun.

"Now or never," Lucy stated.

While she locked up the garage, Gabriel reset the alarm on the house and locked the door. They got into Gabriel's Land Rover and took off.

HONEY, I'M HOME

CAROLINE AWOKE IN HER OWN bedroom, on top of the blanket and with the bedside lamp illuminating the otherwise dark room. For a moment she had the wonderful thought that the last two days had been a dream, until the aches in her body told her otherwise.

She tried to move her arm to her forehead, but found that she couldn't. She was bound around her feet and wrists to the four-poster bed. Looking around the room, everything seemed to be as she had left it last night and she couldn't hear anything from the rest of the house. Going over the scene from the car would've made her feel like an idiot except that she was too terrified to be hard on herself. Caroline's stomach was in knots. Why would Daniel have brought her back to their own house?

She listened hard again, and thought maybe she detected the distant growl of men's voices, but she wasn't certain. She did not want to be tied up alone in her home, but if she wasn't alone, it was most likely her kidnappers in the house with her. Not good either way.

How long had she been here? Her arms and legs ached, but didn't burn from the restrictive bandages, so she must not have been tied up for too long. She had a searing pain emanating from her neck and remembered the Taser. They had been so fast and professional, she hadn't even had time to resist. She hadn't even had time to see whether her dirty rotten husband was amongst them. How could he possibly think he would get away with this? Had he gone crazy? If he wanted to hurt Caroline, why would he bring her to this place, which he hated, to do it? Didn't he know that Lucy and Gabriel would be looking for her? Maybe Sheriff Grier by now too.

Of course, if he didn't think he was under serious suspicion, why wouldn't he just bring her home to kill her?

How could she have been so stupid? Ruefulness hit her as her arms and legs began to ache in earnest. Motive had already been cast as a drug deal gone wrong. The police would have learned that Mathew Wilson was Caroline's lover after they found her address in his pocket and came to question her. In Daniel's mind, it would not be a stretch for the police to believe that whoever killed Mathew had come to collect from his rich older girlfriend and killed her too. But Daniel didn't realize that they were on to him. Caroline, Lucy, Gabriel and Sheriff Grier already knew, and soon the FBI would too, that there was more to the story than that.

The trouble was that all of those things may well send Daniel to jail when all was said and done, but none of it was going to save Caroline's life if Daniel got to her before her saviors did.

As if to underscore the point, Caroline heard the tiny creak, which always let her know someone had come in through the kitchen door.

The door that led from the back of the property into the kitchen opened and Daniel Lamont walked in to find Santana and his merry band of goons lounging around the old table and leaning on the countertops. He sneered at one guy sitting on the counter and the man jumped down, but without apology.

Daniel had texted Santana that he was coming down the old service road and would be there in a minute, so as not to startle the armed men. In fact, he had almost driven by the road because it was so overgrown with kudzu. If he hadn't been looking for it he would have missed it. There was barely a mark where Santana and his men had driven their two SUVs plus Caroline's BMW through. He followed the road down the back end of their property, through the forest of hickory, white pine, eastern hemlock and dogwood, past the gardener's outbuildings and onto the old carriage and stables, which had been converted to an enormous garage and guesthouse in the 1950s.

What the fuck had he been thinking buying this sprawling Southern mass? Actually, he knew what he'd been thinking. He had wanted to install his Southern belle wife here so that she would be happy, and he wanted to launder some of his own earnings through the purchase and maintenance of his enormous new money pit.

The latter had worked just fine, but the former? Nothing made that woman happy.

He had spat on the ground and kicked a chunk of dirt and sod before heading for the back door and throwing it open to reveal the group of totally incongruous thugs who were making themselves comfortable in his giant country kitchen. Daniel was looking forward to this next part.

"Where is she?" he asked Santana immediately after assessing the scene.

"Comfortable. In the master bedroom," Santana replied laconically.

Daniel hid his irritation. Santana had never shown any respect for him. If he had been a greasy Latino with a Cuban accent and a mansion in Miami, Santana would have been obsequious, but even though Daniel was paying him and giving the orders, Santana always looked at him as if he was a fly he'd rather shoo away than have to bother swatting.

He headed for the wet bar in the great room, and while he was there, cut himself another thick line of cocaine from the stash he kept in the ice machine. He snorted half in each nostril and poured himself a tall vodka on the rocks. When he returned to the kitchen, he felt a lot more confident.

Santana knew that Lamont would come back with a drink in his hand and figured he would be a little wide-eyed. Daniel Lamont had been earning himself a reputation for using too much of the cartel's product and washing it down with booze. He'd called the higher-ups yesterday to tell them that Lamont was becoming a little "overzealous", and that his plan to kill his wife had gone from a little well-conceived revenge to hell-hath-no-fury risk-taking. They said to go along for now and they would get back to him.

This morning the second-in-command had called and told Santana to go along with Daniel's plan to snatch the wife, and then kill her and Daniel and make it look like a murder-suicide. Lamont's drug use and erratic behavior coupled with the dead lover would look convincing. Then Santana's team was to sweep the house for anything incriminating and remove it, and leave the property otherwise intact and the bodies for neighbors to discover whenever they happened by. A white-collar guy who was becoming erratic and drug-addled was a liability to the cartel and they would just as soon get rid of him.

This was fine with Santana. He'd wanted to put a bullet in Lamont's head since he'd met him. The guy was a prick, and cocaine made him worse. He was a shit with more attitude than he could justify and he'd treated Santana and his guys like scullery maids since he'd hired them. Santana had a thick skin, though, and he knew that guys like this always got what was coming to them. He was just pleased that he would be the one to put this smug bastard out of his misery.

When he'd walked in through the back door, Lamont looked like shit. He hadn't shaved that day and had a five o'clock shadow that didn't inspire confidence, his suit was wrinkled from the drive and he had mud and grass on his shoes like he'd just had a temper tantrum on the lawn outside.

Lamont had looked around the room like he was watching a bunch of cockroaches scurry around and then gone to get more booze and blow. Santana sighed when Lamont came back with a drink. Frankly, he would be glad when this guy was out of his life.

"What?" asked Daniel belligerently.

"Nothing, man," Santana replied tonelessly. "When do you want to get started?"

Santana's men had already been through the whole house. They'd found hard copies of cooked books for the cartel, and a few incriminating photographs in his office, but nothing anywhere else. More than enough evidence that Lamont was being careless. Another team had been sent to Lamont's condo in Atlanta to make sure there was nothing there that could be traced back to the cartel, and Santana would go through his phone and laptop before they left. The woman was a little bit of a snag, but otherwise, Daniel Lamont's death would be pretty tidy.

"First, I want to see the bitch," said Lamont.

Santana had seen no indication that Caroline Lamont was a bitch. She seemed to be more a casualty of her husband's bad choices. But who was he to judge?

"She's right upstairs. Tied up nice and tight."

Daniel looked at Santana for a moment. Then he gulped down the rest of his drink, went to the freezer, pulled out a full bottle of Grey Goose, and stormed up the servant stairs.

The man who had been sitting on the counter top asked his boss in Spanish, "Should we follow him up there?"

"No," Santana replied languidly in his native tongue, "he won't do anything without us. He can't have a scratch on him when the cops question him. Besides, I think the pretty lady up there who's going to die because her husband is a shithead might want a last word with him."

Caroline heard heavy footfalls pounding up the back staircase and knew they were Daniel's.

Bound hands and feet prevented her from arranging herself in a more dignified position, but she steeled herself from the inside for what was going to come next. If this was the last time she was to see her husband, she was really going to let him have it.

After a few seconds that seemed like an eternity, the door opened and Daniel Lamont came through without ceremony. He looked at Caroline, tied up and lying prone, her head and shoulders propped on a stack of pillows, her body partially covered by the wool afghan that Caroline usually kept at the end of the bed. Her hair was mussed and the covers were a bit disheveled. The top button of her blouse was torn open, revealing a tiny peak at her incredible cleavage. *Caroline has great tits*, thought Daniel a little nostalgically.

With her hands bound to the bedpost over her head, Caroline should have appeared vulnerable, but the look in her eyes belied her position. They were wild with fury and she looked as if, were it not for her bindings, she would have torn him limb from limb with her bare hands.

It took him aback.

He caught himself. Only his princess wife could manage to look imperious with her hands and feet strapped to a bed. God, how he hated her!

He pushed the door closed behind him and leaned against it. "Drink?" he proffered the bottle with a petulant wink. "No? Well, don't mind if I do."

"Fuck you!" spat Caroline, without moving. In spite of the vulgarity, she seemed as entitled as ever.

"Now, now, Caroline. Foul language won't do you any good now. You're going to die a terrible death and you should reserve your screams for the beating." He sat down at the end of the bed, and smoothed the blanket back over his wife's legs in an obscene gesture of mock tenderness. He set the bottle of vodka down on the chest at the foot of the bed and took a sip of his drink. "Last words, darling?" he asked, his voice dripping with sarcasm.

Looking directly into his eyes, she said coldly, "I know all about you, Freddy Selvers."

Daniel's face paled. He had not been expecting that to come out of her mouth. Before he could consider the ramifications, he had slapped her hard with the back of his hand. Caroline's face flew to the side.

"How?" he demanded, wrapping his strong fingers around her jaw and turning her face to his. Blood trickled from one nostril and her cheeks were flushed with rage.

"I know all about the Havana Cartel," she replied in the same cold tone and with the same unwavering stare as before. "I know everything, Daniel. Everything."

BRASS TACKS

L UCY AND GABRIEL PARKED AS inconspicuously as possible down the street from Caroline's home. There were no other cars on the tree-lined boulevard and many of the houses could barely be glimpsed from the road, but without other vehicles there was no anonymity. They would be fine as long as all of the players were already inside, but if anyone new arrived, Gabriel's Land Rover would stand out like a sore thumb.

"We have to take the chance," Lucy stated as she scanned the street. Gabriel agreed. Time was of the essence.

They headed through the front yard along the tree line to avoid being seen, though the house and gardens were completely dark. Lucy stayed behind Gabriel and they moved slowly, Lucy feeling out each step to prevent aggravating her injured leg. Gabriel guided her around low-growing vines and dips and divots in the earth.

Once they reached the house, Gabriel stooped and whispered, "The house is completely dark."

"There is still a lot more house to come," Lucy assured him. "Plus they probably covered some of the windows to prevent light leaking out."

As they progressed along the side of the house and finally made their way around the back, Gabriel saw a sliver of dim light framing a large square window.

"That's the kitchen," Lucy pointed at the window. "They must feel secure that no one is going to wander around back and notice a little light."

Gabriel squinted into the dark expanse of land behind Caroline's home. There were manicured flowerbeds, evergreen bushes, sugar maple and dogwood trees that seemed to go on forever into the night.

"I can see why," he replied. "Who the hell would be wandering around back here without a good reason?" He noticed that the gravel driveway curved around the other side of the home and ended a couple hundred feet away in a large semi-circle outside of what appeared to be an old carriage house. Even in the dark he could see an old, unpaved track heading toward the back of the property.

"Do they use that as a garage?" he asked.

"Yes. Should we chance a look inside?"

"We'd have to use a flashlight to see who's parked inside. I'd like to know what's on the other side of that window before we take a chance on using a light. The best thing we've got going for us right now is that no one knows we're here."

"I'm going to try to look into the kitchen."

"No, Lucy. I'm going to go. I don't want you to trip over something and hurt yourself and alert them to our presence."

Lucy acquiesced. She generally liked to do things herself, but she couldn't argue with Gabriel's logic.

She stayed put while Gabriel crept to the kitchen window. For a strong, tall man he moved with astonishing stealth and grace and Lucy felt an inappropriate little tingle of desire in spite of the circumstances. She told herself to focus and started scanning the rest of the windows for signs of light. Nothing. Either there were no other lights on or someone had taken steps to black out the windows.

Gabriel crept back to her side. "I saw two men and the arm of another. They looked Latino, but that's all I can say about them. I did not see Daniel, but there could be fifteen guys in that kitchen and I wouldn't be able to tell. I heard some faint murmuring, but couldn't make out what they were saying. Something is definitely going on in there. We'd better go check the carriage house for cars and call Grier from over there."

Lucy wordlessly put her hand on Gabriel's chest in agreement and they began walking toward the carriage house. Apart from a few broken twigs and a little shoe shuffle in the grass, they were silent. After circling the gravel car park to the far side of the garage, Gabriel pulled out his Maglite and his mobile phone. He handed the phone to Lucy and shone the light through the row of shoulder-height windows. The first car they saw was Caroline's BMW.

"She's here," said Lucy, as she felt her stomach drop to her knees. She handed the phone to Gabriel and took the high-powered flashlight from his hands. "Call Grier. Please. Get the cops here."

Gabriel dialed 911 first. They needed anyone close to get here quick.

Lucy was searching the garage. The vehicle parked next to Caroline's black car was a large, dirty SUV. She had to go around to the backside of the carriage house to see what was parked on the other side of that. She signaled to Gabriel where she was going by pointing and tiptoed around the corner. The windows were larger on this side, and when she reached the halfway point she again shone the light through the window. Next to the SUV was a smaller sedan, also filthy, and next to that...

Lucy rounded the corner of the garage as quickly as she could without falling over and making a lot of noise. Gabriel was still on his cell phone and she could tell by the frustration in his voice that he hadn't gotten hold of Grier and was leaving an urgent message.

"I told the cops to approach stealthily, but a word from you is more likely to make that happen than a request from a civilian. The house is blacked out except for the rear kitchen window. Caroline's car is here and I saw at least three men in the kitchen—"

Lucy grabbed Gabriel's arm and hissed frantically, "Daniel's car is parked in the garage!"

"Daniel Lamont is here, too," Gabriel said into the phone's receiver, keeping his eyes on Lucy. "We have to go in right now. Get here as quick as you can because we're pretty well armed, but I'd bet the farm that they are too."

He hung up. "Most of the police force is at the crime scene up north. I have no idea when anyone from law enforcement will get here. Let's go."

Lucy dropped the Maglite onto the ground. They needed their hands to hold their firearms.

Gabriel turned first and again led the way back to the mansion. Without a word they both knew that even though it would take longer, it was worth it to approach the house slowly and quietly. They would need to use surprise as a weapon.

In a whisper, Gabriel said, "Don't suppose you have a key to the front door?"

Lucy gave him a little smack on the butt. They stopped a few feet from the kitchen window and this time Lucy crept forward and peeked in. She saw three men, but it was impossible to know if there were more. Plus, she now knew that both Caroline and Daniel were somewhere in the house.

They backed off a bit to confer.

Gabriel said, "I think you should go around to the front of the house, break a window and run like hell. When these assholes go to see what's happening, I'll break in through the kitchen and take them down."

Lucy was already shaking her head. "You go around front and break a window, I'll go in through the back and find Caroline. When they come out you run back here and come in behind them and blow them to bits."

When Gabriel looked like he was going to protest, she went on, "I can't run fast enough to be useful at the front of the house. Plus, I know the layout of the house so I'll probably have better luck finding Caroline."

"And running into whoever they leave behind in the kitchen. And, running into Daniel Lamont if you find Caroline."

"I won't hide in the bushes, and my safest bet is to get in through the kitchen door when at least *most* of the gunmen are in the front."

They faced off for a few seconds, Gabriel having a harder time than Lucy with the thought of her in danger, but he knew that if he wanted to love this woman he would have to accept who she was. And right now, Lucy was Caroline Lamont's hero.

The plan they came up with was solid, considering they were two people against a group of no less than four murderous men.

Lucy tiptoed to the kitchen door while Gabriel made his way to the other side of the house. He climbed the five steps onto the veranda, walked over to one of the blacked-out picture windows and smashed it with the butt of his gun.

From the kitchen, Lucy heard the glass break and saw an instant motion of arms and heads and guns through the crack in the curtain. She wouldn't know for certain whether anyone had stayed behind until she was inside.

She tried the doorknob before breaking a pane and was amazed to find it unlocked. *The gods must be smiling on me tonight*, she thought.

Slowly easing the door open, Lucy led with the end of her semi-automatic Sig Sauer. There was no one left in the kitchen, but no telling when the men would come back. She closed the door as quietly as possible and then dashed up the servants' stairs to the second floor, hoping that Gabriel had gotten away and that Caroline was still alive.

After breaking the enormous picture window, Gabriel had vaulted himself over the porch railing and onto the soft grass beneath. Without even pausing to look over his shoulder, he ran for the back of the house and the woman he was beginning to fall in love with.

He couldn't see through any of the windows as he passed them, but Gabriel heard footsteps as the men ran through the unfamiliar house, dodging furniture and broken glass.

He had two important things on his side. First, the Havana Cartel men would be smart and trained well enough to do some recon before they ran out the front door. The first thing that would have come to Gabriel's mind if he heard a window shatter was that there would be big guns waiting right on the other side of it. He figured these guys would watch out for the same thing and it would take them a few minutes to figure out that there was no one on the veranda.

Second, and perhaps most important, was that even though the antebellum home was far enough away from neighbors for them to overlook something that sounded like glass breaking, no one would ignore the sound of gunfire. It was in their best interest to keep as quiet as possible for as long as possible. That meant they would hold their fire unless they absolutely had to use their guns.

The wild card, Gabriel was thinking as he raced around the corner to the backside of the house, was Daniel Lamont. He was not well trained, and might even be coked up. If he had a gun, there was no telling how jittery his trigger finger was getting.

A sharp pain in her leg forced Lucy to pause as she approached the top stair. She clutched her thigh and held her breath for a split second before moving forward. The door to the hallway was already open and at the other end of the long hall she could see light shining out from beneath the door to Caroline's master bedroom. Downstairs she heard the men moving around and conferring with each other in Spanish, but she couldn't make out what they were saying.

Daniel was nowhere to be seen, which meant he was either downstairs, or cowering in the bedroom with Caroline. If he was standing behind that door with a gun in his hand, she could be in trouble. At the same time, if he was getting trigger happy because of the commotion downstairs, Caroline could be in trouble.

Caroline heard the sound of shattered glass and breathed a sigh of relief. It had to be Lucy. But her relief only lasted until she saw her husband's face.

Daniel was sweaty and panicked. He jumped off of his perch on the foot of the bed and whirled around, then hurried to the door of their master suite and pressed his ear to it, while reaching down to check the flimsy lock. The house seemed to have fallen quiet and Daniel remained by the door for another minute. Then he rushed back to Caroline and slapped his hand over her mouth.

"If your friend causes me any trouble, I'll cut her into little pieces. Do you understand me? Keep quiet."

Caroline nodded and he slowly removed his hand from her mouth. She hadn't seen a gun or knife, or weapon of any kind on Daniel since he had entered the room, but that didn't mean he didn't have one.

If she called out to her friend now, what would happen?

Lucy was midway down the second floor hallway, unsure of what she would find on the other side of the bedroom door, when the quiet intensity that had filled the house since Gabriel broke the front window was broken by semi-automatic gunfire.

She hoped to God it was Gabriel doing the shooting, but in seconds the gunfire was returned and she knew that right now she had to focus on Caroline. Running now, she tucked her Sig Sauer into her jeans at the small of her back and pulled the little twenty-two caliber pistol from her ankle holster and, when she reached the door, immediately shot a round through the wood next to the brass doorknob.

The door flew open and Lucy flew right through it, dropping the pistol and raising her semi-auto into the room. She ignored the sound of gunfire now raging downstairs and focused on the figure of Daniel Lamont. He was turning from the bed where Caroline lay, still alive, and he ran at her with no hesitation. Lucy had never seen a man so full of fury and panic in her life.

She shot him in the leg.

He immediately went down in agony. Cries of pain mixed with obscenities poured from Daniel Lamont's contorted mouth. Caroline cried out to Lucy, but didn't take her eyes off of her husband, who was writhing on the floor.

Lucy kept her gun on Daniel. He was growing

pale, and his flailing limbs were slowing down a bit, but she still didn't want to frisk him. She registered the zip ties binding her friend's arms to the headboard of the bed.

"Caroline, do you have a knife or scissors up here?"

"In the secretary," Caroline replied and Lucy gave Daniel a wide berth as she ran to the antique desk on the far wall. There were two pairs of stainless steel scissors and a menacing-looking letter opener inside. She brought them back and used the larger of the scissors to cut the zip tie on Caroline's left arm. Her friend groaned as her arm fell straight down from the top of the headboard to the pillows. It was completely asleep and totally useless.

Lucy repeated the process on her other arm and then snipped the ties that bound Caroline's feet together and held them to the footboard.

"Shit!" Caroline cried out as she awkwardly twisted her body into a sitting position. One of her arms had begun to tingle and she knew it was going to hurt like hell.

The rest of the house went suddenly quiet and Lucy felt her stomach clench in fear for Gabriel. "Caroline, I have to help Gabriel. Can you use your arm?

Her friend was rapidly wiggling the fingers of her left hand and seemed to have some movement in her left arm.

"Go!" she said to Lucy, "I'll be fine."

Before leaving the room, Lucy picked up the pistol she had used to shoot the door open. It had landed on the threshold when she'd thrown it down in favor of the more powerful semi-automatic Sig Sauer. She gave it to Caroline and made sure her friend could hold the grip before turning to Daniel. She kicked him viciously in the side and when he screamed, demanded, "How many are downstairs, Daniel? If you lie to me I'll kill you."

"Three!" He said it without hesitation and Lucy hoped that meant he was telling the truth because all of their lives might depend on it.

Lucy jogged into the hallway and then tiptoed to the top of the curved grand staircase, crouching low and peering over the banister.

As soon as Gabriel had rounded the house and reached the kitchen door, he threw it open without hesitation. One of the Latino goombahs was backing into the kitchen from the formal dining room at precisely that moment. The man was clearly holding a gun in his raised hands, but he was facing the wrong direction. Gabriel shot him without hesitation and then all hell broke loose.

Gabriel kicked the gun away from the dead man's hands and dove past him, underneath the massive maple table in the darkened dining room.

Pressed up against a wall in the foyer, Santana whipped around to face the direction of the gunfire. He told his other man to stay put and watch the front of the house while he checked out the kitchen. Neither man was panicked – they were professionals – but adrenaline was coursing through their systems, making them sharper and faster.

From under the table, Gabriel Black thought he

heard a footstep and then he saw another of Daniel's henchmen quickly look into the room and then duck back behind the wall. He didn't move an inch, just waited, and as soon as the man edged around the corner, looked around, and slowly entered the dining room on his way to the kitchen, Gabriel took aim and shot the man in the thigh.

Santana fell to the ground, clutching his leg, but he must have been shot once or twice before in his life as a cartel henchman because he didn't make a sound, merely looked for the shooter and began lifting the muzzle of his gun toward the shadow under the table.

Gabriel shot him again, this time hitting center mass, and when the man kept trying to aim his gun, he shot him again.

Lucy was tiptoeing down the stairs, careful to stay near the wall where she was less likely to make creaking noises. When she got to the landing she again peered around the banister, but saw no one in the foyer. Then there was more gunfire coming from the dining room or maybe the butler's pantry. A small, nimble Latino ran into the foyer from the living room toward the sound of gunshots.

Lucy shot at him and missed, but it was enough to get his attention. He dove for cover, and in that moment Lucy shot at him again, this time hitting him in the shoulder. He went down in agony and she said, "Drop your weapon." It was the cop in her, giving the man fair warning, but he didn't heed it.

"Fuck you." He said that with a strong Hispanic

accent while he brought his gun up and pointed it at Lucy. It was too late. She shot him in the neck and he died instantly.

Suddenly the house was eerily silent, the smell of cordite strong in the old mansion. Somewhere behind the scent of discharged guns, Lucy detected the metallic smell of blood as she watched the young man bleeding on the floor.

She waited and then with fear gripping her, she called out, "Gabriel?"

And she heard the sweetest words in return. "Right here, baby." And he came around the corner looking disheveled but unharmed.

"Caroline is safe," she said quietly and was about to run to him but he stopped her with a finger to his lips and pointed into the living room. He looked at the dead man on the floor and held two fingers up, pointing toward the dining room and kitchen.

She understood. He had taken two men down, but they had to secure the house in case there were more than the three he had seen through the kitchen window. And Lucy knew that Daniel might have been lying to her upstairs about the number of gunmen.

Gabriel led the way, ducking low behind his gun, checking every corner and closet. There were no other men with guns in the house.

Finally, Gabriel put his arms around Lucy and held her tightly. "Thank goodness you're okay, Lucy Walker," he said. And she didn't know if she had ever felt so safe.

Suddenly, a gunshot broke the peace and they both began running for the stairs.

The shot had come from Caroline's bedroom. As they walked down the hallway toward the open bedroom door, guns aimed, Lucy did not want to contemplate what might have gone wrong. Instead she focused her energy on the danger that might lie on the other side of the threshold.

Afraid to find her friend hurt or worse, Lucy pushed on the door just as she heard sirens in the distance.

Then Caroline's sultry southern lilt trickled calmly out of the bedroom suite. "Next time, I'll aim for your crotch."

AT EASE

A S IT TURNED OUT, CAROLINE had fired a bullet into the floor near Daniel's head. She was an excellent shot, and Daniel knew it. If she wanted to hit him in the balls, she would.

The police arrived shortly after Lucy and Gabriel stormed the bedroom and found Daniel writhing and crying on the floor and Caroline perched ladylike on an ottoman, just out of his reach.

When the deputies entered the house, they were shocked by the carnage. This was Graceful Bay! The worst thing that ever happened here was maybe a drunken spring break brawl and now they'd had a brutal murder and some kind of shoot-out in just a few days. Gabriel and Lucy left their weapons in the hall and came to the top of the stairs with their hands in the air.

John Lee Harper, the young deputy Lucy remembered from his house call a few days before, belatedly shouted, "Hands up!"

The other deputy rolled his eyes like an embarrassed teenager.

"Miz Walker?" Deputy Harper asked in surprise. "What are you doing here?"

"Just helping a friend, Deputy. May I put my hands down?"

The deputy began to nod but his partner

intervened, saying, "We have to frisk you." Lucy and Gabriel descended the stairs with their hands still in the air. "There is an injured man upstairs and he'll need an ambulance." The other deputy pushed a button on the walkie-talkie on his shoulder and ordered a bus and backup. He kept his gun pointed at Gabriel and Lucy while Deputy Harper frisked them. He did a thorough job on both, removing Gabriel's wallet but finding no weapons. He turned bright red and apologized profusely as he patted Lucy down.

"You two know each other?" asked Gabriel when they were allowed to put their hands down.

"Deputy Harper canvassed my house after Mathew was murdered."

"Ahh."

"Miz Walker wasn't entirely forthcoming with me that day, as it turned out."

"Sorry about that, Deputy," said Lucy with her best look of regret.

The young policeman shrugged, "No hard feelings."

Then the other officer pulled his cuffs off of his belt and, gun still aimed, told Gabriel to turn around and put his hands behind his back.

Gabriel and Lucy exchanged a look and he started to turn around when one of the walkie-talkies squawked and Sheriff Grier's booming voice came over the radio. The deputy who was about to cuff them stepped back to answer the call.

"What the hell is going on there? Is everyone alive?"

"No sir," he replied, "everyone is not alive. We

have two suspects, a man and woman, and at least one dead body."

"Where are Lucy Walker and Gabriel Black?"

Deputy Harper said, "This one's Miz Walker, but I don't know the other guy." Carefully bending down to pick up the discarded wallet, he studied the driver's license and nodded at his partner. "It's him."

"They're right in front of us, Sheriff."

"All right, leave 'em be. They're not suspects. Where is Caroline Lamont?"

Gabriel said, "She's okay."

After conveying that information to Sheriff Grier, the deputy looked at Lucy and Gabriel, "At ease." They relaxed. "Sheriff's on his way."

By the time they straightened everything out it was the middle of the night. Daniel was at the local hospital under police guard. The morgue van had arrived and was waiting for the county crime scene techs to clear the bodies for removal. Caroline had been checked over by the EMT, and was fine, apart from a few nasty bruises and some psychological trauma. They had told Sheriff Grier the whole story and all three had given official statements. With promises to come into the station house the next day, Grier dismissed the trio.

As they turned to leave, Grier put a hand on Gabriel's shoulder and pulled him aside. With a nod in Lucy's direction, he said, "That girl is trouble. Better hold on tight."

EPILOGUE

THREE MONTHS HAD PASSED, AND under Baxter's watchful eye Caroline was packing her suitcases in the downstairs guest room at Lucy's house.

Lucy leaned against the doorframe.

"There's no hurry, Carolina."

"I know, Lucy. But I'm ready, and I bet you and your gorgeous boyfriend are ready to have the house to yourself. Run around naked, make lots of noise, play doctor...." She trailed off with a big grin on her face. "Besides, I'll be living even closer than I was before. My new house is just on the edge of town."

After the shootout at her house with Daniel, Caroline had gone home with Lucy and had never spent another night in the big mansion again. She filed for divorce a few days later, as soon as she could think clearly, but the divorce became unnecessary when Daniel Lamont was shot to death by a sniper rifle on his way to arraignment for charges of murder, murder for hire, attempted murder, drug possession and a host of other felonies and misdemeanors. Santana and his men had tried to hide the evidence of money laundering when they had searched the house and loaded all of Daniel's cooked books, papers, and photographs into the Range Rover, but they hadn't made it out alive and the car was still sitting in the carriage house when the police arrived on the scene.

The bosses of the Havana Cartel decided that if Lamont couldn't testify that the ledgers referred to the cartel's illegally earned money, the Feds would be hard-pressed to make a case for racketeering. Daniel Lamont had to go and they sent their best sharpshooter to dispatch him quickly and cleanly.

When Caroline heard the news, she cried. She was angry that he would never be punished for Mathew's death, frustrated that she'd never be able to divorce him and that she would always be his widow, and furious that he wasn't going to have to spend the rest of his life in jail. And she was sorry that a man she had once loved was dead. The profound sadness and rage she felt at his death surprised her, but enabled her to properly mourn their relationship and the man she had loved enough to marry.

Caroline had gratefully accepted Lucy's offer to stay with her as long as she wanted, and the time she spent at the big beach house had been healing and hopeful. She believed Lucy when she said that could stay as long as she wanted, but Caroline knew that it was time to go.

The recent shootout at her antebellum home had made the mansion only slightly less appealing to buyers. In the fashion of Southern ghost stories and intrigue, a small hotelier with haunted bed and breakfasts in Charleston and Savannah bought the home for a great price and would start remodeling in a week.

Caroline had bought a three-bedroom, very modern, beach house on the edge of town. "Not a built-in bookshelf or lead glass panel in sight and I can look at the bay and walk to LaValle's. What more does a girl need?"

Lucy agreed: the new house was perfect. It was in no way reminiscent of the house her friend had shared with Daniel Lamont. It was smaller, brighter and closer to the center of town, and apart from the bedrooms and bathrooms, the open floor plan gave the sense that there were no secrets hiding there.

Still, she would miss having her best friend in her house. In the three months since the shootout, she and Caroline had never run out of things to talk about. It had been like one long slumber party.

Lucy was back on ninety minutes of physical therapy each day since she had thwarted much of the healing she'd done on her leg while running around with guns trying to save her friend's life. Four days a week, a merciless therapist named Spencer came to the house and guided Lucy through a painful circuit of exercises intended to get her leg back to the strength and flexibility she'd had before being stabbed in Miami. "Returned to its former glory," was what Gabriel called it. Caroline had known Spencer for years from different social occasions in the small Southern town. He was a handsome, homosexual, male version of herself. They had always gotten along well, telling each other bawdy jokes and discussing Hollywood gossip – from Charlie Chaplin and Marilyn Monroe to Denzel Washington and Jennifer Anniston – as if they were participating in a global political summit. Now that they were seeing each other more frequently, their friendship was blossoming and Spencer often came back for dinner after his appointments were finished for the day.

Lucy wouldn't let Gabriel near the house when she did her PT. "You don't need to see that side of me. Not yet, and maybe not ever."

Gabriel replied, "I like every side of you. Even the crabby one," and he poked her in the ribs.

"When have you ever seen me crabby?" asked Lucy, giggling.

Truly, Gabriel had no problem giving Lucy her privacy. He had a new security project keeping him busy from home, and once, when Spencer had just arrived at Lucy's house, he had winked at Gabriel and said, "Run away. This isn't going to be pretty."

Gabriel Black had been by Lucy's side since Lamont had been arrested. He didn't always spend the night, but Baxter and he were a fixture in the beach house and he often cooked dinner for the two women. He was constantly amazed by how natural and easy his relationship with Lucy had become, and how endlessly excited he was by her. Soon, the men who owned Gabriel's rental house would be back and he and Lucy had already decided that he would move in with her instead of returning to his Manhattan apartment for the summer.

That evening, he and Lucy helped Caroline bring her suitcases to her new house. Movers had already delivered a few boxes of clothes, books, family heirlooms and little treasures from the mansion that Caroline wanted to keep, but she hadn't kept much.

Lucy surveyed the sparsely furnished house.

"Why don't we get some take-out and unpack some of your things?"

With a genuine smile, Caroline wrapped her arms around Lucy. After they embraced, she said, "I am going to put my brand new twenty-thousand-thread-count linens on my brand new pillow top bed. Then I'm going to open that bottle of red wine," she pointed, "pour myself a glass and watch *Some Like it Hot* on my laptop. I might not unpack anything at all. I feel really good here, Lucyfer. I promise."

Lucy grinned, "Sounds like a perfect date."

When they arrived back at Lucy's house, Gabriel walked her to the door. When she opened it, Gabriel's big cat was waiting for them in the foyer. He yawned, stretched, and finally sauntered over to be petted. Lucy hung up her coat and turned to Gabriel with a smile.

With a surprisingly shy smile, Gabriel said, "Actually, Baxter and I thought you might want a night to yourself."

Lucy's eyes opened wide when she replied, "I want no such thing!"

Laughing, Gabriel scooped Lucy up into his arms, "Thank goodness!"

He carried her to the great room and set her on her feet by the sofa. "Would you care for a glass of wine before dinner?"

Lucy reached up and tugged on the collar of his T-shirt. "Nope." He leaned into her kiss and lifted her waist to his, picking her right back up. "I want to spend some time naked in your arms. And since we have the place to ourselves –" She lifted her arm to gesture around the great room, but Gabriel was already upon her.

His mouth opened against hers and he pressed her body to his, relenting only long enough to pull the cotton sweater over her head and unbutton her blue jeans. He slid his hand beneath her panties and groaned when he felt her wetness. They finished undressing quickly and found themselves, once again, in the center of the thick Afghani rug.

Gabriel leaned over Lucy, taking a moment to touch her hair, her lips, to look into her eyes. She pulled him over her, inside of her and wrapped her long legs around his buttocks, his waist, opening herself completely to him.

They made love slowly, Gabriel guiding himself in and out of her with intent. He wanted this to last until they were both at their peaks. Lucy pulled him to her with increasing urgency, but he resisted. When the moment came they looked into each other's eyes, letting out sounds of pleasure and delight that went on and on as they shared the rapture of lovemaking.

Lying still and naked on the carpet, with the ambient light from the kitchen and a silvery quarter moon glowing on their sex-slicked skin and glimmering in their eyes, neither moved for a long time. Their breathing softened and they relaxed into each other, arms and legs intertwined.

With a gentle but decisive movement, Gabriel lifted Lucy's shoulders and cradled her head, turning her toward him.

Looking into her eyes, he said, "Lucy Walker, I am completely in love with you."

For a moment she couldn't speak. Her lips parted and her eyes widened but nothing came out. Then, in a quiet voice, choked with surprise and delight, she said, "Me too!"

ABOUT THE AUTHOR

Ava Parker is an author and traveler, freelance researcher and writer. A devotee of love stories, scary movies and popcorn for dinner, she is already penning her next adventure in romance and intrigue.

CONTACT AVA:

Email: bellanovels@gmail.com
Twitter: twitter.com/avaparkerauthor
Facebook: www.facebook.com/avaparkerauthor
Instagram: instagram.com/avaparkerauthor

Website: www.avaparkerauthor.com

www.ingramcontent.com/pod-product-compliance
Lightning Source LLC
Chambersburg PA
CBHW022142170626
46807CB00005B/2035